"Where you gettin' money
to buy a record or get pictures taken or for anything?"

"Got a secret." Tilly winked at her friend. "I'll show you, but you have to promise to never, ever, tell a soul."

"Not even Johnny?"

"Oh, especially not him. He thinks I spend all the money on groceries," Tilly replied. Keeping secrets wasn't something she'd set out to do, but warnings niggled at the back of her brain to save up for a rainy day. These coins might come in handy when there were no more thrown on the bedcovers in the early hours. She rose from the table and headed to the small room off the kitchen, then pulled down the Mason jar from the cupboard. Once back in the kitchen, she stared hard into her friend's eyes. "Promise me."

They linked their pinky fingers together where years earlier they'd made small cuts in their skin, promising to be blood-sisters forever. Rita Mae nodded solemnly as Tilly unscrewed the top from the jar labeled *beans* and tipped it sideways. Coins cascaded onto the table, a couple of pennies even rolling away. She put her hand just under the edge of the table and caught both.

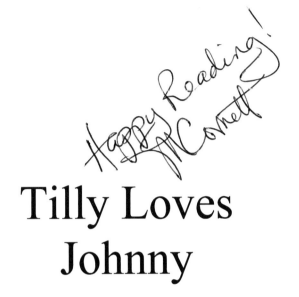

Tilly Loves Johnny

by

Marion L. Cornett

Tilly Loves Johnny

Cover Art by *Tina Lynn Stout*

The Wild Rose Press, Inc.
PO Box 708
Adams Basin, NY 14410-0708
Visit us at www.thewildrosepress.com

Publishing History
First Mainstream Historical Edition, 2016
Print ISBN 978-1-5092-0937-8
Digital ISBN 978-1-5092-0938-5

Published in the United States of America

Dedication

For DC and KC

Chapter 1
In the Depths of Prohibition

1928

Three taps at the front door meant the beginning of another night of drinking, playing cards, entertaining hoary men, and wondering when it was all going to come crashing down.

She rose from the dining room table and adjusted the dress hanging loose from her body. Her clothing had taken on a life of its own—expanding like a burgeoning cocoon. Or, she was shrinking. Even the slightest breeze was probably strong enough to whisk her up into the gathering dark clouds.

The old house was a cacophony of noise—her footsteps made the floorboards groan while fitful gusts outside rattled loose shakes on the roof, air slithering like mischievous ghosts under the jangling clapboard siding. It was a hot, sticky wind. Her stomach churned like a bubbling cauldron as she waited for thunderstorms to assault the area. Maybe then some much-needed moisture would lighten the air.

She paused, with her hand on the doorknob, sighed before sucking in a deep breath of stale air, and plastered a smile on her face.

"Come in, gentlemen." She sighed upon opening the door, stepping to the left as three men from the village slithered past. They ducked into the darkened room, eyes trained on the floor with coat collars pulled upward to shield their faces from prying eyes. Little did they know nearby neighbors were some of her best customers.

Her contempt for them far outweighed the silvers and coppers she'd pocket by the end of the night. But, oh, those coins. She'd gather up every bit of money left behind without an ounce of guilt. Otherwise, she'd be looking for handouts just to survive into next week.

"You're late." She grumbled at a fourth man trailing in a few steps behind the others. He skidded by her to make his way to the other three gathered around the table. None of the men ever made eye contact but, then again, they barely spoke to each other either. At least not until the games began.

"This way." The latecomer took the lead and grabbed the cards and games the old woman had stacked on the table. "Gentlemen, we are conducting our meeting in the stalls tonight."

He didn't have to say anything more. With no further explanation, the first three left the dining room faster than a squirrel treed by a dog.

The old woman lingered a few more minutes to see if anyone else showed up. No one did, so she finally followed the motley parade down the back steps toward the shed at the back of the property. The ground still radiated heat from the afternoon sun even though darkness had fallen long ago. She held up one hand to her eyes, crooked fingers looking more like battered fence posts, dried and rotten from years of abuse. If not for the dull light barely glowing under the barn door, she'd have seen nothing and maybe even thought about being young again, carefree, her hands smooth and her body lithe. But she was old. Used up, after all these years, and this was the only way to put food in her belly and warm her bones come winter.

So she stepped closer to the shed, steeling herself for the evening's festivities. By the time she slid the door open, the first three men already held drinks in their hands and the fourth was clinking the coins he'd pocketed. Under no uncertain terms, she'd be reminding him two-thirds of the take belonged to her.

"You...men...paid...him?" She cleared her throat three times in order to croak out four words while tilting her head in the direction of the last man to enter the house. The three men nodded. "So what's your game...of...choice tonight?"

No one answered but, then again, she didn't much care as long as they paid to play.

"Hear tell the sheriff's been rattlin' back doors," George mumbled, picking up his cards. "Catching rumors of drinkin' in the area." He was the first one having walked in the front door. Older, slightly stooped, with a bulbous gut, he rested both hands on his stomach while holding three playing cards, squinting at them like he couldn't figure what was on them. He looked back and forth from those three cards to the grimy table. They were playing community poker with two cards flipped face-side up on the table rounding out each player's hand.

"Aw, heck, the sheriff's more interested in trappin' speeders comin' through town," the youngest of the three men replied. Del, short for Delbert, was always willing to offer up an answer or opinion in any conversation. He'd tell anyone showing the slightest interest he was born knowing all worth knowing. "We could pour ourselves a ten-gallon milk jug full of hooch right under his nose but instead he'd probably be phonin' the sheriff in Howell to watch for rum-runners on old Grand River Road." He discarded one of his cards and tapped the table for a replacement.

The old woman was most wary of the third man, Oscar. He rarely took his eyes off the dealer, always acting like a spoiled kid about to be wronged. She didn't trust him. Was he about to rat them out or was he in for the big bucks from gambling? He'd hardly drink any of the jag juice offered as part of the deal but showed up nearly week after week anyhow.

The fourth, Sonny, was her kin but that didn't mean she trusted him. All she cared was him doing whatever she demanded. She moved over to his side, putting out one hand for the coins in his pocket. He reluctantly fished out a handful of silvers and coppers and, as inconspicuously as possible, slid them into her waiting hand. They'd settle up for the rest at the end of the night after the poker game was finished.

A few hands were dealt, no one saying a word; the only sound being the slap of the cards on the small table the four men sat around. With each round of cards, piles of coins grew in front of the three players as the dealer's cache dwindled down to one silver dollar—enough for one more call. Players tossed coins to the center after two cards were placed in front of each of them. All three men across from the dealer scowled in unison at their hands. A couple more cards were tossed, face-up, on the table and more bets placed. The dealer threw in his last coin, calling out the players.

And then, the dealer let the slightest smirk curl the

right side of his mouth as he flipped over an Ace and King of Hearts to go with three other red-hearted cards—a flush. He hardly paused for any reactions and, in a grandiose gesture, swept up the pot. He flipped a few coins, gazing over the lion's share of winnings. Silence cloaked the table except for the metallic clink of silvers over coppers. The air stilled, making the hot shed even more stifling.

"Dealin' off the bottom agin?" Oscar spoke, shifting the stub of a cigar from one side of his turned-down mouth to the other. A smoke curl ascended and shaped itself into a question mark above the man's head before drifting upward to the rafters.

All Sonny got back from the others around the table were glaring scowls.

"It was only one hand," George muttered.

"My cards might'n as well been hand-picked to be the worst." Nothing new there. Oscar was always grumbling about one thing or another.

Some nights the old woman handled his surly attitude with a shot of her better gin—not the usual hooch acquired locally—or to place a hand on his shoulder to console him. Tonight, she had nothing for him. If he didn't like coming here, let someone else take his place. Enough other men in town were willing to play cards and have a drink, even if it meant breaking the law, this being a dry country and all.

"No call for accusing anyone of bad dealing." Sonny stood up to stretch his arms overhead. He twisted his head side to side, appearing to ease tension built up in his shoulders. He then walked over to an exposed cabinet, the slider wall having been pushed off to one side, exposing shelves containing more bottles. He

5

poured another tumbler of gin from an already half-empty bottle. His back was to the group, challenging anyone to say more.

A thunderclap resounded off in the distance after a couple flashes of heat lightning seconds earlier. A light smattering of raindrops battered the shed roof like hot popcorn, but the air in the room wasn't cooling off any. Only getting worse. Maybe the mood or possibly the close air was putting the men on edge, but something was hovering over them. Trouble like a festering wound with no hope of healing.

Oscar slowly rose, keeping his glare directed at Sonny, and moved around the table getting closer to the dealer with each step. "Maybe I ain't wrong. Seems my bad luck don't ever change."

Sonny didn't acknowledge the taunt nor even turn around, which only served to make the situation worse. Oscar threw his cards down to the table—not caring whether or not they landed face up, showing a two, three, and nine, all different suits—and clenched his fists. A sneer crossed his reddening face, coupled with eyebrows dipping deep down. He stood only a few feet away from Sonny, never changing his stare.

"Oz, sit down," George nagged. "This won't get us anywhere."

Didn't matter what anyone said, Oscar had entered the house looking for a problem and now he was making it happen. Before anyone stepped in to stop him, he took a long, hard swing at the back of Sonny's head. He missed, with all the gracefulness of a man falling off a horse. The momentum of the misplaced punch into thin air sent Oscar's shoulder plowing into Sonny, taking them both to the ground. The glass of gin in Sonny's hand went flying, splaying the tinged liquid in an arc like the wake from a rumrunner's speeding boat. Polka dots of darkened soil pebbled the dirt floor. As the men tussled, dust rose up like a whirling dervish, swirling around them, partially obscuring the scuffle happening on the shed floor.

"Get off me, old man." Sonny growled the words. He rolled side to side, nearly getting free from Oscar's grasp.

"Cheat." The older man grunted, getting the better of Sonny, seeing as he outweighed the younger man by a good hundred pounds. He pressed one knee into the center of Sonny's chest, nailing him down in the dirt, his arms flailing out like a kid making an angel in the snow.

The older man's face turned nearly purple from rage—or exertion—and stale spouts of breath chugged out of his mouth, the cigar stub long ago lost. With exaggerated slowness, he balled up his left hand and, before anyone reacted, he swung toward Sonny's head, landing a solid punch to the side of the younger man's right eye.

Sonny's head snapped sideways and he crumpled, both arms going limp and flopping to the ground, his legs gone still with his feet splayed outward. He was either dead or knocked out cold. The men froze as if a strong blast of wind had turned them to ice, no one taking a breath until Sonny's chest rose ever so slightly.

One perfectly-placed punch was all it took to end the fight. And, to maybe even ruin the night. Another flash of heat lightning snapped everyone out of their daze, a collective sigh nearly audible as their breathing matched the young man's chest rising and falling, as he lay prone on the dirt floor.

George and Del stood up from the table. They were looking to leave, downing their drinks in quick gulps.

"Now…now," the old woman mumbled, then coughed. The dust hadn't settled much and was aggravating her gravelly voice even more. She came up behind the two men, placing her hands on their shoulders. "Let's…not be…too hasty. There's still lots more to drink."

"Booze ain't no better than the cards." Oscar struggled up from the floor, having slid sideways off Sonny and was now standing. His hand trembled and he kept looking from his fingers to the young man's cheek as if somehow swelling skin had attached to his bloody fist. He ran a sleeve across his face, wiping away sour-smelling sweat, turning the stale, humid air even more rancid.

"No call…to be…accusin' anyone, Oscar." She took a swig of the gin to get her voice back. "You know the rules here…pay so's you can play poker and we give you somethin' to drink. Why'd we go cheatin' on ya?"

"I ain't sayin' I won't be back, but you might want to talk to your boy here 'bout how he deals them cards." Oscar pounded at the film of dust covering his pants, some fragments filtering down to the still-unconscious Sonny.

A clap of thunder brought the men to attention just as the shed door was rattled.

"Well, well, what d'we have here?" A voice behind them boomed.

Those in the shed turned as a bolt of lightning lit up the doorway, backlighting the person standing at the threshold. He nearly filled the entryway, the perennial plaid scarf draped over his shoulders, even if the woolen fabric was out of sorts with the stifling elements.

Ah, a new arrival. This was the one person she loved seeing. Nothing better than a big spender to line her pockets with coins and make this night go from bad to profitable. She abandoned the worries of the lost battle to concentrate on beguiling her newest guest, not giving a rat's ass whether Oscar decided to stay, go, or to ever return again.

She pulled in the stale air, expanding her decrepit lungs, hoping to calm her insides, and plastered the same smile on her face as when the three men first walked in through the front door.

Chapter 2
Tilly Loves Johnny

November 30, 1928

Rays of sun streaming through the east bedroom window warmed Tilly's face. The sheets were cold, though. She slid her hand over to Johnny's side of the bed.

Empty. He never came home last night.

"Here we go again," she whispered into the pillow, still warm from where she'd laid her head. They'd been married only a few months and this was the second time he left long before dark the day before, then stayed out all night.

The first time—barely a week after their wedding—she'd been in a panic, rushing from the bedroom down the stairs to the parlor, into the kitchen. Even poking her head out the back door of the house like a chicken with its head cut off, running to Rita Mae's down the block, then sitting at the kitchen table for hours on end. Her vigil ending as he strolled in the back door twenty-four hours later. He'd feigned surprise and confusion by her questions, intimations, and finally, directed anger at her.

His fury scared her into silence.

She never did find out what happened during those nighttime hours and then nearly all of the next day. He was righteous in his wrongness to mind her own business. He had every right to do whatever he *damn-well* pleased, and she better learn to deal with it. But then, he turned on the charm, erased any hurts faster than her next heartbeat.

She'd been so befuddled by his range of emotions, she never even asked how he got a bruise alongside one eye. Below his right eye, a bluish shade spread out from a bump the color of purple morning glories, pushing out his cheekbone so far the skin looked to explode any second. At first, he grabbed Tilly's hand as she reached up to caress the spot but then allowed her to run fingers down the side of his face. She didn't dare press too hard on the spongy flesh for fear of hurting him more.

He winced and turned his back on her, stopping all inquiries. The most she'd been able to do for him was give him a cold water-soaked towel to press against the side of his face.

But now, only a few weeks later, was she supposed to treat this morning like any other, forget the fact he wasn't lying in bed, warming her back? Again. Or, be at the ready with a towel for maybe the other side of his face since the old bruise had faded to varying grades of green and yellow.

"I love you, Johnny," she spoke aloud to the empty bedroom. "But, oh, whatever this is you're doing, I hate it."

She wrestled her legs out from under the sheet and debated about using the chamber pot or running to the outhouse. One involved work later on and the other insured she'd end up with a few mosquito bites, seeing as a hard frost still hadn't come to the area. She opted for the pot, knowing full well her best friend, Rita Mae, would brag how all she had to do was pull the chain alongside the water tank before crawling back under warm covers. Her friend's family had installed an indoor toilet and sink, after enclosing their back porch a few years back. Mrs. Osborne boasted of the luxury as often as possible. Tilly's parents hadn't wanted to spend money on something so frivolous.

After the wedding, Johnny joined her in the big old house her pa built years ago when they settled in the small village. He'd promised her all sorts of updating would be done in the old place—especially a toilet—but she was still waiting. Johnny was four years older but sometimes those years felt like a generation. She was getting smarter, though. She kept wishes to herself, thoughts under control, and bided her time to get what she desired while figuring out the man she married.

Johnny was Johnny, to be sure.

What she was realizing, he moved at his own sweet pace and nobody was going to budge him faster or slower. So, she held her tongue and waited, even if it was sometimes difficult. Rita Mae was always expounding on how nice padding down to the bathroom and then crawling back into bed felt without barely having to open her eyes. Someday, Tilly'd have the same luxury.

Johnny's ma claimed he turned out the way he did—mainly stubborn—mostly because of articles she clipped from the newspaper. Hardly mattered she couldn't read much more than simple words, she said. Mostly made up stories on how to be a man. On the day before his birth, she taught him about being bull-headed, which came natural for Johnny. The woman even gave her a story as proof, even though the real evidence was more in how she constantly showed a stubborn streak far longer than her son's. His ma was one tough cookie and had a way of intimidating Tilly like no other.

So now, was he being stubborn in not coming home because of how she reacted the last time? Or, should she be worried? Well, her dear mama—long gone from the flu epidemic in 1918—used to tell her worrying only made the sun shine a little duller and the moon hide behind the clouds. And she wasn't about to fret, not on this sunny day in November. Before too much longer the days would be so short, she might as well not even open the drapes. Winter would be upon them for months on end. Time to head outside and make the most of the warming sun rising high in the morning sky.

Chapter 3

The Next Morning, December 1, 1928

"Hey, *doll-face*? I'm home!"

Johnny slammed in through the back door, but she wasn't so sure about acknowledging him. He'd been gone—by her calculations—twenty-two hours and five minutes. For each hour he'd been missing, she'd labored to come up with a good reason they'd gotten married in the first place. So far, she'd failed on twelve of the twenty-two counts.

But, oh, those first ten were actually pretty good.

To begin with, he was so very good looking with his dark hair, sultry eyes, and casual smirk of a smile gracing his face all in deep contrast to her fair hair, deep blue eyes, and an aloofness some found disconcerting. Secondly, he could make her laugh 'til tears fell, while third, he made her cry. Sometimes, crying was as cleansing as those carefree moments when laughter would bring on salty tears. In order of importance, the fourth count included his patience. Tilly was always finding something to be upset about while he found a way to calm her.

Five, six, seven, and eight culminated in those sweet moments before sleep or upon opening their eyes. Oh, to be a woman married to a man like Johnny.

Nine made her pause for a few minutes as she

considered a conversation they'd had a while ago. About having children. He was lukewarm on the subject, growing up fatherless but with a controlling mother. At the same time, he'd wondered aloud how being a father intrigued him. His wavering was all so confusing.

Ten, oh ten. Their future. She wanted their life together to continue so she held her tongue. The other twelve reasons were best forgotten. Her dear mama had always told her *the heart wants what the heart wants and there's no arguing its choice.* And her heart clearly wanted this man. For better or for worse, in sickness and in health, 'til death do they part; her love for him blossomed from his vulnerability and the sweetness only she knew.

"Shush," she whispered, but only loud enough for her own ears. Johnny was downstairs, she was still in bed. And, hope upon hope, her father hadn't roused himself from his bed yet only to find out the truth about her husband's malingering.

Money—short for Monroe, as his cronies called him—had moved to the third floor of the house after the wedding. They had as much privacy as could be afforded on the second floor, with the first where family would gather.

But, was there enough privacy? Maybe Johnny felt overly cloistered, crowded, with her pa under the same roof. It wasn't what she wanted, but families took care of each other. Her pa was lonely, they had no extra money to speak of, and all three needed a roof over their heads. He'd become increasingly more quiet as the years advanced, especially after the flu epidemic of 1918 left him a widower and herself motherless. Tilly hoped, at some point, she and Johnny could fill the house with the laughter and noise of young children.

But, for now, she slaved after two men, cooking meals at least three times daily, often more, keeping up with mending and ironing brought over by neighbors, and falling into bed late at night. Half the time, her dreams had her waltzing the night away wearing some of the long, flowing dresses worn by actresses dancing up on the movie screen. Some mornings, she'd wake up tired and a little sad her life wasn't filled with parties and social events. She and Johnny had talked with him making big promises of laughter and adventures.

"Hey, didn't ya hear me?" Johnny burst into the bedroom, mindless of keeping the noise down, never wondering she might still be asleep or even her pa might not have risen with the rooster's crowing.

"Mornin,' Johnny," she mumbled. "Gone a bit, eh?"

He stretched out on the bed. She was still under the covers, him now on top of them, smelling of the night air and *hooch*. Her questions were quickly answered. He'd been out all night, indulging in his favorite hobby. Prohibition hadn't slowed him down one bit. The saloons may still be closed but he'd somehow found a way around the law. He loved playing Black Jack, Dominoes, and sometimes Mahjongg and betting a few coins along the way, and no doubt someone came up with some *giggle juice*. Or, oh, what else did they call rye mash? *Jag juice.* Such odd names.

"Definitely long enough." He dropped a handful of silver and copper coins onto the spread. A ray of sunshine glinted off a single gold coin, reflecting a yellow oval onto the cream-colored wall opposite their

16

armoire. The clinking continued as he picked up a few and then let them slide from his palm.

Tilly couldn't think of anything to say so she started to slide out from under the cover but Johnny was quicker. He grabbed her arm to pull her close. His breath reeked but he seemed unaware of her discomfort as he kissed her soundly on the mouth. Within seconds she was responding—maybe against her better judgment—but how she craved his touch. Anger and passion raged like a thunderstorm within her thoughts, wanting to push him away yet draw him closer.

His hand slid under the covers so his fingers could travel up her rib cage. His right hand came to rest on her left breast where he held on tight, slowly pulsing back and forth, kneading her with his fingers. Her back arched as his left hand found her other breast and mimicked the same dance.

She pushed down the covers and let her anger dissipate up to the ceiling, finding the passion so much more pleasurable. Before long they were skin to skin, wrapped in a lust to burn off the morning haze.

The coins were easily forgotten, scattered amongst the tangle of sheets, yet occasionally clinking under the rhythmic rocking of their bodies.

****

Tilly padded barefoot down the steps and into the kitchen an hour later.

Since one desire had been satiated, she was hoping to quench another. If she had any luck, Mr. Andrews would have delivered at least a couple bottles of milk, as was their usual morning order. Sometimes she was up early enough for a quick conversation with him before he headed on to the next house. The clip-clop of

17

Brown Molly's hooves on the pavement, as the old horse pulled the milk wagon, always sent Tilly scurrying. That is, if she was up in time.

Thad, as he was always reminding her to call him, couldn't be too much older than she was, but his years out in the weather had worn him down. Gave him a bit of a hangdog look with those drooping eyelids and tanned, wrinkled skin.

How she loved their few lively words together. He was always ready with some stimulating tidbit of news or a funny story about someone from his deliveries. And, she was usually ready with a bit of carrot or apple for Brown Molly.

She missed him today, nearly running into her father's back as he sat hunched over the kitchen table, his elbows bookending a bottle of milk and an empty plate. The half-empty glass container stood at attention as if challenging him to drink the remaining.

"Mornin' Pa. Sleep well?"

"As good as expected." A frown creased his already wrinkled brow. "You?"

Tilly didn't answer right away. Her lips still tasted of Johnny, their time together vanquishing any thoughts of last night's sleep.

"Probably not," he continued. "Heard Johnny come in 'bout an hour ago. That boy needs someone…"

"Father, please, Johnny's no boy, he's my husband." The hackles rose on her back faster than a dog's as this old argument had been played out once too often. "Johnny's a grown man."

Money shook his head, starting to respond but this time Tilly wasn't in the mood. She pulled a handful of coins from her housedress pocket and dropped them to the table. She'd managed to gather up a majority of the money, including the lone gold one, leaving a few for Johnny to find upon waking. She figured the pile was adequate payment for him being gone twenty-two hours and five minutes.

"Ill-gotten gains, I'm sure." Her father sputtered. He got up from the table, grabbed hold of his cane leaning against the wall, and headed toward the front parlor. "I'll stoke the fire before leaving for the shop."

Oh, a few minutes talking with Thad would've been so much nicer than dealing with her pa's perpetual anger. She didn't totally disagree, but Tilly was caught in the middle between his need to deride her husband and of Johnny's actions out of her control. She sat down and drained the remaining milk from the half-empty bottle, not even bothering to go in search of a glass.

A mistake, since a small chip in the rim caught on her lower lip and split the tender skin already swollen from her husband's passion. Immediately, the metallic flavor of blood soured on her tongue. She spit the mouthful of pinkish milk onto the plate, hoping there'd be no chunks of glass left in her mouth. The bleeding didn't last long once she dabbed the spot with a handkerchief, but her lip already ached and was tender to the touch.

To get her mind off the nick, she counted out the coins and found there to be over twenty dollars. A fortune.

She quickly gathered up half of the money and hid those coins in a Mason jar she'd stowed on the top shelf of the pantry, one she'd labeled as *beans* after lining the inside with some leftover chicken feed bag fabric.

Someone curious or suspicious might check out such an inconspicuous jar but probably not Johnny. The coins clinked against a few others she'd pitched into the jar a week earlier, after a long day of taking care of someone else's clothes. Maybe once the jar was full, she'd figure out what to do with the cache. A new dress, for sure. Perhaps store-bought instead of handmade. Oh, what a luxury.

The remaining money left on the kitchen table would be used for restocking flour and sugar and possibly even some real coffee. Maybe she'd even try to catch Mr. Andrews the next morning to see if he had any sweet cream butter in his wagon. Tilly's mouth watered at the thought of the yellow substance melting down the sides of warm biscuits. She savored the thought of not having to churn a batch, for a change, but to lay down coins for store-bought butter.

"You ain't mad at me, are ya, doll-face?" Johnny leaned against the doorframe leading from the front parlor into the kitchen with all the casualness of a man happy in his surroundings. She startled at his voice, lost in thought of heading to the local grocer for much-needed supplies.

"You know I can't stay mad at you, Johnny."

"Taking half the money probably helps, too. Right?" He winked.

"I assumed you left it on the bed for me. You know. Make up for being gone last night, and all." The vein in her forehead pounded. So sure it was visibly pulsating, she took deep breaths trying to calm her nerves, hoping he hadn't been watching while she'd stashed away the coin-filled Mason jar. She made her way to the table to retrieve the remaining full bottle of milk. The container shook in her hand.

"Here, let me put the bottle away." Johnny stepped forward. He released the latch on the heavy door of the refrigerator and placed the milk on one of the wire racks. At the same time, he flicked his fingers on the motor clattering away on the top of the box. The box rattled while the engine sputtered to life a little louder than before. "Guess we'll call this morning even. You make me breakfast, and I won't ask what you're doing with all the money."

"Buying us food, if you need to know." Anger had resurfaced as the glow from their early-morning passion cooled further. Bitterness was slowing to a burning within her, what with her father always irritated and Johnny getting more sullen with each passing week since they'd married. There was no question she loved her husband to the moon and back, but marriage was different than she'd imagined. He'd changed, or maybe she was finally seeing him for the man he really was and she'd been oblivious. "Father's gone to the shop this morning and I'm going to Mr. Navarro's. I'll make you a couple of hotcakes before I leave. Sound good?"

Johnny nodded but didn't bother offering up what he'd be doing today once she left for the grocer. What he did instead was come up behind her, wrap his arms around her waist, and nuzzle her neck. Tilly went weak in the knees, forgetting the Mason jar, building resentments, or even how to make the hotcakes.

****

Wives Are Quite Necessary

"My wife's been away 10 days out of a three-week vacation she is taking," said a Richter street resident, "and, exhilarated as I was when she left at the thought

of freedom, now I'm longing for her return. Every dish in the house is piled up in the sink and there are enough empty milk bottles around the place to run a good-sized dairy for a long time. My sheets haven't been changed, there's an inch of dust on the piano, and the lawn looks as ragged as a plot of marshland. Funny! But a man certainly does get shiftless when he's alone. And, in nothing short of a few days of the single 'blessedness' to make him wish for the 'yoke' again."

****

"Johnny, you here?"

The house was quiet. Not an answer nor even a creak of a floorboard above. He was obviously off doing something on his own and she'd be cleaning the house, once again. Numbers ran through her head of how much money she'd spent and, especially, how little was left.

Snow White Lard...2 lbs for .25
Maxwell House Coffee...1 lb can for .45
Jell-O...4 pkgs for .29
Pure Cane Sugar...25 lbs for 1.49
Gold Medal Flour...45 lbs for $1.95
Scot Tissue Toilet Paper...3 rolls for .25

Tilly pushed her way through the back door, carrying a large box containing all but the much-needed flour and sugar. Mr. Navarro offered to deliver those large bags later in the day, after he closed up the shop. She was grateful for his help.

Because of his generosity, she splurged on a few goodies. Maybe the Maxwell House coffee was two times as much as Eight O'Clock, but each cup was also twice as tasty. An extra dime for the softer Scot instead of Waldorf toilet paper would be well worth the few pennies. Anyhow, she saved by getting lard instead of the pricey new Crisco. All in all, she was feeling a bit like the necessary wife she read about recently. Especially now, with her ever keener eye for grocery shopping.

Mr. Navarro's thick German accent had such a commanding tone, he could talk her into most anything. At least, until the coins were exhausted.

She'd then stopped by the blacksmith shop to visit with her father for a few minutes. He seemed in a better mood until he looked directly at her.

"What the devil happened to your face?"

Tilly's fingers flew to her lower lip, having mostly forgotten how much the cut hurt, except for remembering to purchase a small bottle of Listerine to clean the wound. All the advertisements were now touting how users would no longer offend others with sour halitosis, but she still thought of the yellow liquid as the same old antiseptic her mama always used. "Cut my lip on the milk bottle you half drained."

"That all?" Money scowled but kept other thoughts to himself.

Tilly nodded and ducked out of the shop before they could talk more. He was busy shoeing an old, sway-backed horse he'd admonished a few times and needed to give his undivided attention, even having to growl the horse's name—Rocky—under his breath a couple of times. Tilly knew of only one horse by that name in the area belonging to a woman living north of town. No one had proof but there was definitely talk, gossip, and rumors of why she kept to herself most of the time. The two women were probably pretty close to the same age but Tilly couldn't guess, never having shared a conversation.

Which, they almost did. Both women happened to be in Mr. Navarro's grocery store at the same time, eyeing the same freshly-butchered chickens. But, as hard as Tilly tried catching her eye, they never even nodded a cordial hello.

While Tilly stocked up on staples, the woman filled her box with herbs and spices. There'd been talk around town—especially from a couple of biddies Thad Andrews had no time for but at least told her about— there was a lot of bootleg gin being made outside of the village. Tilly figured she might have to quiz him if he knew anything more about this woman. In particular, was she using herbs and spices for something illicit?

Maybe she was the one supplying hooch to some local drinkers. Johnny also? Tilly wouldn't be surprised to find out someone was doing this right under the sheriff's nose. Deputy Sheriff Calkins seemed more apt to be in town, talking with shop owners, than driving around the countryside. He seemed like a good man but more interested in talk, gossip, and rumors.

With the box half empty and most of the food stashed away, Tilly finally twisted the dial on the radio, hoping to fill the silence. Maybe even listen to the *Aunt Sammy* show. Sure, they were always trying to sell something and they never played enough romantic music, but she'd learned to make meatloaf, hadn't she?

"Meatloaf's one of the easiest dishes to make." A snort came out of Rita Mae's mouth, kind of like a laugh, but then she shrugged her shoulders. "Even if Ma's always saying no one's compares to hers."

Tilly hadn't cared when her friend made fun; at least she was trying and Johnny had loved the recipe she used. Maybe she was getting this wifely job figured out. If she worked hard to make her husband happy—with new meals and tender moments—she could spend the rest of her days doing what she wanted to.

As Tilly was walking home with her box of goodies, she passed by the newspaper office and stopped in to see Mrs. Harbinger, her former teacher at the Coghran school. Years earlier, Tilly had been so begrudging for the walk to the outskirts of town, but now she held a special place in her heart for the woman. Although Tilly didn't feel she and Johnny could spend the fifty cents each week for a paper, occasionally she would pick one up, mostly so she could say hello to her old teacher. They chatted for a few minutes and, as the box became heavier with each word, Tilly paid for the paper and headed home.

The box ended up even a little heavier by five weeks' worth of papers since Mrs. Harbinger wanted to get rid of back issues. Of course, Tilly couldn't refuse.

So now, with a few quiet minutes to steal away from chores, Tilly made a fresh pot of coffee from the newly-purchased beans and sat down to the kitchen table. She piled the newspapers by oldest date on top so she could catch up on all the news chronologically. Always so much gossip to read about and she was excited to have something new to ponder over with Mr. Andrews. And then, lo and behold…

October 31, 1928, Hallowe'en Issue

Thad Andrews played a nice little joke on himself on Wednesday. He came to the village and hitched his horse near the Palmerton block and later had occasion to move the rig across the street. He purchased a new coat and finding a rig hitched where he first left his rig, he absentmindedly put the coat in the carriage. Later he remembered what he had done and went after his coat, but the rig was gone. A little later S.S. Abbott telephoned to Jesse Miller's shop, where the coat was purchased, that upon reaching his home and unloading his purchases from his carriage, he found himself in possession of a new coat.

"Oh, Mr. Andrews." She giggled out loud. "Looks like you played a trick on yourself for Hallowe'en."

"You talkin' to the walls again?"

Tilly jumped up from the kitchen chair, rattling the china cup causing a few drops of coffee to splash onto the tabletop as her knee made contact with the edge.

"Johnny, you scared me," she scolded, realizing his habit of soundlessly appearing in a room jangled her nerves but also left her a bit excited. Felt slightly illicit.

"Came back to see what you bought." He ignored her flustered state. "Need something to eat anyhow."

Since Tilly was standing and knew she wasn't going to get back to the newspapers for a while, she carefully folded the first issue back to its original size and gathered up the entire pile to tuck away in the back room. By the time she returned to the kitchen, Johnny was rooting through the box, pulling out and inspecting each item she'd brought home.

"Looks like you did pretty well with the money I gave ya, doll-face," he finally said.

"I did," she answered, lacking any enthusiasm, absentmindedly fingering her lip. "After this morning, all I could think of was some warm biscuits covered in fresh butter."

"I'll leave you alone then." He headed for the back door.

"Hey, Johnny," Tilly said, making him pause halfway out the door. "You ain't—I mean aren't—doing anything to get us in trouble, are you?"

"Now, doll-face." The smile on his face was more a smirk and Tilly's stomach flipped. "You know me. You've known me all your life. Would I do anything to harm you, us?"

She shook her head side to side but her thoughts muddled like eggs curdling against the whipping of an apple-twig whisk. Something didn't feel right. He seemed different, or maybe she'd changed, but something tainted and swirled around him. His hair had grown a bit shaggy and his gorgeous blue eyes were hooded more often than not by half-closed eyelids. He definitely didn't look her square in the face much anymore, rarely making eye contact. Didn't even notice her swollen lip, even if the Listerine had actually helped the swelling go down.

And, this morning. What had happened? Yes, they were together but his need overpowered her body, leaving her unsettled. Maybe he figured her lower lip was slightly puffed for reasons in bed.

"No, Johnny," she finally replied. "Just don't like being left alone all night."

His answer was letting the screen door slam solidly against the frame, never looking back, while a picture rattled against the wall. It was the final note before silence.

****

"Now we're talking," Johnny mumbled through a mouthful of warm pan bread, a stream of melting butter sneaking out of one corner of his lips.

"They are good," Tilly replied, "aren't they?"

"Thought you'd mentioned biscuits."

"Had more lard than butter so I made these." She was going to stretch their staples as long as possible since who knew when more coins would appear on the kitchen table, or in their bed. "Any luck talking with Mr. Straws about giving you a job?"

Johnny looked down at his plate of pan bread and frowned. He pushed back from the table and stood up.

"Thanks for nothing, woman." He scowled. "Can't a man enjoy a little breakfast without being grilled like a criminal? Didn't I leave enough on the bed for ya?"

Tilly reached out, hoping to grasp his hand but he pulled away. He moved close enough to the table to grab a handful of pan bread, leaving without another word. Well, she'd caused yet another problem—made Johnny mad at her and didn't understand how or why. She craved conversation with him, not petty arguments, but they were falling into a rabbit hole of circling accusations and questions.

He was out the door faster than she could think of a reason for him to stay. She wandered into the front parlor to catch a glimpse of him. Her heart yearned for his lonely figure as he hunched his shoulders to ward off the stiff wind. He was heading west toward town, but then where to? And why? Had he changed so much since their wedding day? That much since her own mother died?

At the time, she was six, he was ten; children thrust into the world of grown-ups. As her mama took her last breath, she and Johnny huddled behind the shed in her backyard, where no one thought to look, him hardly saying a word. He held her hands, not trying to fix anything because nothing could ever be the same. He let her tears flow, drops falling from her cheeks wetting the ground between them, a few marking his pant leg. Eventually, he placed his thumbs on her wet cheeks, so gentle she thought butterflies had landed there. He then wiped away the tears with all the seriousness he could muster, until he surprised her. He'd pulled back his hands, licked each thumb, and winked at her, a sly smirk crossing his features.

"Gonna call you my umbrella girl…you know…the one from the salt box, if you don't watch out." He laughed. "Raining salty tears." He made her giggle. Maybe for an instant both pushed aside their loneliness with a connection forming like a rubber band that could stretch out but always return to this original moment.

As the sun winked one more time before setting in the west that long ago afternoon, they found the words to encourage each other. Him without a father and now her without a mother, but they'd always have each other. But could a bond made so many years earlier hold strong enough while she figured out exactly what was pulling them apart?

The young boy was now her husband whom she loved. To all others, maybe he still wasn't much better than the ruffians wandering through town, stealing beans or peanuts or pickles out of the grocer's barrel. He'd swagger through town, concealing this softer side for fear of unwanted pity. And, maybe, his haughty attitude was doing more harm than good.

But now, he was pushing her away, treating her more like a neighbor down the street.

She couldn't remember the last time he wiped away her tears and broke the tension by licking his thumbs. She moved away from the window, one lone tear landing on her morning dress and her wishing the Johnny she so dearly loved would come back to his umbrella girl.

Chapter 4

December 8, 1928

Tilly believed her life was comprised of vignettes of threes and quickly admitted to being superstitious. *All things thrive in thrice*, her dear mama used to whisper and gaze skyward. Maybe three lovely events would happen, once in a while bad, but most often a little bit of both.

Wasn't she proven right when Rita Mae was named valedictorian of their class the same week her friend found a pile of coins dusted over on the road? The money was nearly invisible but once she'd gathered them up and counted out the total, there was enough to go buy a container of Calumet baking powder for her mother. Then she entered a contest with Calumet and won a pair of the latest and greatest silk hosiery stockings now available at Hamilton's. Rita Mae turned the twelve cents in pennies and nickels into a gift plus a pair of $2.75 stockings, and the whole adventure felt pretty darn nice.

So now, Tilly was counting her blessings in three. A bit of a change had come over Johnny. Their petty arguments were long forgotten, especially once he'd returned late in the afternoon a week ago with a new job and a smile on his face. Put a smile on her face also.

The second was Pa. Maybe Johnny's lighter

attitude had brushed off, but whatever the case, her father actually offered up a compliment or two this past week. Those had always been few and far between.

And lastly, this morning, she was actually at the back door as her favorite milkman came 'round the corner, Brown Molly pulling the laden wagon, snorting streams of misty white air. Freezing temperatures were more common now than not. A small American flag, attached to the buckboard seat, was frozen as stiff as a cardboard postcard, flapping in the breeze instead of gently fluttering as fabric usually moved.

"Top of the mornin' to you, Miss Tilly." Thad laid on thick his normally subtle brogue to greet her, tipping his tam in greeting.

"And to you, Mr....I mean, Thad." Caught in the middle of three men in her life making her happy, her heart felt light as a feather.

"And what delights will you be making with some of this milk ye've ordered?"

"Well, first off, more butter…" She paused. The wool coat he was now wearing reminded her of the newspaper article. "Oh, I see you have a new coat."

Thad smoothed his hands down the dark lapels.

"You're rather fortunate to have such a warm coat since winter has finally arrived." She let her gaze travel over the coat and then offered up a bit of a frown.

"Aye, Miss Tilly." He puffed out his chest a little farther, obviously prideful of the fact someone had noticed.

"I'd heard a coat had been stolen from Mr. Miller's shop." She egged him on and slowly measured out her words for effect. "And seems I heard that particular one looked a lot like what you're wearing."

"You've heard no such thing." He scowled. "This coat was bought with me hard-earned money."

"Or, maybe I heard Mr. Abbott had lost a new coat." She placed a finger on one cheek and looked skyward as if in deep contemplation.

Thad snorted nearly as loud as Brown Molly would with each plodding step pulling the wagon. And then, his laughter echoed from the back porch across the yard.

"Oh, ye had me going there for a second," he said. "Ye've been reading the newspapers agin."

"I have, and how funny to read my favorite milkman played a trick on himself. You should be more careful where you leave your rig."

"Aye, Brown Molly must've also been insulted as the old gal's gotten louder with her snorting whenever I come out any building or house."

"Such a smart horse." Tilly smiled, wrapping her housedress around her body a bit tighter as the morning's brisk air seeped through. She stood a moment longer, watching as Thad climbed back onto the buckboard seat and tipped his tam one more time.

"Walk on." Thad urged Brown Molly on her way with a quick flick of the reins.

She gathered up the carton with the bottles of milk and turned to head indoors. Just then, the back door swung wide open, with Johnny standing at the threshold. Tilly startled and nearly dropped the precious milk.

"Here, let me help." He snarled under his breath. He took the container, turned to move back into the kitchen, not even waiting for Tilly.

Maybe her imagination was running wild, but the

temperature inside felt as cold as the outdoors. Without a word, she began stacking the bottles in the refrigerator, keeping her back to him, waiting for whatever was going to be said.

Her stomach roiled like a bubbling cauldron. She was caught between wanting to be happy with him and her pa and enjoying a few pleasantries with Thad, yet having to worry about breaking Johnny's happy mood as quickly as someone crushing eggshells. Their shaky truce had been broken as he continued to scowl.

"Johnny, what did I do?" A whine never before coming from her mouth left her puzzled. This was not who she was. Yes, she'd shed more than a few tears in her short life but never cowered or felt cowed by someone, anyone, and was now especially surprised Johnny brought this sound out of her.

"Seems to me our milkman likes to linger at our back stoop a bit long."

Tilly's head whirled with retorts but none would help and probably only make matters worse. If she mentioned they were talking about an article in the newspaper, he'd want to know how she got her hands on the paper. If she told him about complimenting Thad on his new coat, would he think of her actions as flirting? If she thought this way, might he also?

Instead, she kept her thoughts sealed away and went about the task of making breakfast. Pa hadn't come downstairs yet, so making enough coffee for the three of them was her first chore. But, by the time she'd stoked the coals and sprinkled a few granules of sugar over the small flames to encourage them to flare higher up, she was too late. Johnny left and now an answer wasn't necessary nor a need to make coffee.

"Yoo-hoo," came Rita Mae's shrill greeting, followed by the slam of the back door. Well, Johnny will definitely stay out of the kitchen now. Rita Mae lived down the road a couple blocks eastward. The two of them had the kind of friendship where neither knocked first before entering each other's kitchens. Usually a quick *yoo-hoo*, then in through the back door was plenty. Even Johnny had finally conceded he couldn't roam around the house in only his long underwear. Just in case.

"Morning. I was about to make some coffee. Do you want some?"

"Real coffee?" Rita Mae plopped down to one of the kitchen chairs.

"Why, yes, thanks to my husband." Tilly pulled another cup and saucer from the sideboard and placed the set in front of her friend.

"Huh?"

"I haven't told you…" She was almost back to her good mood, having some news for her friend.

"Are you sure I want to hear?" Her friend interrupted, never missing a chance to show doubt where Johnny was concerned. Although months had gone by since unkind words were spoken.

Rita Mae had blurted out how Johnny's mother must have the longest apron strings in the whole village, hurting Tilly's feelings more than even she wanted to admit, and their blow-up nearly cost them their friendship. They hadn't spoken for almost a week even after nearly bowling over each other in the corset aisle one afternoon in the dry goods store. They'd nodded as stiff as soldiers at attention but by evening, they were hugging one another. Tilly's front porch was the scene for the reconciliation as they rocked back and forth, swearing they would never fight again. As long as Rita Mae couched her words when Tilly's love for her man came into question.

"Oh, don't be such a grumbler. Johnny got a job with Mr. Straws."

"So, can we go to the movies instead of you always ironing and sewing? The Vaudette is showing *Our Dancing Daughters*. You know, the one with Joan Crawford. She talks just like Mrs. Harbinger. Remember how she'd stand in front of the class telling us to sharpen our *t* in the middle of words and drop the *r* at the ends. All the actresses talk like that now. So, let's go tonight," Rita Mae rattled on.

Tilly pressed the coffee grounds through the water she'd heated, then poured a cupful for each of them, finally sitting down across from her friend.

"Heard there's more talking in this movie than almost any other." Tilly leaned forward as if she were imparting some great secret. Better to concentrate on their conversation now instead of the past. "Read in the newspaper Joan Crawford's voice is smoother than three-minute whipped frosting."

"I want to see the dancing." Rita Mae slowly stirred a little sugar into the steaming coffee.

"I don't think Johnny would want to see the movie," Tilly began. "Let's only you and me go."

"Aw, be*t*ter by me, my noble*r* friend." She accentuated the 't' and nearly dropped the 'r' like their former teacher taught them, while flipping back her hair, similar to a classic Joan Crawford move.

"Rita Mae, I swear you want me all to yourself," Tilly stated, only to get a snort from her friend rivaling

Brown Molly's best. "Johnny's a good man, maybe a little lost right now."

"Not from what I hear," Rita Mae finally said. "Heard tell he's found exactly what he likes doin,' but I'm not talking."

Tilly waited for more from her friend, but nothing was forthcoming. Especially since Johnny quietly appeared at the kitchen door, his arms folded in front of his chest, his face closed tighter than the Mason jar full of coins. Then a smile spread across his face, yet his eyes didn't sparkle in their usual way.

"Any coffee left?" He didn't wait for an answer as he took four steps across the room, grabbed the pressed coffee, and poured some before Tilly could even stand up. "Maybe even some of the precious cream your milkman left you."

Rita Mae raised perfectly arched eyebrows in Tilly's direction and silently mouthed, *trouble?* Usually, they pretty much spilled even the most intimate details of their lives but her friend didn't need to know Johnny might be changing into what had been predicted right along. She slowly shook her head.

"Hey, doll-face, this is actually some good coffee. Wise choice for some of the money you've been hoarding."

Tilly cringed. Did he know, or even care, how crass he sounded?

"Aw, come on, Johnny." She hoped to pacify him by offering up a wide smile. "You know we're in this together. Whatever I can squeeze out of our money, share."

"Yea, sure," he agreed, even if he did seem distracted. "Hey, listen, doll-face. I'm going to be late tonight."

Well, she'd been forewarned for a change. *Late tonight* probably meant she wouldn't see him until at least the next night. Oh well, then a change in plans was in order—no pining away at home alone. Tilly suddenly had the bright idea to dip into the Mason jar for enough money to go with Rita Mae to see *Our Dancing Daughters*. Let him have his fun. She would too, so tired of sitting home alone or, worse yet, listening to her pa rail against her husband.

****

Barely a few hours later, Rita Mae and Tilly settled into two rather stiff chairs smack dab in the middle of the theater, empty seats surrounding them fore and aft, and side to side. Mr. Peek had ushered them down the aisle, shining a beam toward the floor in front of the three of them from a small flashlight. He'd pointed the light at slim cushions which had been added to the seats and backs. "Want to fill the house," he'd said, tapping the leather bill of a well-worn soldier cap he never was without, having served in Europe during the Great War, and headed back up the aisle to assist more movie-goers.

Tilly looked around at others settling in. She was about to comment how empty the theater seemed when the lights flickered off and the screen lit up with the Movietone newsreel. Diamond Head on the Island of Oahu could be seen in the background, with guys and gals, no older than Tilly and Rita Mae, sitting on the beach wearing bathing suits, laughing, nary a care in the world.

"Oh, wouldn't you love to be there?" Tilly whispered, leaning toward Rita Mae. "We're going to be freezing before long."

"Shush," her friend chided. "The movie's 'bout to start."

****

They walked eastward along the deserted road toward Tilly and Johnny's house; she and Rita Mae dissecting the movie.

"Immoral," Rita Mae continued. "Totally wicked, all the lies and deceit to get a man. I'm not sure if I even like Joan Crawford anymore."

"Oh, it wasn't so bad," Tilly replied. "She obviously loved the guy. Don't we all do whatever we can when love is involved?"

"So you believe love can make us follow the wrong path?"

"Yes, well, no. Oh I mean…I know you're thinking of how Johnny treats me."

"You let him leave without an explanation…" Rita Mae began, picking up the tenuous thread of their earlier conversation.

"Wait a minute. Are you saying he should tell me where he's gonna be every second of the day?"

"Well, maybe not when you repeat my words, but don't you think he owes you at least some reason why he's leaving and doesn't say when he'll be back?"

"Rita Mae, you're my friend. You won't ever forget, right? We talk about almost everything but I'm not sure talking about Johnny like he's a bad man is right. He's not, things just aren't…oh, see? There, I'm saying too much."

"Let's talk about something else." Rita Mae wound her arm through Tilly's, pulling her close. "You know you can tell me anything, anytime. Maybe someday, but not right now."

The house came into view and the only light visible was coming from Money's room on the third floor. A soft, yellow glow faded into thin air. Johnny obviously wasn't home unless he was sitting in the dark, which wasn't likely.

"Want me to come in with you?"

"Thanks, I'll be fine." Tilly untangled her arm from her friend's. "See you tomorrow?"

"I'll be by in the afternoon to help you with the ironing," Rita Mae answered, as she headed across the road toward home. "And maybe to start making those bags?"

"Are you sure your ma won't need your help instead?" Tilly called out.

Rita Mae didn't even bother to turn around, waving a hand in farewell, leaving Tilly alone and a little hesitant to head into the dark house. She was beginning to feel like she was holding her breath too long under water, waiting for Johnny to come back home, safe from whatever he was getting involved in. So many unspoken words were growing between them like a hedge of holly, taller day by day, prickly and unbending.

Chapter 5

December 15, 1928

Days bled into weeks. Especially with a strange and uncomfortable truce hovering in the air between her and Johnny.

Tilly reached down to the floor, her palm landing on the cold wood. Her fingers finally found the fireplace poker she'd taken to hiding next to her side of their bed. It had become her routine after enough nights without Johnny by her side. She felt a little less vulnerable. The metal stung her hand like a frozen flag pole, nearly causing her to drop the poker. Oh, the clatter would have awakened even the sleeping mice usually scurrying in the attic.

Johnny didn't know—or hadn't paid attention—of her need to keep something at close range for ease of mind. But now, she wasn't thinking of him, even with his rhythmic breathing in and out reaching her ears.

Something, or someone, was downstairs and either she was going to have to wake her husband or investigate the noise alone. Sam Gillam didn't normally deliver coal to their chute before light and Mr. Andrews wouldn't show up with Brown Molly so quiet. Yet a loud clunk had most definitely found its way into her dreams and, then, a scraping sound repeated over and over again. She was wide awake now.

Tilly finally opted to slip noiselessly as possible out from under the covers, barely moving the mattress even if the springs did groan a bit. Johnny was leaving an invisible cloud of alcohol vapors as he snored in and out, in…out, in…out. He pretty much fell into their bed hours after she'd given up lying in bed awake, waiting. He rolled to his side, settled deeper into the covers, and then released a stream of putrid gas.

She barely held back a giggle. She was so nervous of what might be downstairs yet here she was listening to her husband unwittingly relieving himself like a slow-dying balloon. At least she felt ever-so-slightly safer with him lying there, even if he was peacefully oblivious.

Another scraping sound reached her ears as she slowly pulled open their bedroom door. Embers from the living room fireplace cast a slightly orange glow up the staircase, shadows dancing as the drafty house made small flames repeatedly flare up and die down.

"Pa?" She'd about decided he must be downstairs looking for something to settle his constantly upset stomach. Money was certainly drinking more milk than before and she had to up their order a couple of times in the last week.

But, only silence.

Tilly gripped the poker a bit tighter and edged toward the top step. At the same time, she looked up the narrow staircase to his bedroom door on the third floor. The darkness and quiet made her legs go wobbly.

Now she was scaring herself, letting her mind play tricks. As kids, she and Rita Mae would tell each other fantastical ghost stories of how souls not yet welcomed into Heaven had to stay in the third floor attic, floating around waiting for their names to be called. To this day, she imagined meeting up with a wispy being when delivering her father's laundry to his room. She wasn't positive, but there was always some unexplained clunk, chatter, or scratching.

But the sound came from downstairs, at least this time. She had two choices. Concentrate on what's below or go back to bed and snuggle up against Johnny's back. A sigh escaped her lips. Her husband wasn't going to wake up, and she might as well take care of business, clearly like she'd been doing more and more of late.

"Pa?" she called out a bit louder, descending the staircase step by step, cold treads stinging the balls of her feet. The gas lamp by the stove cast a white apron of light into the hallway. Her heart slowed a beat or two. Someone breaking in wouldn't announce his presence, and what ghost ever needed light?

"Till?" She easily recognized her father's raspy voice. A sigh of relief whistled through her lips. He was sitting at the kitchen table, his back facing Tilly as she crept into the room, still not wanting to make any extra noise. She hoped Johnny was still asleep. "Sorry if I woke you."

"Have to admit, you scared me a bit. You doin' okay?"

"Dang stomach," he said. "Woke up when Johnny came home and couldn't get back to sleep."

So, nobody breaking in or delivering anything, but now she'd come downstairs to get an earful from her pa. The warmth of her bed and Johnny's back beckoned Tilly. She nearly turned toward the stairs to head back to bed but then Money gave her an apologetic smile and a quick wink.

"Sit down, please?" he asked quietly, taking another sip of milk. "Let's talk while I finish this."

"Only if you aren't going to rail against Johnny."

"Can't promise," Money began, "but I would like to tell you something."

Tilly had caught the chilly air of her and Rita Mae's imaginary ghost moving through the kitchen, so she walked over to the stove, stoked the coal in the lower bin and waited for a couple sparks to ignite. Mixing up the egg-shaped bits added some oxygen in between the pieces and, before too long, the coal caught fire. A circle of warmth fanned out toward the table.

She pulled out a plate from the sideboard and found a couple biscuits from yesterday's breakfast, placing them in front of her father. He smiled at her while she settled in across the table from him.

"Pa, I'm always defending my husband. Why?"

"I'm not here to tell you I'm a little disappointed in him. Something you already know. But, I'm thinking this dang stomach of mine is telling me to warn you. And Johnny."

"Warning? You're not making much sense."

"Johnny's getting in too deep in something that isn't going to end well."

"Pa, I know he runs with a troubling crowd but he finally got a job—a real job—with Mr. Straws and he's making honest money." Tilly noted that annoying whine creeping back into her voice.

Money stared down at the half-empty glass of milk and slowly shook his head. Tilly fidgeted with the scar on her lip, waiting for some substance to his accusations.

"This whole Prohibition thing isn't helping anyone," Money continued. "Ever since your ma died, I've merely wanted to live out my life without fuss. I ain't never wanted to cause a problem for anyone, but Johnny is pushing too hard and making the wrong people unhappy."

Tilly hadn't ever heard so many words come out of her father's mouth, ever. So far, all he'd said was common knowledge, if she were to believe Rita Mae.

"When you and he got married, he told me, no matter what, he'd take care of you," Money said. "I believed him."

"And, he has," she argued, even though a picture was forming of what was becoming of their marriage. He was finding ways to make more money while she was hiding away as many pennies, nickels, and dimes as she could for when their good fortune came to a screeching halt.

"He's doing something many see as just plain wrong."

Tilly pulled her robe tighter around her chest, a chill going so deep it would take the summer heat to bring relief. She broke off half of one biscuit and spread a little of the cream butter across the top. Her mouth had gone dry as his word sank in, causing crumbs to stick when she tried to swallow. Money continued to sip on the milk like anything else would do more harm than good. The acrid black smell of coal hovered in the kitchen as light began filtering through the windows, the sun low in the south but still rising on another day. Normally, this time of day comforted her, but Money was trying without success to give warnings. She wasn't cooperating.

"Until you want to tell me outright what is going on, leave me be," Tilly countered, coughing once to dislodge some dry biscuit.

"Mark my words," Money said, not letting her off easy. "Bad days are coming and I might not be able to stop what is already in motion. Tell your husband to forget everythin' else and work hard for Mr. Straws. There'll be enough to take care of you and him."

Finished, her pa stood, drained the last few drops of milk in the glass he gripped as if his hands were stuck to the same cold flagpole she'd thought of earlier, then turned and headed back to his room on the third floor. The rhythmic scrape of his cane and each thump of his foot on each stair tread finally faded and the click of his bedroom door closing was the last sound to end their little meeting.

Tilly was left with the empty glass, one and a half biscuits drying out on the plate, and a stove going cold until she went to the basement to retrieve more coal. Instead, she laid her forehead on the table and nudged her toes closer to the poker sidled up to the chair legs. She now viewed the metal rod more as armament against a shadowy enemy than a tool to spark a flame.

Chapter 6

Later That Same Morning

Two weeks to Christmas and Tilly didn't care what season they'd entered into, who needed her, or what she was supposed to do to be the perfect wife, or the necessary wife with the husband *longing for her return*, or whatever she'd read in the newspaper. She was right here but would never be perfect what with all the anger and resentment floating about the house, and unasked questions resulting in no answers. Quite honestly, thoughts endlessly swirled in her brain how to make right what she hardly understood to be wrong.

Her pa came downstairs and acted as if nothing unusual had happened. He acted like his cryptic warnings never happened. Was she supposed to pretend this day toward the end of 1928 was like any other in the life of her, Johnny, and Money?

Her husband finally made an appearance around nine in the morning—long after Money left—rubbing sleep from his eyes. Tilly suspected he'd been awake for a bit, waiting to come downstairs after the coast was clear. He'd strolled into the kitchen like last night was nothing unusual. Late, no explanation, smelling like one of the long-ago shut-down saloons, and snoring as if he hadn't a care in this whole wide world. He then up and left without a word of where he was off to or when he'd return.

Thad Andrews dropped off her order of milk and butter sometime between her giving up on worrying to refilling the stove with fresh coal. The milk stayed cold on the back porch but her mind had not been stimulated by any new conversation.

Men—they all had their own needs and wants but could care less what she thought, cherished, or craved. She was starting to feel like a ship left in the middle of some ocean, sails ripped and useless, waiting for some giant whale to take pity on her and maybe help her back to shore.

Tilly grabbed her coat and hat, buttoned and pinned in place what was needed, and headed out the back door, no thought of direction or length.

What happened was she ended up at the cemetery, ten blocks to the east, staring hard and fast at her mother's crude headstone, and absolutely chilled to the bone. But nothing registered, except for the chunk of discolored marble. Her mother's marker was at least half the size of most others in the cemetery, her pa skirting any additional expense. So, at no more than a couple feet tall, the stone was scarcely visible behind weeds swallowing it up like a hungry monster, etched with *Theodory Monroe, beloved wife of Silas Monroe and a Gift of God, b. 1.6.1889, d. by flu 1918.*

How sad this represented the whole of someone's life when there'd been so much more.

Nothing about how her ma held Tilly close all those years of growing up only to be locked away during the flu epidemic, no one to hold her dear mother in the last few hours and minutes of a shortened life. *Gift of God*—how her pa had whispered the Polish translation for Theodory over and over as his wife lay dying. But, why, oh why, had God taken back his gift, stealing her mother away when she was so dearly needed?

Tears pushed hard against her eyes and she snuffled loud enough to awaken the dead. Sadness weighed her shoulders like an oxen's yoke.

But, like nearly every other woman in this small village making her way as a young bride, how was her life any better or worse? So many others had perished during the epidemic, fracturing whole families. Rita Mae lost a brother, leaving her folks bitter. Mrs. Osborne changed from a loving woman, ready to help anyone, to a nasty gossip who'd probably even started some of the most destructive rumors. Did these actions make the woman feel better by looking down on others, so her own pain was pushed aside?

Tilly longingly looked a few more minutes at the headstone, wishing time spent with her own mother hadn't been cut short. The pain was almost too much to bear, contemplating the trek back to the house where she was out-numbered by men who treated her more as a servant than a member of their small family. She reckoned men would always be more of a mystery than even one-side conversations with her mama could glean.

As it was, her lot in life was to stay on an even keel and help her pa and Johnny. Calmed by the belief her mother kept watch from those Heavenly clouds, Tilly made her peace. She resolved to be the bright spot in the house and wait to see if Money's warnings amounted to anything, choosing not to upset Johnny with unsubstantiated rumors and gossip.

Chapter 7

Christmas Eve, December 24, 1928

Inspiration struck like a blue bolt of lightning from amassing clouds. Tilly was going to upset the stagnant current in this house and do something unexpected and maybe a bit costly. Otherwise, why was she secretly saving money in the Mason jar tucked in the back room, labeled *beans*, and thus ignored?

Why not have Mr. Jensen take a portrait of her and Johnny, frame the picture for their living room, and years later look back at how young and in love they were? Tilly ran up the stairs, skipping a step or two, once tripping as her housedress caught between her legs, but ultimately making it to their bedroom door. She burst into the room but stopped short by what was before her. Johnny was sprawled across their bed as if it was made solely for him. After a moment of enjoying the sight of him so innocent and without worry, she soundlessly knelt down next to the side of the bed closest to his head. She placed her hand on his cheek to wake him.

"Hmmm?"

"Johnny, let's do something special," she blurted out before he even cracked open an eyelid.

"Hmmm?"

"Get dressed. Let's go to Jensen's and have our

portrait taken."

"Huh?"

"'Tis nothing to bother about." Tilly tugged at his nightshirt sleeve as he finally opened both eyes and gazed at her with a questioning rise of his brows. She kissed him on one cheek and pulled back some of the covers. "Come on."

For once, unexpectedly, he acquiesced. No comeback of this being a waste of money or time, or even questioning such frivolity. He pulled her close and they lay in bed, trading warmth from one to the other until she couldn't wait any longer. She wrestled away from his arms, rose from the bed, and flung open the armoire doors so their clothes were on display. Both looked at their slim choices of finer wear and she fell back into bed.

"Looks like I have a couple choices and you're wearing your wedding jacket." She giggled as Johnny wrapped his arms around her shoulders. She held still as he kissed the top of her head.

Finally, the time arrived to get dressed. Tilly slipped on a slimming off-white shift beautifully accentuating her waist and Johnny did, in fact, put on his wool wedding jacket. She even grabbed a simple bell-shaped hat, with a broach pinned at one side, wondering if she could incorporate her mother's favorite going-to-church headwear in one of the pictures.

They looked so very smart, as if they were heading to repeat their own wedding. Oh, what a lovely day the ceremony had been late in Indian summer, when the air hung heavy and the nights cooled off. Her nerves sparked like a thunderstorm about to burst from polar opposite energies. But, how she could be both happy and so sad, at the same time, had puzzled her. This was her wedding day and she was about to cleave to the man who let her glimpse at his failings as well as his passions, to be his partner. Yet her beloved mother could not be there as a witness to their moment of happiness.

As Mr. Abbott, the Justice of the Peace, solemnly intoned the words to commit her and Johnny to each other…to have and to hold…'til death do they part…she'd looked to the heavens and had hoped for a message from her ma. None had come except for a cool breeze lifting the few tendrils having worked loose from her braided hair, caressing her face as soft as the touch of butterfly wings. She imagined her mother's fingers blessing their union. Someday, she might tell Johnny; he would understand.

Here they were, months later and dressed in their best going-to-church clothes with the December air brisk, a dusting of snow to cover the grass. The cold hardly bothered her what with her inner boiler working on high. Even a rosy glow of her cheeks heightened her self-confidence after taking a quick peek in the front hall mirror upon leaving the house.

They marched down the main street of Cedartown as if they were grand marshals of some parade, pausing momentarily to witness their reflections in the large windows set on each side of a large door before heading into the storefront housing Jensen's photography specialty. Anyone paying attention might have wondered what was going on. If anyone had bothered to ask, she'd have replied they were merely recording a moment in their lives.

"Well, hello you two," Mr. P.J. Jensen greeted them with his usual formality, bowing slightly at the waist, then waited for them to continue.

A rotten-egg odor hovered like an umbrella above them, no doubt from all the flashbulbs popping and burning with each picture taken earlier.

"Do you have time to take our photograph?" Tilly asked, immediately intimidated by all of the equipment in the studio wondering who the devil lit a fire under her this morning. Were they worthy of being photographed? But she wasn't given time enough to back out.

"Ah, yes," Mr. Jensen spoke. "Here, here, let us not delay. I've always wanted to take pictures of the two of you together. Oh my, such a beautiful couple…" He sputtered, he started and stopped, then hurriedly gathered equipment together as if they might disappear faster than a white-tailed deer bounding into the woods.

Mr. Jensen ushered the two of them into a back room separated by a long, dark curtain. A large window stood at the opposite side, a couple of chairs placed in front of the draped fabric, and a myriad of stands and braces available for cameras. The photographer moved with surprising quickness as he attached a large box to one of the stands and encouraged them to sit down, stand, do whatever, because he was planning on taking numerous shots.

"Mr. Miner, stand behind your wife," the photographer said, directing traffic like the local deputy sheriff. He stepped behind one of the cameras and placed a big cape of cloth over his head. His voice was muffled as he spoke, "Tilt your head up, now hold still. I'll tell you when you can move."

A flash went off while Mr. Jensen continued to hold up one hand. Johnny and Tilly remained as still as possible, freezing their expressions as best they could.

"All right, relax." He stepped back from the camera. "I'd like to take more. Here, here, come take a little walk around the studio to see other photographs I've taken. Then, maybe you can hold still for more?"

They both nodded.

After a short break, they repeated the process. Once again, the flash went off and the two of them remained as unyielding as statues until the photographer released them.

"Stunning, fantastic." He gushed. He flittered around them, tucking in a corner of fabric, fluffing Tilly's dress at the shoulders, gently lifting her chin, brushing an invisible piece of lint from Johnny's lapel. "You two should be in the movies; oh my, why have you never, ever, come into my studio before?"

Johnny started to answer but Mr. Jensen wouldn't be interrupted. "Please, please, let me take more pictures of you. Now, now, Mrs. Miner, stand behind your husband, put your hand on his shoulder. There, there, Mr. Miner, look a little bored or maybe more interested in something off into the distance. Perfect, perfect."

Tilly sneaked a look at her husband and they both smiled, obviously wondering if they'd gotten in over their heads when, in fact, all they wanted was to have their portrait taken. Each time, the bright light momentarily blinded them, white spots obscuring their vision.

"Mr. Jensen," she began, "we want a gift for my pa and maybe even Johnny's ma."

Mr. Jensen shook a hand at them—shushing them—and continued slipping trays in and out of his camera. More pictures, more poses. By the time the hour had exhausted itself, she hoped he'd captured their best angles and not unsightly hollows or imperfections.

"When will the pictures be ready?" The day had turned into an unexpected and delightful adventure. Maybe this was how Maude Adams or Joan Crawford, or all the lucky actresses, felt while being fawned over. A mixture of egotism, anticipation, and fear.

But for Tilly, all this attention and glamor was short-lived. She would soon be back stoking the fire, baking biscuits and taking care of laundry, and her best dress would go back to hanging in their armoire. Her shoulders slumped ever-so-slightly inside her woolen coat.

"Soon, soon, my lovely dear," was all Mr. Jensen would say.

****

"Having our pictures taken was wonderful this afternoon, don't you think, too?" Tilly settled in next to Johnny on the loveseat with their backs to the front window in the front parlor. She tucked her legs under her dress and leaned farther into him, feeling his answering nod. "I think we should have our pictures taken every five years." She sighed. "Don't you?"

"Wasn't too sure at first but, you know, doll-face, I'm curious how we'll look when we get those portraits. That's what he called them, right?" Johnny ran a finger down her cheek. "Promise me, you won't turn into one of those movie stars you're always talking about."

"Do you think they'll turn out looking like us? Good, I mean."

"More than good. How could they not, you and me?" He paused and settled in lower so she could lay her head on his shoulder. "Don't know I've ever had my picture taken."

"I think there are some pictures of me somewhere when I was a baby," she replied, "but I'm not sure what happened to them."

"My ma probably wished she never had me so why have any evidence?"

"Oh, Johnny, I don't believe you."

"Why not?"

"Whether or not you wonder, I'm glad she had you." She squeezed his arm. "I can't imagine life without you."

"Well, no need to worry. Not planning on leaving my umbrella girl for a long time."

He hadn't called her his "umbrella girl" in so long; she scarcely dared to breathe, letting her heart flutter in love. They remained close for a few minutes, both quiet and lost in thought, until the scrape of Money's cane broke the quiet. He came into the room, raising his gaze up from the floor to shoot a grimace across the parlor.

Johnny readjusted himself slightly away from Tilly, pushing her slightly to sit up straight instead of falling farther into him. She'd have loved to stay nestled close but their moment together had ended. Even though embers in the fireplace still glowed, a chill snaked through the room faster than an icy draught. Money's cane scraped along the wood floor, the only sound until he'd settled into a chair close to the hearth.

"Cold tonight," was all her pa said, picking up the poker so he could disturb the embers. The very same poker Tilly would grab later in the evening to hide by her side of the bed. Money pitched a chunk of wood on top of the fire causing flames to scatter upward like a fireworks display.

The silence, other than a few snaps and crackles from the fireplace, was driving Tilly crazy. It was Christmas Eve, after all. Had the tentative truce been broken and no one bothered to inform her?

"Who would like some egg milk punch?"

There was milk in the refrigerator, a couple of eggs to thicken up the mixture, as well as the sugar and some cinnamon sticks Mr. Navarro had talked her into purchasing a month or so ago. Maybe a few tongues would loosen up and there'd be a bit of laughter. She didn't wait for an answer from either of them, but instead, jumped up and headed toward the kitchen.

Knowing Johnny, he'd probably want a little something stronger poured in with his serving, but tonight she was setting the tone. Of course, nothing stronger than milk resided in this house, plus she was getting tired of the sour rye mash odor clinging to him. Tonight, egg milk punch was being served. She also had the small gift she'd labored over for months and was finally ready to present to him.

This way, too, she'd leave her two men in a room alone to either talk or ignore each other. It was their choice. She wasn't going to let their bitter relationship affect her Christmas Eve, especially after having so much fun with the picture-taking this morning. Mr. Jensen had finally assured her and Johnny the photographs would be ready in a couple of weeks and she was already counting down the days.

Once in the kitchen, Tilly went to work preparing the mixture while hoping to hear some sounds from the parlor. A disquieting pall had settled over the house. *Merry Christmas to me*, came the unbidden thought of how happy this holiday season should have been with them not even married six months, yet already finding obstacles nearly too lofty to hurdle.

She poured the egg and milk mixture into three cups and sprinkled some additional cinnamon and sugar on top of each, placed them on a small tray where she'd already arranged some shortbread cookies, and headed back toward the parlor.

"—and, you know damn well what I do is none of your concern." Johnny's voice assailed Tilly's ears before she was halfway out of the kitchen. She paused.

"I've already warned my daughter."

"You have no right interfering, old man." Johnny's voice had a disturbing harshness as he measured out each word as if her pa couldn't understand plain English. "If I had my way, we'd have kicked you out when you gave us this house as a wedding gift. Doesn't mean I can't do—"

"Hold on." Money growled. "Stop before you say something you're goin' to regret."

"I'll say and do whatever I damn well please." From the sound of it, Johnny had stood up and walked toward the kitchen, as these last words might as well have been yelled right into Tilly's ears. His tone alarmed her. This was not the sweet man who moments earlier caressed her cheek. "Consider this a warning— you tell your old cronies to stay out of my business."

Before Tilly could step back into the kitchen, Johnny came barreling out of the parlor, nearly upsetting the tray she was carrying. He skirted around her, took long enough to grab his overcoat and hat hanging on a hook by the back door, and left without another word.

Merry Christmas to me.

Johnny wouldn't be back for a long time, at least until he figured Money had retired for the night. Maybe he wouldn't be back until sometime tomorrow. If she were a drinking woman, she'd probably have spiced up one of those cups of egg milk punch but, instead, she continued into the parlor, only to find the room unoccupied. Money had either left through the front door or headed up to the third floor while Johnny was still yelling.

Tilly returned to the kitchen, set the tray on the table, and promptly drained two of the three cups of punch and jammed a couple cookies into her mouth. The house was so quiet—one minute soft murmurs between them, to the next full of yelling maybe even the neighbors heard, then her own soft sighs in and out.

She tucked the small gift she'd planned on giving to Johnny back behind the Mason jar in the back room. A few more sips of the punch to finish off the third cup of milk. Then, once she'd extinguished the lamp over the sink, she made a detour into the parlor to check the fire and grab the poker. The sour mood had returned, with emotions on fire between Money and Johnny so, for now, there was nothing else to do except retire.

Maybe, the morning sun would bring change. At least, she could hope.

Chapter 8

Christmas Morning, 1928

Tilly rolled to the center of the bed and promptly bumped up against Johnny's back. Well, what a nice surprise, especially after last night's fireworks. Johnny let out a loud snore and rolled toward her.

"Merry Christmas, doll-face," he whispered, slowly opening his eyes, giving her a lazy, half-asleep gaze causing her toes to curl forward.

"Merry Christmas, Johnny."

They continued to lie facing each other, otherwise wordless, both hesitant in their wait for the other to make a move. Johnny finally leaned in and kissed Tilly slowly at first then with more urgency. Her body instantly responded. *If only we could always be like this.*

Unwise to think, just let these moments happen. Tilly quickly pushed any thoughts aside as he started exploring, his fingers encircling each side of her slim waist. With slow deliberation, he then began undoing the dozen or so small buttons up the front of her nightgown. His hands pushed the nightgown open and he took each breast in hand and slowly, rhythmically pushed and pulled. He gently fingered each areola until her nipples were as hard as fresh spring peas while her stomach clenched in a most pleasant way.

Don't stop.
Don't think...

He urged her back to the cool sheet so he could slide atop her, both now looking deep into the other's eyes. Maybe Johnny could see to the depths of her soul and how strong their love held her captive. She'd remain loyal no matter what he was involved in, and she'd accept his erratic behavior. Her feelings would never change. They moved as one, animal instinct equally taking over as they strove for the most basic of human needs.

A few minutes later, he grunted, then rolled off of Tilly. She remained still, allowing her simmering insides to slow to soft waves undulating from her breasts down to tingling toes. Hardly a few more seconds and Johnny's breathing slowed to a steady rhythm. Tilly stretched the luxurious lengths of an awakening feline, then slowly realigned her nightgown back down across her ankles and secured about half of the buttons in place before quietly slipping from the bed. She'd let him sleep a bit longer—having absolutely no idea when he'd crawled into bed last night—and then maybe they could have some breakfast together.

This was the man she loved, as she gazed down at his face. The few creases he had around his eyes and on his forehead smoothed out while his eyelids fluttered a bit. He must be dreaming of something pleasant as his lips curled slightly upward.

Was it only last spring, as buds were barely speckling all of the tree branches while crocuses and daffodils were poking their heads through the brown dirt, they'd gone on what she thought was an impromptu picnic? She'd hurriedly packed cheese sandwiches, grabbed the two last apples left in the root cellar, and made tea sweetened with sugar. Upon her opening the front door, she found him laden with a blanket over one arm and a shy smile creasing his face, a few lines visible on his forehead as if he was burdened with some worry. The air had been crisp, the sky a robin's egg blue, and the sun warmed their winter-white faces as they'd eaten their lunch in the park behind the lumberyard. He'd been a bit quiet and she soon discovered why. When he finally took her hand in his and asked her to be his wife, and she squealed and nodded so there'd be no mistaking her answer, Johnny let out a long sigh like he'd been holding his breath under water.

Of course, they talked of a million wishes for once they were married. He eventually stretched out on the blanket as she rattled on. At some point, sleep overtook him, even with the sun moving over his face. A sleep so deep he'd let out a couple loud snorts. She'd gazed down at him then as now, the same blissful feeling engulfing her. Oh, how she loved this man lying asleep in their bed and yearned he'd allow the world a glimpse of his softer side. But he wouldn't. He might let her glimpse the loving, caring man but, to outsiders, he was tough, someone not to be taken lightly.

She leaned over him and slowly ran a finger along his stubbly cheek. Her foot slipped, causing her big toe to nudge the poker on the floor, bringing her all too quickly back to the here and now. She was beginning to believe the ever-present poker had taken on a living, breathing life; mysteriously rolling underfoot as a reminder to be picked up and returned to its rightful spot.

"I love you, Johnny," she whispered as she exited the bedroom.

The house was cold, the fire in the parlor having gone out, yet the heat their bodies had generated still warmed her. She descended the steps and found only a few embers glowing in the fireplace. Tilly gingerly poked those coals with her weapon of choice then piled three logs on the grate. The way they were going through wood and egg-rock coal, she'd either have to bother Johnny or haul some wood in from the shed herself. A soft crackling came from the fireplace once the wood caught on.

After she was satisfied the parlor would be heating up soon, Tilly headed to the kitchen. The hour was too early for the morning sun to do its magic warming up the back of the house, but putting a match to the stove would soon help. Her thoughts were jumbling with all she wanted to do for Johnny, their morning together so far giving her a burst of well-being and energy.

And then…she didn't have even one foot firmly planted across the threshold when she spotted lumps resting in the center of the table, blackening liquid oozing from whatever lay there, a puddle long-ago formed, then eventually seeping through a crack in the tabletop, pooling on the floor.

A single ray of morning sun spotlighted the mess. Her eyes focused on what looked like soup cooling into a gelatin glob, gray lumps and slimy cords curling like snakes, and oozing marbles; her brain couldn't process what she was seeing. A sour odor assailed her senses and sharp pinpricks of light pierced her peripheral vision as her breathing came in short, shallow gasps.

She was becoming light-headed as her mind realized what had been displayed like a centerpiece on their breakfast table.

Tilly covered her mouth with one hand while grabbing for the doorframe with the other. She was either going to throw up or scream; either one a violent reaction in sheer contrast to moments earlier lying next to her husband.

"J-O-H-N-N-Y, come, come quick," Tilly finally screamed. "Oh, God." She moaned, crumpling to the floor.

****

"She'll be okay," Money said. "Leave her be."

Tilly didn't move a muscle, merely cracking open one eyelid wide enough to see her Pa standing in the doorway of the parlor. She was now stretched out on the horsehair couch, her head braced up by one of the lovely brocade pillows her mother made years earlier. Quite seriously, she was more concerned about throwing up all over the pillow than even thinking about what had been smeared all over the kitchen table. Although, at the thought of blood slithering through cracks like slimy snakes or puddling where plates were usually placed, her stomach somersaulted like an acrobat spinning through the air and she swallowed down some bile.

"Tell me," she could hear Johnny demand. "Tell me who did this. You make this happen?"

There was a long pause.

"I've already told you, I can't stop what's put into motion." Money dodged Johnny's question. "You're gettin' in too deep."

"Money, ya gotta tell me who's behind this,"

Johnny said. "No one comes into this house and leaves a pig snout, intestines, and eyeballs bleedin' all over the table without me doin' something 'bout it."

All things thrive in thrice…ugly times three on their kitchen table.

The floor creaked as someone moved closer to Tilly. She closed her eyes, not wanting to let those two know she'd regained consciousness. A warm hand caressed her forehead. How often had she watched her own mother butcher a chicken or turkey and nary flinch at what needed to be done to feed their family but, oh, how she so badly wanted to erase the image of those parts of a pig obscuring the top of the kitchen table. Thank God, those guts weren't desecrating the gift she'd so lovingly created, wrapped, and finally hidden behind the Mason jar last night. The gift would have been ruined.

"I don't have to tell you anything." Money's voice still came from across the room. So, obviously, her concerned husband was the one checking to make sure she was still breathing. Or, at least, allowing himself to show concern in front of his father-in-law. "But, consider this a warning. Take it serious."

Consider this a warning. She'd heard those same words not too long ago and now they whirled through her thoughts around and around again.

Tilly groaned ever so slightly causing all conversation to cease. She slowly reached shaky fingers to her forehead to find Johnny's hand still there. She opened her eyes and looked upward. Barely an hour earlier his gaze had burned into her very being as they'd coupled in their wedding bed. But now, she stared up at a man nearly foreign by his actions. Someone who may possibly have caused such ugliness to enter their home.

"Johnny?" Tilly's voice cracked.

"Doll-face…hey, you're still with us." He gave a seldom-heard nervous laugh. "Thought you'd given up the ghost and we'd have to take care of ourselves this Christmas day."

Johnny was on edge. In all these years, ever since she first recognized there was this boy always hanging around her, making sure she was safe, happy, whatever; she'd never, ever, heard him so panicky. This was not her usual Johnny, not her husband. Maybe there was more going on than she'd been willing to admit, even with Rita Mae asking questions and early-morning conversations.

"Would you mind terribly if I go back to our bedroom for a while?" Tilly needed some time alone to think about all she'd heard and to figure out her pa's warnings, her husband's nervousness, her having to defend him, and, in particular, what to do next.

She sat up and Johnny started to help, but she waved him off. On wobbly legs, Tilly made her way up the steps and then slid under the covers still smelling of their morning love-making. She turned her face into the pillow and waited for tears to soak the fabric.

Merry Christmas to me.

Chapter 9

The Next Day

"You're awfully quiet this morning," Rita Mae said, after they each took a sip of tea. They were standing next to the stove, working as an assembly line of ironing and folding handkerchiefs and doilies.

From all appearances, the kitchen looked as normal as ever. The mess had been cleaned up but definitely not by Tilly. She wanted nothing to do with what had been brought down on them, staying in the bedroom until she couldn't forestall a trip to the outhouse any longer. By the time she came back into the house, by way of the front door so as to avoid the kitchen, Johnny was waiting. Avoiding him would have worked so much better, but he'd been insistent. Christmas dinner was going to happen.

The meal was a solemn combination of focused chewing and lack of conversation for the three of them. She prepared clam chowder a couple days earlier for their Christmas Eve dinner. The meal which never happened that night. They ate at the kitchen table, a cloth thankfully covering the stained wood. She kept her eyes closed most of the time, yet imagining burgundy soup in place of clams in white sauce.

No centerpiece nor anything festive for the birth of Christ decorated the room. It was like the spirit of the holiday had dripped through the cracks of the table riding on the crest of red blood.

Tilly recalled the words of the famed actress, Maude Adams, which wandered through disjointed thoughts as the day wore on. We were only on this earth for a short time and one's happiness depended on living a life devoid of complaints, anger, and spite, while accepting our station here on earth.

Sad as her situation seemed, Tilly had come to such a conclusion—to settle into the lot in life she'd been dealt—while lying in bed Christmas Day. Hey, if someone famous could be happy with the dealt hand, why not her? She and Rita Mae had gone to see Miss Adams in a silent movie being replayed because Mr. Peek hated—to use the term lightly—the latest movie sensation, *Plastered in Paris*, a story of two Army buddies and their adventures after the Great War.

"Those hotshots in Hollywoodland making such a movie—shenanigans of those two men in my Army—just awful," he'd muttered to Tilly as he led them, once again, to the center of the theater for optimum viewing. The beam from the flashlight bobbed up and down as if in agreement. "How's my Johnny-boy these days? Haven't seen him in a dog's age."

"Doing fine. Just got a job with Mr. Straws. I'll tell him you asked on him."

"Always liked that boy." Mr. Peek tipped his hat in her direction. "I'll never forget his help after the fire in the projection room. He spent more time helping me clean up than I could ever pay him and we were back in business lickety-split. Well, you ladies enjoy the show."

Tilly looked over at her friend hoping these nice words had echoed through the entire theater.

Compliments were few and far between these days, and she was going to bask in the glow while waiting for the movie to start.

And, as far as she was concerned, thank goodness Mr. Peek never received the reel. Luck was on their side all 'round. Romantic shows were the *cat's meow*. And, especially, Maude Adams. She was so gorgeous and had such a presence on the big screen, they'd sit and stare, dreaming of how they might imitate such a lifestyle. Following movie stars and watching films became her great diversion from a life she was barely coping with.

"Wouldn't you simply love to be a movie star?" Tilly said, surprised the words actually escaped her lips even after having thought them so many times.

Rita Mae didn't reply right away, but only looked in her direction. Then, "How are you, Till?"

"Oh, you know me. I'm always working out something."

She hadn't told Rita Mae yet about the pig snout, entrails, and eyeballs. Until she found out who did this or why, or her stomach didn't flip as the ugly sight was remembered, she'd keep this secret hidden away. Rita Mae held some unwarranted prejudice against Johnny. Tilly, in her most stubborn moments, wasn't going to encourage a debate on whether or not her friend had been wrong by last summer's lovely wedding.

Tilly handed Rita Mae another pile of handkerchiefs and doilies for pressing with the hot flatiron. Once the task was completed, they folded and stacked each one in a box for delivery later in the day. Oh, how an electric iron would be so nice, especially now with the first floor wired for a few lights. Until then, she'd continue heating the old, heavy iron on the stove. The only real advantage with a flatiron on the stove was the fact the kitchen was warm and cozy while she and her best friend chattered away.

Little successes, like being able to ignore the cold wind and swirling snow, became more important than slights and arguments.

"So, Till, when are you going to start making those purses you've talked about for so long?"

"I did," she simply replied. "But, first I experimented on something for Johnny. I was going to give them to him Christmas Eve."

"Was?"

"Oh, we were busy," Tilly hedged. "Want to see?"

Tilly headed to the backroom and opened a cupboard before her friend could say more. She pulled out the small package behind the Mason jar. She turned the present over a couple of times and then slipped her thumb along the ribbon holding the paper closed. Two tan calfskin gloves were centered on the paper, thick matching beige fur peeking out from the cuffs, finished off with contrast stitching on each finger and thumb with additional detailing on the palms.

"Oh, Till, where, no, how did you afford these?"

"I made them," Tilly answered.

"You made these? I've never seen anything so gorgeous," Rita Mae exclaimed, turning one of the gloves over and over.

Tilly nodded, tears threatening at how thrilled she was with the gloves. "Johnny's gift, but I didn't have a chance to give them to him yet. Maybe tonight."

But, it wasn't to be.

Chapter 10

Two Days after Christmas

To Clean Up On Klan Demand
The fiery cross of the Ku Klux Klan is concentrating its rays on this area and the rest of the county. Following a silent invasion of secret agents of the order, law officers suddenly began a sweeping drive against bootleggers, gamblers, keepers of disorderly houses, and particularly blind pigs. By 6 o'clock Sunday morning, the local lock-up was filled with prisoners, both men and women. And, as they were being dumped before the sheriff's door, a large group of Klansmen as well as state and village police and members of other secret societies, gathered at the local Presbyterian church to pray, sing hymns and cheer on speakers.

The only cloud eclipsing the burning rays of the fiery cross was the 'tip.' Someone blundered, knowingly or unknowingly, for the keepers of well-known roadhouses and other places of unethical amusements had removed most of the liquid evidence before the raiders arrived.

Public officials of the county deny responsibility for the tip and the Klansmen charge the officials are hiding proof. There has been no announcement the Klan intends to start another clean-up but ample circumstantial evidence exists.

Trooper Thomas S. Sykes, pastor of the Presbyterian church, is supposedly the chief figure behind the crusade. Yet, he has disclaimed all knowledge of the Klan and emphasized he was getting wonderful cooperation from the sheriff. He said further the cleanup was being made by means of a fund supplied by citizens. This whole sorry situation started a short time ago when money was raised by Pastor Sykes to pay for secret, private detectives of the Klan to enter the territory. True espionage methods were used and then, again, pitting neighbor against neighbor, as when a new member bought a quart from someone who had known him for some time.

Local authorities deny they are giving the Klan's full details but have been told raids will continue. The blind pigs, on the whole, have been closed according to the Ku Klux Klan.

Tilly couldn't read any further. She didn't want to. Now she was sorry Mrs. Harbinger had given her the latest issue of the newspaper. Even the brief mention of blind pigs brought back the sour stink of the pig snout. Blind pigs, blind tigers, and even blind monkeys—places of ill-repute—gained their strange names because of some fellow in Maine charging customers money to watch sightless animals hapless in their cages. On top of making fun of the poor creatures, these same gawkers were given a complimentary tumbler of hooch.

This article was hitting too close to home, and making her fixate on trouble. Time to give up and go to bed. To, at best, get a few hours of sleep before the nightmares started up again.

Johnny had been gone two nights, not one, as

before. As happened the first time, she vowed not to question him or get mad, but should she start counting again the reasons she loved him? Repeat her little game of tally like the last time she'd lain in bed alone?

The next morning, long before the sun brightened the day, she was beyond caring by the time she found him sitting at the kitchen table. She'd startled at the sight of his still form, his head braced up by his hands.

Johnny finally looked up as she slid by him, making her way toward the stove. She barely acknowledged him, not knowing what could be said. His beard had grown in thick over the last forty-eight hours and his eyes were surrounded with a gray shadow as dark as storm clouds. Basically, he looked as if he'd been put through the washtub wringer with nothing left to be squeezed out.

"Mornin' Johnny," Tilly eventually greeted him. "Coffee?"

"Money around?"

"Ain't—haven't—seen him yet this morning," she replied.

"You here all night by yourself?"

"Guessing Pa's upstairs. Why so many questions?"

Johnny didn't have a chance to answer.

A loud knock came at the back door, making them both startle at the suddenness of the sound. Tilly cringed. Was Mr. Andrews wanting to get paid for the milk he'd delivered before Christmas? Household money was dwindling and she balked at digging into the canning jar to pay for milk. But, the thought of avoiding the one person who'd engage in light conversation, unlike her own husband, made her involuntarily rise. She'd depart with precious coins if need be.

"M-I-N-E-R, open up."

Balled fists striking the back door rattled Tilly's insides. Couldn't possibly be their gentle, soft-spoken milkman. He'd never be so aggressive.

Johnny finally stood, positioning himself between her and the back door. He grabbed her arm, steering her in the direction of the parlor. His pull on her arm stung like the hard pinch they'd tease each other with as kids. But they weren't children and this wasn't looking like a game.

"Johnny." She gasped. "What are you doing? Answer the door."

"Don't have to. I know what it's about."

"Miner! I know you're in there." Whoever was on the other side of the door jangled the handle hard enough, Money was either now awake from all the noise, maybe dead, but more likely not at home. Tilly half expected to hear his bellowing complaint cascade down through the stairwell and was surprised when nothing happened.

"Doll-face, wait here," Johnny said, once they were in the parlor. "Guess I better take care of this."

"Then you can come back here and explain what's going on." She'd caught early on the only time he called her *doll-face* was when he wanted something. Or, was in trouble. Pretty sure, trouble had landed at their back door.

As soon as Johnny left the room, Tilly made a decision. She rarely headed to the third floor but, if something bad was going to happen, Tilly wanted her father to be of some help. Anything he could do. She mounted the steps and knocked on the bedroom door.

No response. She knocked harder, causing the unlatched door to slowly open. Tilly peeked inside to see a bed—made and obviously unused last night—and her pa nowhere in sight. So, he wasn't in the house.

Tilly turned away from the bedroom, headed back to the parlor, and grabbed the fireplace poker. This little weapon might come in handy. She marched back to the kitchen, only to find the room empty. The back door was wide open and cold air was blasting in. Tilly approached the doorway, wielding the metal rod in front of her like a sword.

"Johnny?" Her voice was nearly lost to the howling wind. "Johnny!"

"Till, get back in the house."

Clouds briefly separated and the full moon illuminated the backyard. She could see all the way to the shed at the back of the property as well as two figures standing half the distance between. One was her husband, with his back to the house, blocking most of the view of the person he was talking with. She couldn't guess who the other man was. He was a bit shorter, maybe barrel-chested, and something familiar in his stance. Going against Johnny's wishes and getting involved could make the matter worse so she stepped back through the doorway and headed for the parlor. Better to let him take care of whatever was happening.

A couple of minutes turned into a few more and then, finally, the back door crashed hard against the house frame, probably caught again by the stiff wind. Someone stomped their feet on the small rug. Tilly waited. The poker was on the floor, at her feet, in case a reason to defend herself arose.

"Close your eyes, doll-face," came Johnny's voice from the kitchen.

"Not in the mood for games. What's going on?"

"Close your eyes. I know Christmas was a few days ago," Johnny continued as if she hadn't even spoken, "but I couldn't forget. Ready? Are your eyes closed?"

"Yes."

His footsteps were heavy on the wood floor as he strode across the room. The air moved around Tilly as he moved closer.

"Okay, you can open them." He stood before her like he didn't have a care in the world or that someone had not just been yelling and pounding at their kitchen door. He held a rather large wooden box in his arms and wore a crooked, almost shy smile. The flickering embers from the fireplace lit him from behind like a ghostly aura was shadowing him. "No time to wrap this." Johnny stepped closer to the couch and sat down, the glow behind him dissipating. He set the item between them.

She knew immediately what he was giving her—a Victor Talking Machine.

"Oh, Johnny," she squealed. "You got me a player?"

"Knew how much you wanted one. Can we count this for both Christmas and your birthday? See I remember."

"And, here I thought you never noticed any of my hints," Tilly exclaimed. She jumped up from the couch to give Johnny a hug. "Where's the megaphone? Oh, oh, Rita Mae and I are going to go to Mr. Jensen's. I remember seeing he had some records for sale."

"Whoa, hold on…" Johnny started to speak as Tilly ran out of the room. "You can't go now. He's not goin' to be open yet."

"No, no, wait, I'll be right back." Tilly skirted around the kitchen table, heading toward the back room. She grabbed the wrapped package tucked behind the Mason jar and hurried back to the parlor. She presented the present. "Here. Merry Christmas."

"Till, what's this?"

"Open and see."

His eyebrows knit together, a solemn look creasing his features. She was about to grab back the gift and do the honors, when he finally slid the ribbon to one corner and let the paper unfold. He slowly held up the gloves she'd labored over for weeks, each stitch perfectly lined up with the last one, while each finger obviously the exact length to match her husband's fingers as he found, once he'd slipped them on. He'd been sound asleep as she'd traced his hands onto a piece of paper, creating the patterns for gloves to slide on and fit like a second skin.

"Oh, baby," he murmured. He gently rubbed her cheeks with the gloved thumbs, his eyes glistening. "Never had anything this nice."

If only they could freeze this moment. She loved his touch, the glistening in his eyes, the soft tones of his whispered words. Between their portraits taken a few days back and now a beautiful Victor phonograph player and gloves to keep those strong hands warm, this Christmas had turned out to be almost perfect.

Well, of course, minus the pig snout, entrails, and eyeballs, someone scaring her by banging on their back door and demanding her husband's appearance, and maybe even how in the world he ended up giving a Victor as a belated Christmas gift.

This time, Tilly ignored the questions in deference to what was right in front of her at this moment. Better to remember *all things thrive in thrice*; sometimes good, sometimes bad, and maybe even a combination. An ugly centerpiece and an unexpected visitor were the first and second, but the one she'd concentrate on was the third—gifts given in loving reverence.

The New Year was only hours away and 1929 was going to be their year. They were going to be happy.

Chapter 11

January 2, 1929

"I've got a crush on you."

"Ah, Till, we'll always be best friends." Rita Mae smiled over the top of her coffee cup.

"No, I want my first record for the Victor to be *I've Got a Crush on You*. You know, the one—"

"—the one by Gershwin!" Rita Mae laughed, as she finished Tilly's sentence.

"I wonder if Mr. Jensen has his store open today," she pondered. "He sells records, you know. He was open Christmas Eve so Johnny and I could have our picture taken. Oh, oh, maybe we could go buy a record and see if the photographs are ready."

"Where you gettin' money to buy a record or get pictures taken or for anything?"

"Got a secret." Tilly winked at her friend. "I'll show you, but you have to promise to never, ever, tell a soul."

"Not even Johnny?"

"Oh, especially not him. He thinks I spend all the money on groceries," Tilly replied. Keeping secrets wasn't something she'd set out to do, but warnings niggled at the back of her brain to save up for a rainy day. These coins might come in handy when there were no more thrown on the bedcovers in the early hours.

She rose from the table and headed to the small room off the kitchen, then pulled down the Mason jar from the cupboard. Once back in the kitchen, she stared hard into her friend's eyes. "Promise me."

They linked their pinky fingers together where years earlier they'd made small cuts in their skin, promising to be blood-sisters forever. Rita Mae nodded solemnly as Tilly unscrewed the top from the jar labeled *beans* and tipped it sideways. Coins cascaded onto the table, a couple of pennies even rolling away. She put her hand just under the edge of the table and caught both.

"Where did you get all this money?" Rita Mae gazed down at the glittering mountain of copper pennies, silver nickels and dimes, even a couple half dollars. Those had such a severe-looking Pilgrim stamped into each one as if the scowl meant one better think pretty hard before spending so much money. She picked up one of the coins for closer inspection. "I've never even seen half dollars before. You takin' to holding up banks?"

"No, not exactly," Tilly hedged but then smiled. "But maybe taken to make sure I get what's due me. Johnny's working for Mr. Straws but he's getting money from somewhere else. I don't know he cares when I grab some of the money as long as I don't ask questions."

"You're kind of scaring me, Till," Rita Mae said. "This doesn't sound like you. Keepin' secrets, you know."

"People can change. Ever since Christmas, Johnny's been different, so why can't I?"

"But, you're only talking a week ago."

"I know, but he's been home more'n he ever used to be since…"

"Since what?"

"Oh, never mind," Tilly said a bit quicker than she should have, the memory of an oozing pig snout dribbling through her thoughts like the rivulets of darkening blood.

"Oh, no you don't. No never mind me," Rita Mae came back equally as fast. "Since what?"

"Okay, you have to promise you will never, ever, say anything to anyone," Tilly whispered, leaning in as close as possible across the table. She paused and took a sip of her coffee, and then started gathering up the coins.

Johnny had left a few hours earlier but who knew when he'd return. And then, there was her pa. He'd been working late hours at his shop and coming in looking bone-tired, yet somehow with a glint of excitement in his eyes. Something had changed since she'd fainted at the horrible mess in the kitchen, a scene of blood and guts no one should ever witness. Her mind still couldn't wrap around why someone would put such a horrific display of animal parts in their kitchen. And, of course, no one was saying anything, clammed up faster than those slimy oysters Mr. Navarro would sell fresh, floating in a fish tank at the back of his store, until someone ordered up some for a meal.

Rita Mae stacked a few coins one on top of another, obviously waiting for Tilly to continue.

"You ever seen a pig snout?"

"Well, of course." Rita Mae scoffed. "Who ain't seen a pig?"

"No, I mean just the snout, not the rest attached?"

"You mean no face, no ears?" Her friend shivered.

"And eyeballs," Tilly said. "Eyeballs lying next to a snout, no face, no ears. The eyes pointing in opposite directions."

"Sounds disgusting. I never look at that bloody stuff at the grocer's. Not sure why anyone would want 'em although ma says usin' all of the animal makes soup better. But what are you talking about?"

Tilly scooted her chair around the table, sticking her face mere inches from her friend's. "No, this wasn't at Mr. Navarro's. They were here. I only saw them for a second, but they were right here on this table a week ago."

"Go on, *dry up!*" Rita Mae's hands shot up into the air, knocking over the stack of coins, horror dilating her pupils to large brown orbs. She was poised as if held at gunpoint. But then she startled Tilly by placing one hand on her forehead like a mother checking a child's fever.

"I'm not sick." Tilly gently batted her friend's hand away. "It's the truth. I walked in here and found a snout, some innards, and two eyeballs placed on this table, like someone had been trying to arrange a centerpiece. Blood seeping away from the mess like little ribbons."

"Now you're scarin' me, Till. You act like this happens all the time."

"Oh no, I fainted," she replied, keeping her voice monotone for affect. Her lack of emotion held Rita Mae completely transfixed, stringing her along, while the cuckoo clock in the parlor chimed the top of the hour. Albeit morbid, this was turning into a bit of fun. Normally Rita Mae was the one weaving fantastical tales but Tilly was pretty certain nothing could top this story. "I woke up a little bit later in the parlor—Johnny must have carried me in there. So romantic, don't you think? Just like Mary Pickford in *Daddy Long Legs*. He must have picked me up, oh-so-gently into his arms, and…oh, if only I could've seen the look on his face."

Rita Mae started to interrupt.

"Except," but Tilly continued, raising one hand, "when I woke up, Johnny and pa were arguing. I listened but couldn't figure out what they were talking about. But since then, Johnny's been so agreeable, nicer than ever before, coming home at night, giving me the player and all."

"Why didn't you tell me any of this before now? He's been stayin' out all night—doing what? And, why aren't you worryin' more about what you've told me? Did you even find out who put the mess here?" Rita Mae lifted up her hands from the table a second time as if she couldn't fathom the surface could ever be clean enough to touch.

"Johnny told me the whole mess was a joke, and I believe him," Tilly quickly replied, now a little sorry she'd told her friend. Rita Mae was asking all the questions she couldn't think about or else the unimaginable would make her nightmares even worse.

Sure, the whole muddled mess had been ugly and creepy and left her oddly hyper-vigilant, but a shift in moods had changed things for the better. Johnny had laughingly explained away what happened, blaming his friends on the prank; her pa started being a little nicer and less demanding; and, best of all, she didn't have to do any clean up. Now, there was a surprise. Actually, this was the first time the burden of cleaning wasn't placed on her shoulders since her ma died.

She still found a spot or two of blood, dried to a blackish burgundy, sometimes when she was wiping up crumbs on the floor. She pretended the dried drops were something else. Maybe red gelatin wiggling off someone's spoon.

"Till, you are crazy if you think blood smeared all over a table where you serve food was meant as a joke. Were you amused? Were Johnny or Mr. Monroe laughing? I'm fairly certain no one found any part funny." Rita Mae paused, then added in a quiet voice, "Johnny's getting into trouble, ain't he?"

"Don't you dare..." Tilly exclaimed.

"I hear talk around town," Rita Mae began. "Rumors..."

Before another word could be spoken, they heard the front door pushed opened and then slammed nearly as quickly and strong enough to rattle the full jar on the table. Or so Tilly imagined as she grabbed the container and lid and ran to the backroom.

"Doll-face," Johnny yelled. "You here?"

****

"You have to promise to keep..." Tilly began as soon as she'd scurried in through the back door of the Osborne's house. But she'd stopped mid-sentence. Rita Mae's mother had been stirring something at the stove and turned around, spoon now held up in the air, pinkish liquid dripping back into the pot. Apples bubbling in sugar hovered in the kitchen air like a sweet walk through an orchard.

"My, my, young lady." Mrs. Osborne turned her attention back to the hot applesauce. She then wiped her hands across the front of her apron, leaving behind a streak of sugar crystals brightening faded flowers on the fabric. "Here, let me strain this—had to use up apples found in our cellar before they turned mealy. Then you can tell me what has you so upset."

"Oh, don't stop what you're doing," Tilly replied, not wanting to let slip why she had rushed over.

"You were saying…promise? To keep what? Maybe a secret?" Rita Mae's ma was being friendlier than her usual severe self and a bit too interested by the way her eyebrows peaked halfway up her rather large forehead, wrinkling like ocean waves.

But Tilly didn't reply. She needed her friend, not Mrs. Osborne. No less than an hour after Johnny came home, then left again for who knew how long, Tilly grabbed her coat and boots and waded through six inches of fresh snow to the Osborne house. She had to find out what Rita Mae meant by *rumors*. She also had to make sure new gossip didn't start circulating around because of their earlier conversation. And now, here she stood in front of the one woman who most delighted in blowing a secret out of proportion and making sure word spread like wild fire in a dry cornfield.

With each step she took through the new snow, a poem her mother used to chant kept running through her muddled thoughts.

> *Don't be in a hurry to tell it,*
> *The tale that was whispered to you;*
> *Just wait till you find out about it,*
> *For maybe it will not prove true.*
>
> ~*~
>
> *And if it be false, think a moment,*
> *Will you add to the cruel wrong?*
> *For falsehoods, like snowballs grow larger,*

The farther they travel along.
~*~

But if it be true, just forget it,
For why should your lips e'er repeat,
A tale may ruin another,
And end all his hopes in defeat?
~*~

So, don't be in a hurry to tell it,
The tale that was whispered to you,
For here is one thing to remember,
Because whispered tales seldom are true.

Funny thing, Johnny had actually been a bit talkative while she bounced from one foot to the other, only half listening to him prattle on about Mr. Straws, his new boss, and of a customer accusing Johnny of doing something wrong. Instead of paying attention, comments she'd overheard while in the newspaper office the other day circulated through her thoughts. How Johnny might be involved in some *wrongdoing* once again. Those words kept coming up a bit too often.

"I can't believe it." He grumbled, as his speech sped up. He was a bundle of nerves.

"Believe what?"

"The man said I stole his scarf. You know I don't steal." He shook his head but never offered up anything more.

"Maybe the same thing happened to this man as with Mr. Andrews," Tilly mentioned, remembering the article of their milkman mistakenly placing his new overcoat in the wrong rig. Johnny hadn't seemed to register she'd even spoken.

Since Johnny hadn't removed his outerwear, he was then quick to leave the house before Tilly could ask further questions. She'd looked across the parlor room and spotted her newly-installed Victor phonograph player and remembered the conversation she and Rita Mae hadn't had a chance to finish.

Now, with him out the door again, she hurried over to her friend's house, hoping Mrs. Osborne wouldn't ask any more questions. Tilly sometimes wondered if many of the town's rumors were dreamed up in this house and scattered haphazardly from village residents to farmers and back again. The woman did act superior, what with her being the leader of the women's temperance movement and living the pious life, as she liked to remind any and all on a regular basis.

Tilly needed to make sure the chat she and Rita Mae were having an hour earlier wasn't going to be the latest fodder. To make sure her friend hadn't told her mother. *Because whispered tales seldom are true.*

No one needed to look at her and Johnny's home imagining pig snouts, intestines, or slimy eyeballs. As a matter of fact, she was going to suggest she and Rita Mae bundle up and walk to Mr. Jensen's to see if he had the record somewhere on his shelves. Then, maybe people would hear lovely music emanating from her front parlor instead of mulling over unfounded gossip.

"Is Rita Mae home?"

The old woman shrugged her shoulders, pointed up toward the second floor to indicate the bedroom, and went back to her task. Dismissed, Tilly ran upstairs.

****

"Anything to get away from her," Rita Mae said, referring to her mother, as soon as they were at least two houses closer to the downtown. More giant snowflakes started falling, gently coming to rest and coating their woolen coats and tams with a white glow. The air was as still as an expectant mouse while gray clouds obscured the sun, creating an eerie quiet. As if Rita Mae thought her voice would travel miles over open fields, she whispered, "All she does is talk 'bout getting some big, important speaker to come here an' straighten out the *whales*, as she calls 'em. The heavy drinkers, you know."

This gave Tilly a chance to broach their earlier conversation.

"Rita Mae," Tilly continued whispering, taking her friend's arm, and leaning in closer. "You have to promise me not a word to anyone of what we were talking about."

"Who'd ever want to talk about cut-off pig snouts, bloody intestines, and loose eyeballs?" Her friend's dark brown eyebrows bounced upward like dancing caterpillars. "But we have to talk about the rumors."

"Rumors," Tilly repeated. "Doesn't mean anything is true. Someone is making up lies and half-truths to cause problems."

"But, if you hear them often enough, don't you think there might be a smidgen of truth?"

"Johnny is Johnny, he ain't…isn't…bad." Tilly defended him once more. "Folks 'round here love to blame the bad on someone so their lives look better."

"Ma…" Rita Mae began, "…Ma says there's a lot of bootleggin' goin' on and it ain't right. She says bootleggin' is gonna get someone killed."

"Maybe there's bootlegging going on but don't accuse Johnny unless you know for sure," Tilly said. The metallic smell on him some nights did bother her, but she had to believe he wasn't involved in making illegal hooch. Maybe he could get some, but where would he hide the mash? And, he certainly wasn't making any at home. Granted, she couldn't remember the last time she ventured out to the back shed, but had Johnny?

"You ever heard of blind pigs?"

Rita Mae's question caused Tilly to stop in her own tracks, her boots sinking farther into the snow than when they were quickly walking along the road. Whispers of paying money to get in somewhere, play games, and gamble, and get free alcohol trailed her like a preying coyote. She didn't know anything else about them; not where or if there were any, but yes, they surely existed. Men needed their drink. Maybe these activities described Johnny's favorite past time a bit too close.

Rita Mae tugged on Tilly's arm and they picked up the pace again. The snow muffled any sounds. No one had their *autymobiles*—as her father would snuffle over the uselessness of horseless carriages—out in this weather and yet, hopefully, horses were tucked away, warm in their stalls.

Grand River Road was deserted. Probably a good thing since the roads undoubtedly were slippery. As a matter of fact, a couple days back, Judge Cole had the misfortune of being in the wrong place at the wrong time. He found himself flat on his back in the middle of the road after losing his footing on an icy patch. The driver, desperately trying to turn the skinny tires on the frozen road, came to a skidding halt mere inches from the good judge. Townsfolk were still abuzz how this could have gone so much worse, but all he ended up with were a couple of bruises and one little cut on his forehead.

"I have," Tilly finally answered. "I was reading how some are being shut down by the Klan. How Klansmen are acting like the police and raiding suspicious locations."

"Do you think Johnny might be runnin' one?"

"No, he works for Mr. Straws," Tilly simply replied. "I'd know if he was doing something illegal. Rita Mae, if I didn't know better, I'd think you are the one starting the rumors."

Her friend pulled away and stuck her hands into the deep pockets of her coat, a look of surprise on her face like she'd been caught snatching a warm biscuit before dinner. Tilly wasn't going to let Rita Mae off easy, so she kept her mouth shut. But no more accusations, at least not yet.

"Till, I ain't the bad one here," Rita Mae began. "I'm just asking questions. I hear talk in town, never saying anything to anyone. Someone is makin' and sellin' hooch to someone runnin' a blind pig. Ma hates how these men get around the law by chargin' to get in to play cards and then being able to drink. Drinkin' is agin the law."

"But, how'd you get from what some men are doing to figuring Johnny is running one of these?"

"People are sayin' all this stealing is part of the blind pigs and someone is going to get tossed in the lock-up, or worse."

"Stealing? Johnny's no thief." But Tilly only half-listened to Johnny's short conversation earlier before leaving again and now her thoughts were all jumbled up. Was he trying to tell her something she couldn't understand? If he didn't steal a scarf, was this more about someone running a blind pig? But all of this made no sense at all.

"I also heard there could be a tar 'n' feathering if they find out who's runnin' the blind pig." Once Rita Mae started talking about all of the gossip and rumors circulating throughout the village, she was a wealth of information, sounding too much like her mother. "Oh, hey, look, Jensen's is open."

Tilly was startled out of her thoughts with her friend's sudden change in topic. Almost felt like they were playing an old walking game from years earlier when they'd stroll to a corner and take turns shouting out whether to go left or right or straight across the street. An hour later, they might find themselves at the end of town or back home. Always an adventure to get them giggling.

For now, they'd made a beeline from Rita Mae's house to the photography studio. A soft glow of light shone from the two front windows of the studio. A few other storefronts had lanterns lit or electric bulbs burning to show they were open on this somewhat gloomy day. A small number of shoppers were scurrying from one building to the next and at least half a dozen rigs were secured to the hitching posts. Horses were pawing at the hard ground and releasing impatient, loud snorts, all in an effort to stay warm and, no doubt, wishing they were back in their warm barns. Rita Mae and Tilly ducked into Mr. Jensen's studio, a bell tinkling over the doorway as they pushed open the door.

"Ah, Mrs. Miner." Mr. Jensen brought his hands together in a soft clapping sound. "And, fetching Rita Mae. What brings two such lovely ladies out in this cold weather? Are you here to check on your pictures?"

Tilly reached deep into an inside pocket to retrieve her change purse. One she'd made recently from the leftover calfskin after finishing the gloves for Johnny. She pulled out three coins from the jar, hoping that'd be enough for at least one record, maybe even two. She was so excited to finally get a chance to see how the Victor sounded.

"I'd like to buy a record. Do you know the one by Gershwin?" Tilly asked and then began humming her favorite tune. "But are the photographs also ready?"

"Ah, alas, they are not finished but how lovely you want music in your house," he exclaimed, continuing to bring his hands together in delight. "You have a Victor now? So many more phonograph players are now in the village."

Tilly nodded and followed Mr. Jensen to walls lined with shelves, black cardboard sleeves standing in a row like soldiers at attention. There had to be *I've Got a Crush on You* in one of those sleeves. She'd buy the record and hope Johnny listened to the message when the music echoed through the parlor. She'd sit next to him in their parlor, snuggle tight under his arm, and quietly tell him about her day until they retired to their bedroom…

"Miss?" Mr. Jensen said, then louder, "Miss. Here's the record. Do you want to make a purchase today?"

"Oh, yes," Tilly replied, startled out of her dreams. She hurriedly pulled coins out of her purse and handed them over, cradling the record like a newborn baby.

"Where'd you go?" Rita Mae asked as soon as they'd left the store. "You looked miles away."

"Oh, thinking about how I can't wait to play this record." She didn't need to say more, especially about how Christmas was such a disaster, or how maybe she needed to help Johnny in celebrating her birthday, or how voicing any hard feelings only made their lives challenging.

But, maybe, just maybe, she'd broach the subject of blind pigs and bootlegging. No…she had to stop thinking along those lines. But, unfortunately, since Rita Mae had put these notions in her head, other thoughts kept bubbling like hot stew.

Marion L. Cornett

Chapter 12

January 10, 1929

...I've got a crush on you... music filled the parlor. Tilly wanted to shout *sweetie pie* every time she heard the words crooned by the singer. But, instead, she hummed along while the Victor phonograph player offered up the lyrics.

Gershwin was amazing. The composer had managed to pluck desires right out of her deepest thoughts...pardon her mush for she had a crush...on her husband. Oh, Johnny, *could you coo, could you care?* She had a crush on him.

Johnny had surprised her—his birthday present for her—attaching the megaphone and, ever since then, she'd been playing the only record in the house over and over again. She knew all the lyrics, where each downbeat and upbeat came in the four-minute song, and when she should swoon. Which happened pretty much every time *my baby* came out of the singer's mouth. Instead of those two words, she'd overlap Johnny's *hey, doll-face.*

She'd bought the only copy Mr. Jensen had and now treated the ten-inch black disk as protectively as the few remaining porcelain pieces from her mother's china. Never did she leave the record sitting in the Victor. She'd slip it into the dust-free sleeve to then be

94

stored flat on top of the closed Victor.

She snuggled closer to Johnny's side while he read the latest newspaper she'd picked up earlier in the day from Mrs. Harbinger. Tilly also brought home more papers from the previous five weeks but tucked those away for looking at another day. She wanted to savor the news alone, something she enjoyed almost as much as when Johnny was being attentive.

"Thinking you like the new player, hey, doll-face?" Johnny interrupted her thoughts with his question, gently raising her hand to softly brush his lips on her opened palm.

"The best," she replied, chills running up her arms, savoring this perfect moment.

And then, the clunk and scrape of Money's cane sounded at the top of the stairs.

"Looks like your pa's gonna join us this evening." Johnny shrugged, moving away from Tilly ever so slightly. He carelessly folded the section he'd been reading before tossing the newspaper to the floor.

An idea then struck. She took her husband's hand and hurried them toward the door to the stairway, figuring they'd pass Money but only nod in greeting. No conversation and they'd make their way to the room behind the kitchen.

Ever since the snout incident, he'd been away from the house more often than not and any contact had been short and stilted. At first, she wondered if the fault was hers but, after Rita Mae's insinuations, she'd been pondering the relationship between the police and the Klan. If anyone had gotten wind Johnny was possibly involved with a blind pig, had a Klansman been the one to sneak into their house to deposit the rancid animal sections on their kitchen table? And was Money trying to find out the culprit? If answers to these questions even came close to yes, some of the conversation she'd overheard upon waking from her fainting spell might make sense.

Consider this a warning. Take it serious.

Money's words had reverberated through her head too many times since their early-morning talk. And, now Johnny seemed different. Yes, maybe he'd leave for hours at a time but overnight disappearances had ceased. Each night, sometimes long past dark, he'd crawl in beside her, and they would hold each other close until heat from their bodies warmed the sheets. Sleep came as they hung onto each other.

Johnny had become her gentle yet urgent lover— she secretly smiled how many mornings they'd awaken and then explore. If her pa, in his bedroom above them, heard the bed springs creak, she no longer worried. Months of shedding a lingering shyness because of her inexperience had finally been overcome by the sheer need to match her husband's lead. But as time moved on, she pushed aside her vulnerability and opened up to him, tried not to think, and worked at making him happy. Sometimes, their time together was rough and basic, like the time he'd thrown the coins on the bedspread. Other times, he was quiet, slow and thoughtful, and would allow her to discover.

Tilly was happy. Maybe not completely secure, but she believed with all her heart Johnny loved her. And she would love him until death parted them.

"Pa," Tilly said, as she and Johnny turned toward the kitchen. "Good night."

"Early, don't you think?" Money commented, but

didn't stop moving. He kept taking each step one by one, placing his cane down on the next tread, and then moving both legs to line up side by side. He was slow going but mostly steady.

"Busy day," Tilly answered, acutely aware for the first time what an old, old man he'd become. "You can crank the Victor some more if you want to hear the record I bought."

"Heard it enough times." Money dismissively waved his hand and continued on his way down to the first floor. "Thought I'd get some milk."

"Oh, here, let me get you some," Tilly replied, remembering she'd better arise early enough to catch up with Mr. Andrews in the morning. She couldn't keep putting him off paying for the deliveries, plus too long a time had passed since they last spoke, depriving her of his stimulating conversation. "You could maybe take the milk to your bedroom."

Pa's bushy right eyebrow rose ever-so-slightly, but he bore whatever she was suggesting. He paused on the third to the last step and waited. Tilly danced around her husband in the kitchen, as he stood either unusually patient or curious as to what she had in mind. Between her father's acceptance and her husband's tolerance for what she had in mind, delight tickled her senses.

"All right, Pa's on his way upstairs." She hurried back into the kitchen, muttering more to herself than to Johnny. "I've been wanting to do something nearly since we married."

"Huh?" This time, it was Johnny's not-so-bushy left eyebrow arching upward in question.

Tilly rooted around in a drawer below the cupboard where she kept the Mason jar labeled with *beans*. She was looking for a pencil and ruler.

"I want to measure how tall we are," she told him. "Aha, here's the pencil. Now, you go stand next to the wall and I'll place this ruler on your head, then make a mark on the wall."

He cooperated and she did exactly as she'd said. She then pulled out a cloth measuring tape conveniently tucked in her dress pocket. She placed one end on the floor, unwinding the rest until the length measured three feet up the wall. She did the same, now placing one end where the first height was noted and stretched it up to the mark on the wall. It was three inches short of another three feet.

"Johnny, you're five feet, nine inches. Remember those numbers and I'll take my turn." She handed the ruler and pencil to him, then turned around and placed her back to the wall where he'd stood moments earlier.

He repeated what she'd done and then they both looked at the mark he'd made. Without hesitation, she measured from his full height down the mark she'd made earlier and found the difference to be about seven inches.

"Looks like I'm five feet, two inches."

Johnny came up behind her and wrapped his arms around her waist and she laid her head back toward his shoulder. "Never thought about how short you are." He gently moved her thick braid to the other shoulder so he could nuzzle her neck. They stood, warmth from their bodies intermingling, while cold wind rattled loosening shakes on the outside of the house. The only sound in the otherwise quiet moment.

How to tell someone you'd like to freeze a moment? To stop all of the outside influences from interfering with the love between a man and a woman? To simply let measuring each other's height be the best part of a day? Tilly pressed a little deeper into his chest but then the moment was over. A gust of wind swirled snow and ice up to the small window, sounding like a handful of pebbles hitting the house. They both shivered from the cold seeping in.

****

"Top of the mornin'." Thad's voice echoed across the side yard, even sifting into the almost quiet kitchen where Tilly had thrown a bit of sugar onto the egg-rock coal, encouraging the flames to flare up higher. After last night, she so wanted her single phonograph record playing softly so she could sway to the dulcet tones and pretend her husband's arms were still wrapped around her waist. But, instead, she responded to Mr. Andrews' greeting by throwing on her heavy coat and slipping into Johnny's boots. The ones left by the back door.

She ventured out to the back stoop. She'd gotten up early enough to get downstairs, stow away the fireplace poker—even though Johnny slept by her side all night—and count out enough coins from the Mason jar to pay up their debt to Thad. She was even able to give him a little extra for this week's dairy order, dreading having to approach her father about adding a little extra money to their stash. He was now drinking more milk than she and Johnny combined. For now, she didn't want anything getting in the way of having a chance to talk with him.

"Good morning, Thad," she replied, once she was standing on the back stoop. Cold was already seeping through the soles of Johnny's boots to her otherwise bare feet. She moved from one foot to the next. Even

Brown Molly looked to be suffering from the cold. She was covered with a blanket across her back, what with the temperatures dipping down so low even the horse's eyelashes were frosted white.

Mr. Andrews stepped closer to accept the coins. He cocked his head sideways. "Do I hear sweet music on this cold mornin'? Warms me heart and surely scares away this boundless frost."

"Johnny gave me a Victor," Tilly blurted out, so happy someone else now knew. "I only have one record but I'm saving up for more."

"But you have a radio."

"And now I have both." Tilly laughed for no good reason other than she loved music and the movies, the morning sun, a contentment greeting her upon rising, and she wished to twirl around if only Johnny's boots weren't so big.

I've got a crush on you…

Strains of the chorus drifted from the parlor to the back door. Thad's smile, once so wide, faded slightly as he set three bottles of milk at Tilly's feet on the stoop.

Chapter 13

February 16, 1929

Time is fluid, always moving forward, and yet some moments freeze.

Some days were exceptional but others piled up and dragged on, with cold, snowy days forcing residents inside—some huddling close to the fireplace—yet Tilly kept busy making warm meals for the three of them, ironing and mending neighbors' clothes, and hoarding precious minutes to work on purse and glove designs.

Rita Mae was the only one in on Tilly's secret. How she hid away at least an hour a day sketching, cutting fabric, then working tiny stitches into the materials to create exquisite accessories. She painstakingly sewed hundreds of tiny seed beads to fabric purses, creating the illusion of high fashion. After the great success in making Johnny's gloves, Tilly used her own delicate, long-fingered hands as templates for women's gloves, once again adding beads at the cuff. Purses and gloves were paired as sets. Maybe she'd hit upon what the women in this farming community needed. A little bit of elegance to cover their hands and fingers roughened to the bone from hard work.

The best part was she could sell these for less than what Mr. Hamilton was offering. A pair of suede gloves cost $1.25 at his store. She could make them for 15-cents and sell for a dollar. Thinking of more money for the canning jar pushed her along to keep creating more.

And now, the movies beckoned Tilly evermore. She studied the fashions worn by the ladies up on the big screen, her mind working overtime on how to replicate the same look.

Her favorites to watch were Delores Costello, Greta Garbo, Dorothy Gish, and Clara Bow, to name a few. Each of those ladies always had a clutch in one hand and most oftentimes a cigarette holder in the other. They balanced the gold-tipped rod between slender, elegant fingers, looking worldly and sophisticated. Ruby red lips book-ended by cheeks sucked in as they took a pull from the cigarette.

One snowy afternoon, she and Rita Mae stole away to see a matinee of another Greta Garbo movie at the Vaudette. For once, much to Tilly's delight, the newsreel before the movie showed stars of Broadway, including Maude Adams and her impish portrayal of Peter Pan a few years earlier. The actress was making the news of how she was now helping to develop better lighting for the movies. Tilly hardly paid attention to the movie, dreaming of how she actually had something in common with a woman as glamorous as Miss Adams. They were both creating ways for women to be more attractive and alluring.

If only Miss Adams would make a movie but, the gossip was, she'd never do a "talkie." Too crass in the actress' opinion to have such noise while watching a film. Plus, voices sounded like cheeks full of air squeaking out through pursed lips.

Life was all so much fun lately. Johnny came home

each night, sometimes weariness ringing his eyes but most evenings a willing partner in her interests. He even gave her a Valentine's card a couple days before. *My thoughts are all of thee* had been changed, with him adding an *r* in *thee*. Maybe he was taking to heart Tilly's suggestion of filling up their home with the laughter of children. Even if she was adding unwritten words into the card, was dreaming such a bad thing?

Dream. That's what was bothering her. She slowly opened her eyes to a still-dark bedroom. But she was confused. A movie had been playing through her thoughts, but something was off. The world decided to spin in a different direction. Johnny was up on the screen, dancing with one of those ruby-red lipstick actresses one second then wandering off into a smoky darkness leaving his partner to sway back and forth.

She was the entire audience, reaching her arms toward his retreating back. Her words were lost in a song echoing from a radio. He never heard her; never turned back.

Letters marched like soldiers across the screen, forming words. Words she read but could hardly make sense of…

If he'd been an inch shorter, the bullet may have passed through his shoulder and he could have dropped to the brown, dead ferns below offering a shield. But 'twas not the case. Instead, the bullet pierced his heart and the slight sting was probably the last thing he ever felt.

If anyone had witnessed his last living moment, they would have marveled how a lock of shiny brown hair had gracefully brushed his forehead. How his blue eyes remained open, the light extinguishing by each second, yet still catching a slight glint from the moonlight above. How his body folded in on itself like a marionette having its strings snipped all at once. Or, how the motorcycle leaning against his hip had toppled in slow motion and came to rest over his now-still form.

But no one saw what happened, except for the lone figure poised next to a large elm tree across the stream. Within a few heartbeats, the stranger sloshed across the shallow water, stripped calfskin gloves from the dead man and then disappeared into the woods.

Her mind waited to see the words "the end" but the screen faded to black and she opened her eyes. She wasn't in a theater, as she gazed around the cold room. Moonlight was coming in through the single window and she barely made out the bulk of their armoire. Her robe hung on the bedpost like a deflated doll while the other half of the bed proved empty. She'd fallen asleep by herself and was now awake and alone.

"And now," Tilly whispered, the trembling in her legs working its way upward. "Because I've thought about it lately, *it* has happened again."

Three, no four, weeks had passed with her and Johnny living in some kind of blissful world of newlyweds. She'd somehow suspected their good times wouldn't last, though. And by all appearances, last night was the ending to another chapter. Tilly slid her hand over the cold sheets on the right side of the bed. Her husband had not returned last night and she'd slept alone, the fireplace poker her only companion.

She recently read an article in one of the back issues of the newspaper about—what was the term—oh yes, "already seen." Some doctor came up with a French term—*déjà vu*. Yes, a feeling of one already having experienced or known something. This morning was all too familiar. But, as before, she'd wait for Johnny to come barreling up the stairway, bellowing *hey, doll-face*, not caring if he woke her or Money. He'd placate her by tossing a handful of coins on top of the bedcovers and then they would make sweet love, never worrying of the clink of silvers and coppers beneath them.

She'd forgive him, as always. Then, when all was said and done, she'd grab at least half of his bounty and head downstairs to store some away in her favorite Mason jar. *Déjà vu.*

A smile crinkled her face at the sequence of events about to unfold, her body actually responding in kind to the caresses she constantly hungered for. Tilly ran her hands from her shoulders down over her breasts to her hips, eventually finding her fingers moving toward the center front of her nightgown. She slowly, and with great deliberation, released each little cloth-covered button, thinking of what Johnny would do. She started at the neckline and continued all the way down to her waist, until her chest was exposed to the cool morning air.

Goosebumps peppered her arms and legs as quickly as when she'd hear the first few strains of *I've Got a…*

Minutes passed and the sun peeked through the cloud cover briefly but not for long. Although her nightmare had somewhat faded, unease hovered around the edges of her mood. Why would she dream of her husband up on the silver screen? Why would she dream of someone falling to the ground, those lovely calfskin gloves being stripped from male hands?

She waited but the cuckoo bird in the parlor clock chastised, announcing the lateness of the morning hour.

Oh well, maybe he's not going to stride into the bedroom this morning after all. Maybe she and Rita Mae should go see more comedies and romantic movies and pay less attention to the newsreels showing so much wickedness in the world. Maybe then dreams wouldn't turn nightmarish.

Tilly had lain in bed long enough; she was getting a bit stiff and definitely cold. Time to give up expecting him to waltz in. After pulling on her heavy woolen robe, she headed to the kitchen. The outhouse would be her first stop before breakfast.

Clouds fully obscured any sunlight from filtering down; in fact, gloominess greeted her as she grabbed the little lantern stored by the back door, lit the wick, and headed outside. She tentatively tip-toed down a narrow path of packed-down snow, slipping and sliding most of the way to the little building behind the garage shed. Even though she had to concentrate to stay on the walkway, she still looked up long enough to notice the doors to the garage were partially open.

Odd…she'd have to check inside the old shed after taking care of more urgent needs.

Tilly was glad she had the lit lantern upon approaching the slightly-cracked open doors of the building. The darkness spooked her as bad as a loud noise scaring a horse. When she and Johnny were kids, his favorite place for hide 'n seek was inside those dark confines. She'd figured out early on, if she was "it" during the game, she'd leave Johnny to his own hiding place because he loved to hide in the shed. There'd be no good reason to go inside looking for him. Especially after the first time he'd jumped out at her—a whoosh of cold air blasting her face and scaring her enough she soaked her pants—while he ran off laughing.

But now, her curiosity was stronger than any long-ago frights.

Two narrow tire tracks led out the doorway, packing down the inch or so of snow. Nothing else looked disturbed. The white surface was pristine of any footprints, whether man, bird, or animal. The single line of tracks leading away from the building, stillness in the air as if she wasn't alone holding her breath, quietness surrounding her, and the remaining untouched white blanket of snow all sent a shiver up her spine.

Johnny rode his motorcycle on dry days and when he could fill the gas tank but he never, ever, rode when there was snow on the ground. He'd choose to walk in the rain before getting mud caught in the spokes. When her pa told Johnny he could have his old Norton—a war relic—shipped over from Europe when Money came back from serving, her husband spent long hours taking the engine apart to clean and polish each metal surface so it'd purr like a cat. He sanded and painted the gas tank until the surfaces shone like crystal. Johnny used the garage on his ma's property but once Tilly and Johnny married, he'd been explicitly clear the motorbike would be used only by him and only when he wanted to show off his handiwork.

She shuddered as the image from her dream returned—a motorcycle toppling over.

Tilly tentatively reached her hand, the one holding the lantern, in through the archway. As her eyes slowly adjusted to the poor lighting, she looked for the motorbike. Her elbow grazed the frame of the shed, causing a shower of snowflakes to fall from the roofline. She looked up, spotting where some snow had caught in carved lettering on a slate of limestone nailed to the shed—Monroe. Her pa made the plaque so long ago, she never knew of a time the siding was blank. The little shower of flakes left a couple of the letters blank with others still waiting to release a flurry.

She placed one foot inside the shed. A breeze kicked up and extinguished the lantern's flame, plunging the shed into darkness. Something or someone pushed past her legs and she stumbled backward, half-expecting her husband to rush by at any second, scaring the bejeebers out of her, yelling "you're it" as he ran off.

Without a second thought, she lurched away from the entrance, started to run through the yard while ignoring the narrow path, training her gaze on the back door. Partway to the house, her left foot slid out awkwardly to the side, causing her to slam hard down to the ground. Right on her bottom. She scrambled up and made her way to the steps, her nightgown and robe soaking through as the clinging snow started to melt. Tilly tumbled over the threshold, plopping hard on the old linoleum, and kicked off the wet boots. A puddle formed on the floor as more snow trickled down from her robe. She gulped in warm air, displacing the cold that had invaded her body while she surveyed the backyard as a foreign land.

A black cat sat at the corner of the shed, nonchalantly licking one paw without a care in the world. Although feral cats roamed around the village, this one seemed a bit too comfortable, obviously claiming the shelter of the garage. Had she startled this animal from its hiding place? Was this what bolted past her? She shivered as if ghostly whiskers had traveled up her spine.

After stripping off the soggy robe, she ran up to their bedroom.

Her own imagination couldn't distinguish between a strong wind, an animal, and Johnny jumping out at her; they all felt so much alike. Tilly plopped down on the bed, waiting while her breathing slowed and her heart returned to a somewhat normal beat. Minutes ticked by, maybe even half an hour. She sat there so long, time was lost.

Tilly kept thinking about the tire tracks in the snow. Had Johnny taken the motorcycle out of the shed or did someone steal his most prized possession? Talk of stealing swirled like a whirling dervish these days as shop owners repeated tales of items gone missing.

Thad recently told her how one customer was upset with him for not leaving their usual order. He was adamant about delivering two bottles of fresh, cold milk. He made up for the thievery, by giving them four the next morning. "'Tis not right," he exclaimed. "No one need steal from my customers. Jes' come ask me for milk."

She agreed with him. But milk could hardly be compared to a motorcycle. Tilly finally calmed down enough to head back to the first floor. After a quick detour into the parlor to crank the Victor, it dawned on her, the usual couple of bottles of milk were absent from the back stoop.

"Ah, Mr. Andr...Thad..." she called out, upon opening the door to find him about to set the containers next to the house. "You're a little later than usual."

"Ma'am." He handed over the bottles. "Busy mornin' especially with me Brown Molly having a bit of a lame leg. Must be gettin' on. I'll collect on the morrow."

Tilly took the two proffered bottles, smiled at Thad then looked toward the shed. His gaze followed hers but instead of saying anything more, he touched his fingers to the edge of his tam in farewell and walked away.

She frowned. Had he started believing the rumors?

Chapter 14

The Next Morning

"Johnny leave early?"

Money sat at the kitchen table across from Tilly. His fingers twitched even though he'd clasped both hands together. His cane leaned at the edge of the table like a sentinel ready for battle. Its blackened handle oiled from dirt on her pa's hands rubbing the wood to a dark patina. Looked more like a snake ready to strike than an innocent shepherd's hook cane. He was never without this third leg anymore.

His question was disconcerting, seeing as she was deep in thought of exactly where to look for her missing husband. Or, if worry was even necessary.

Johnny had stayed out two nights before and then gently placed his hands against her cheeks and swore to never let it happen a third time. Again, his tender gesture had surprised her but, oh, how he could even stand the smell of himself—the vapors coming off him nearly gagged her. Sweat, dust, mash, but always man. Her senses blurred, always stopping her from pressing for an explanation. She needed him.

"No, Pa, he ain't...isn't...here." She stood up to move over by the stove. "You know he's been gone two nights."

Tilly wanted to rage at her father to stall this

innocent act. She was well aware he kept track of her husband's comings and goings. She was fairly certain he knew the exact number of hours since the last time Johnny had been in this house.

Instead, a different tactic might work.

"Pa," she began. "Can you go out to the shed with me? I need to find something, and it might be heavy."

"What d'ya need?"

She hadn't thought far enough ahead he could actually be curious enough to ask. Tilly only wanted to get a look into the garage after sunrise to see if the motorcycle was there or had, in fact, been wheeled out. The tracks in the snow already told her the truth, but maybe the motorbike was back in there since another night had passed. But then, wouldn't her husband have crawled under the sheets and lain next to her?

"Uh," she stammered. "Oh, I know, I've been looking for a box left behind when ma died. You remember those nesting dolls she'd let me play with."

Yes, those half dozen dolls, each one larger than the last one. All except for the littlest one, the rest were split at each waistline so they could be pulled apart. Then each smaller doll could be nestled inside the next bigger. Her ma brought those dolls from the old country, tucked inside the only suitcase she carried when she and Money traveled halfway around the world to seek a better life. When Tilly was eight or nine, she spent hours sitting on the rug in the parlor, nesting and splitting open the dolls, dreaming up stories of six little ladies. One was the mother, maybe one was an aunt or a nosy neighbor, the rest were children, the baby's name Tuesday or Tilly. In her young life, growing up as their only child, these dolls became a major part of her imaginary family.

But when Theodory died, Tilly never played with them ever again. She didn't want to. Her mother had left forever and no amount of imagination could substitute the largest nesting doll from being the mother to now act as the father. What she wanted to do was crush the largest doll into a million pieces but she missed the chance. All she could figure, her pa must have rescued the nesting ladies before Tilly could do them any harm.

And now, even though she only dreamed up the excuse to check out the dark carriage house, a desire formed so deep inside, her stomach cramped. She truly hoped there was a box tucked away holding some precious and nearly forgotten memories. She wanted to crack open each lady and trace her fingers along the intricate detail of their outfits painted into the wooden dolls, right down to baby Tilly.

"Funny thing to be worrying 'bout," Money finally said. "Shouldn't you be more concerned about where your husband might be?"

"Nothing I can do about him," she answered. "You know he'll come home when he's done with whatever he's doing."

She was tired of being on the defensive, but she also wasn't about to let worry creep into her words. The nightmare played again this morning shortly before waking. This time, the cat entered the scene and wandered past the fallen motorcycle. Chills ran up her spine as fast as the whoosh of air flying out the shed entrance yesterday morning.

Both father and daughter looked out the kitchen window as if Johnny would materialize before their eyes. The snow had stopped falling, but a thick cloud cover remained, shrouding the trees, bushes, and dead grass in a grayish tint. With just enough light, they'd be able to swing open the large door and inspect the garage, leaving the lantern behind. This wasn't necessarily something she wanted to do with him but she wanted—no needed—answers.

"Yoo-hoo," came a call from the back stoop.

Tilly jumped up.

"I'm so glad you're here." Tilly greeted Rita Mae with a quick hug. "Pa, you don't have to come outside after all."

Before Rita Mae could get one foot into the kitchen, Tilly grabbed her coat and slipped her feet into a pair of boots, not even bothering to button them up. So what if the sides flopped back and forth and snow might get her feet wet. She much preferred escaping the kitchen than trying to resolve unanswerable questions.

"What's goin' on?"

"I need to do two things, and you're going to help me with both." Tilly grabbed her friend's hand. They waded through the fresh snow, making a new path of footprints. "The first is you need to help me look for something in the garage."

"What could possibly be out there you need? And, what's the second thing?"

"After we look in there, will you go with me again to Mr. Jensen's?"

Tilly had become so wrapped up spending time with Johnny, she'd completely forgotten about picking up the photographs. Granted, for a couple of weeks, all she'd thought about was the fun time they'd had posing. But now, so much time had passed, she was surprised

Mr. Jensen hadn't come by the house.

"Don't you want Johnny to be the first one to see them with you?"

"Oh, Rita Mae, you are such a romantic…after all," Tilly replied, as they reached the front of the shed. "But, no, Johnny'll see them after you and me."

The garage door was still partially open since Tilly had not braved to go back there after the little mishap with the lantern, the rush of air, and then falling. Both of them pushed the door the rest of the way open so what little light there was could help them.

The building was as old as the house but not nearly as well taken care of. It was a mystery how the wood hadn't been splintered and swept up by a strong wind. Dried and cracked vertical planks helped to create a checkered pattern with the horizontal boards forming the outer layer of siding. When the sun was shining, beams of light would stream through the cracks like spotlights on a stage. No wonder the flame in the lantern had blown out, creating the sensation of a mob of ghosts whooshing past.

Yesterday morning was still fresh in her mind. Tilly shuddered for the hundredth time at the cold rush of air scaring her more than when Johnny jumped out during games of hide 'n' seek.

"What are we looking for?" Rita Mae stood in the center of the near-empty shed, her arms akimbo as she slowly spun like a top.

"See any boxes?" Tilly already knew there wouldn't be anything of importance stored in this garage, but at least this gave her a chance to look around. An old workbench—the top covered with long-ago rusted tools—took up most of the back wall.

Another side had ropes and useless harnesses hanging from pegs, and, from the ceiling by the south wall, pulleys and hooks draped down looking like some medieval torture devices. On occasion, her pa hung dead animals from those hooks, ripped the skin off their bodies, and made money selling the fur and meat.

With the door wide open, a breeze caused the pulleys to slowly swing back and forth, an occasional clank and clatter as they came together sounding like wind chimes. It's a wonder she never burned down the shed to get rid of such gruesome memories.

But, no motorcycle. The tracks had not lied. Reality slapped her square in the face, the motorcycle along with Johnny both were missing. What was she going to do next?

Chapter 15

Two Days Later

Fifty-six hours since Johnny stepped out of the house. Twelve hours since Tilly and Rita Mae checked inside the garage—one looking for a motorcycle and the other thinking a lost box was their mission.

And now, half a dozen photographs covered the bed, faces staring back at Tilly. Some solemn, most with uncomfortable smiles, but a couple showing her and Johnny almost happy. Those two faces were now hardly recognizable, caught in a moment of doing something out of the ordinary. She mulled over how single seconds of that day had been stamped onto cardboard like tiny insects frozen in amber.

Maybe she'd been urged on by troubled feelings based on her pa's warnings and Rita Mae's comments. And now, her husband had been gone longer than ever before and all she wanted was to peek her head in the garage and maybe feel the air whoosh past, as if he'd been hiding behind the motorcycle all this time. He loved to startle her, have her flinch in surprise and squeal, then he'd wrap his arms around her to save them both.

"Tilly!"

Pa sounded more impatient than usual this morning. She slowly gathered up the pictures and slid them into the top drawer of the armoire. The essence of her husband assailed her senses; the musky smell still on a pair of pants he sometimes wore working for clothier Mr. Straws, the subtle scent of Kirk's Flake white soap they'd scrub with, and the pomade oil coating the rims of the two fedoras stacked on a shelf.

Tilly sank back down on the bed and ignored any demands placed.

****

Johnny Miner, 29, of Cedartown is reported missing, leaving no trace of where he might have gone. He's been missing one week, after reports of him being seen in town earlier in the evening. State police are searching the surrounding area for any trace of the missing man. Reports say snow is falling heavily in the area covering tracks of any kind. If you have any information on the whereabouts of Johnny Miner, report to Sheriff Claude Calkins immediately.

Johnny had now been missing for a total of seven days.

Tilly sipped warm milk, hoping to settle her upset stomach. Her whole body felt like a loaf of bread dough with the yeast gone bad, languishing on a cutting board instead of rising in celebration. She was becoming nothing more than a blob of emptiness, with worry and anxiety her constant companions.

"He's dead," Money blurted out.

"No," she eventually replied, ready to shout, if necessary. "Johnny is not dead. Something or someone is making him stay away."

"There's been no trace of your husband." Sheriff Calkins twisted his official cap between gnarled fingers. "Can't follow when there aren't any leads."

"Claude," Mr. Peek spoke up, "you can do better than that. Tell Tilly here there's at least something to hang onto."

The kitchen was starting to feel more crowded than Tilly could handle, with her and Money sitting at the table, while the sheriff and Mr. Peek stood by the entrance to the back room.

"Thought I did putting that notice in the newspaper," the sheriff replied. "If anyone knows his whereabouts, they'll come forward."

"Not with so many in the village thinking they'd get in trouble talking about him running a gambling house and such." Mr. Peek tried again. "Johnny wouldn't just up and leave. Why aren't you talking with his ma, Calkins?"

"You questioning my investigation? Peek, you might have fought in the war, but don't go thinking you can order me around." The sheriff straightened up like he'd been slapped. He crammed the hat back on his head and glared.

"Like I said before," Money butted in, "he's dead."

"Pa," Tilly cried, covering her ears with shaking hands.

"How can you be so sure?" Sheriff Calkins moved closer to the table and leaned down, getting eye-to-eye, nearly nose-to-nose with Money. "You know something?"

Money shook his head and started to open his mouth but Tilly interrupted.

"Don't listen to him. I would know in my heart otherwise." She swirled the remaining bit of milk in the glass as if there might be tea leaves to help her see into the future. Instead, words came back to haunt her…*consider this a warning. Take it serious.* Her body shivered as if trying to slough off her father's words. She couldn't have him saying something in front of the sheriff and Mr. Peek, getting himself into trouble. Better to change tactics now and question him later. "Don't you remember how ma used to say *the heart wants what it wants*? My heart hasn't changed, and I believe he's out there somewhere."

But where? No response from the three men filling up her kitchen.

"I'll run the article a couple more times," Claude begrudgingly continued, "but I've got more things to worry about than some husband running off."

"No use sitting here arguing," her father finally said, struggling to stand. He leaned hard on his cane and headed toward the parlor. "Sheriff, I'll walk out with you."

Once the two men left, Mr. Peek sat down across from Tilly.

"Tilly," he started, his cheeks bright red like he was either about to burst from anger or say something sweet. "I know there's not much I can do, just argue in your corner. In the meantime, come to the movies anytime you want. Save your pennies, they're on me."

She nodded in his direction, unshed tears swimming in both eyes to the point Mr. Peek was a blur. In that moment, someone believing her helped and she pulled in large gulps of air. At least one person in this village was willing to stand up for her.

Chapter 16

Thirty Days Later

Tilly swiped at some bile dribbling down the left side of her chin. She'd emptied her stomach for the fifth time since the nausea hit around seven in the morning. She was a bit afraid to have breakfast, let alone even think about food. Her legs were as wobbly as over-cooked noodles. Maybe some fresh air would help.

Spring was trying to come, in fits and starts, and Tilly hoped filling up her lungs with something other than stale parlor air and her pa's angry words might settle the turmoil. She'd hardly been out of the house for weeks.

Sheriff Calkins carried on an investigation to find Johnny as he'd begrudgingly promised but, so far, not a clue. No one knew anything, or at least they weren't talking. He'd vanished faster than smoke caught in a strong wind and everyone, including her best friend kept insisting he was dead. Tilly was sure he wasn't. He'd been taken away—but, by whom? Or he'd run away—but, why?

With no thought of any destination, she ended up smack dab in front of her ma's headstone. Tilly bent down and brushed away some brown grass and leaves flattened by the winter's snow. The marble stone had weathered another season, bleaching the marker a bit whiter with each passing year. The earth was wet and cold, preventing her from kneeling down close to the small stone. Instead, her gaze scanned the rest of the cemetery while she gathered aimless thoughts.

"Found the nesting dolls." She spoke so soft the words barely reached her own ears. Tilly had taken to walking the ten blocks to the cemetery two, maybe three, times a week and found having a one-sided conversation worked to her benefit. "You will always be…"

She couldn't finish as tears streamed down each cheek and her voice choked with emotion. Tilly knew for certain she was going to be a mother. Wife of Johnny, alone with no sign of her husband, was going to have a baby come this fall, whether she wanted a child or not.

The night before Johnny disappeared the two of them had spent an hour in bed talking about the future, holding each other close, and then finding the best in each other. She hung all her hopes and dreams on an hour of whispers much like a drowning person clutching a lifesaver ring. She never knew him to be so vulnerable, loving, and kind. No one was ever going to convince her he ran away. They didn't know the man she loved. And *thee* would soon be *three*—exactly like the card he'd given her.

So now, here she was, certain as the sun would set each evening, with child. She raised her hands to her cheeks and ran a thumb down each one, the same he'd do when tears left salty lines on her face. His umbrella girl…

"Ma," she cried, dropping down to the wet earth, her coat sponging up moisture.

"Thought I might find you here," Rita Mae whispered.

Tilly flinched. She'd heard footsteps approaching, but why bother getting up? Why not lie down next to the weathered headstone and let the earth draw her in like quicksand. Without Johnny, her life might as well be over. Her whole body rebelled in a shudder—*no, no, no, no, cannot think he's gone. Johnny is alive and he will come back.*

"You all right?" Rita Mae tried another approach, rattling on. "No, my guess is you are doing awful. I can't even imagine. If my husband, if I had one, if my husband died…"

"He is not dead," Tilly interrupted with a growl. "Johnny is not dead. He will come home."

"But, Till…"

"Don't you 'Till' me." *Déjà vu* assailed her senses again, and she remembered the last time her friend kept saying something she didn't want to hear. This time, Tilly was adamant. "Johnny will come back when he can. Something or someone is keeping him away from me." *Lie down, sleep, forget…no, I need to be strong. He will return to me.*

No one knew of the baby she was carrying, not even her best friend. The clues were right in front of Tilly, but she chose to ignore them. But, between feeling sick in the morning, her breasts as tender as when Johnny would pleasure her, and the slight thickening below her navel, she couldn't deny her condition.

And now, because their lives weren't just about the two of them, he had to come back. That was the only solution she'd entertain.

"Let's go home," Rita Mae commanded, not waiting for an answer or resistance. She slipped her arm around Tilly's elbow and pulled her up. "Catching your death of cold is not going to help anyone."

Chapter 17

June 15, 1929

Four months—over one hundred and twenty days. No Johnny, no arms encircling her waist, no nuzzling her neck as he moved aside the long braid, nor any thumbs to wipe away tears.

Well beyond twenty-eight hundred hours, Tilly gave up counting out the good about Johnny for so many hours missing. For the first couple of months, when she wasn't sitting in the parlor numb from raw emotions, she wept, ripped precious copies of the newspaper into shreds, fell asleep and would awake cramped from some odd position. She never considered doing anything else.

The last two months, she'd done nothing. Merely existed; ate once in a while, wandered aimlessly throughout the house, and kept heading out to the garage to peek into the darkness, wondering if the motorcycle had mysteriously reappeared.

Her nights were restless. If she fell asleep, the same nightmarish movie replayed over and over again. Gloves stripped off the fallen body, weeds beginning to grow between the spokes of the motorcycle wheels, and only the birds and squirrels curious enough to venture close except when the cat would appear. Then all sounds disappeared.

She even stopped walking to the lock-up to rant at the sheriff for not doing his job. He was a patient man, but that only fueled her anger more. Rita Mae eventually acquiesced and went on Tilly's behalf to plead for action. None came and she sank deeper.

"Not today," Tilly whispered, as she slowly opened her eyes on a new day. Then with a bellow, she added, "Not tomorrow either."

She moved her hands downward to her stomach and slowly rubbed the skin below her navel which was starting to stretch tight. Changes were happening with each day's passing. Her ankles, once so slender, now swelled with extra fluid undulating like waves when she walked. Her skin tingled as if ants were making paths down her arms and legs. But, there were times also, when a blanket of peacefulness worked as a barrier between her and all of the minor irritations of the day. Today was starting out as one of those days.

Her lips were shrinking to a thin line as the corners of her mouth turned downward. But this morning felt different. She woke with a new verve, a sense of hope, and motivation. Today she would find a reason to smile.

Johnny was not dead, he was somewhere else and would be coming home soon, and she needed to take care of herself and their child. For him. Rita Mae was the only one who knew Tilly was carrying a baby, having not even gone to the doctor yet.

Today, she would make a dress—something with a dropped waist, loose fitting, and maybe a couple rows of large ruffles. She was tired of moping around the house in the old ill-fitting housedresses, not caring how she looked. Didn't much matter before, since she stopped going into town, or to the movies with Rita Mae, or doing hardly anything. Except listening to the only record she had for the Victor phonograph...*I've Got a Crush*...not today, though. On this day, she would start fresh.

Tilly slid out of the bed, swung her robe over her shoulders, grabbed the fireplace poker to put it back in its rightful place, and headed for the kitchen. The sun hadn't come up yet so maybe she'd be in time to see Thad. Since Johnny left, Tilly had taken to staying in bed well into the morning, forestalling any interaction between her and the ever-faithful milkman. Today, a little light conversation might work some magic. Possibly even counteract dealing with her pa's perpetual anger.

Money left early most mornings and came home long after dark. For the last four months, their contact was always brief and non-descript. He was avoiding her, which suited her just fine. He stopped asking if her husband was home and was probably even a bit disappointed he didn't have someone to rail against. He even took to acting like he had one foot in the grave, leaning more on his cane, deeper wrinkles creasing his face, all the while putting on the face of someone who didn't care anymore.

"Morning, Thad." Tilly opened the back door wide enough so she could take the three bottles directly from him, instead of having them deposited on the stoop. "So good to see you."

Mr. Andrews tilted his head in greeting but was otherwise silent.

"Oh, and look at sweet Brown Molly," she continued. "Such a patriotic horse with those flags in

127

her bridle."

The horse snorted so loud—as if she understood the comment—even Thad jumped a little bit, his lips tweaking into a slight smile.

"Good day, ma'am. You're up with the sun this bright mornin'."

"I am," she stated. "And, with so much to do, I didn't want to waste another moment in bed."

If Tilly didn't know better, a blush rose up Thad's cheeks. Or, maybe the cold breeze was playing tricks. Didn't matter. For whatever reason, she was happy to chat with him for a few minutes. Did he think she was flirting with her mention of being in bed? *Heaven's no!*

Without another word, Tilly started to head back into the house.

"Ma'am." Thad tipped his tam. "Any word on your husband?"

And then, once again, all came crashing in on her and there was no forgetting her husband was missing. All she could do was shake her head. Her mood and motivation slithered away faster than a garter snake caught sunning on an open pathway. All she'd thought about doing today would now wait for another day. The mere mention of Johnny sent her into a tailspin, knocking her world off kilter. Who was she kidding?

She needed to continue her vigilance, waiting and watching for him to return. If she stopped, she'd be admitting the naysayers were right and he'd abandoned her or was dead. And, he wasn't. She wasn't ready to give credence to the rumors or gossip. Otherwise, she was widowed and their unborn child had no father. Might even be considered a bastard in this town full of women the likes of Mrs. Osborne. Oh, wouldn't she celebrate?

"Tilly?" Her father greeted her, as she sat down at the kitchen table. She put two of the bottles of milk in the refrigerator, then flicked a finger at the ever-rattling motor same as Johnny would do whenever the grinding gears would get to rattling.

"Pa," she replied, a little discombobulated seeing him sitting there as if he'd been invited to a cordial little tea party. "Aren't you going to be late getting to the shop?"

"We need to talk," he answered.

"And, what would you do if I told you I didn't want to?"

"I'd still ask you to listen." He took the bottle of milk she set on the table. He poured some into a glass in front of him. "You're my daughter, Tilly. I might not be the best pa in the world, but I love you."

Tilly stood, turned her back on him, and retrieved a glass from the cupboard. She might as well sit down with him and listen to what he was itching to say since he wasn't budging. Plus, she didn't have anything better to do. And, him mentioning how much he cared had set her roiling stomach on a high boil. Maybe, a small glass of milk would help.

"Seems the stealing in town has stopped," he continued.

"So?"

"Thought you'd like to know."

"You thinking Johnny had something to do with the stealing, after all?" Typical of him. "So now you're sayin' since my husband's been gone for months, he was the thief?"

Money nodded slowly but didn't say anything. He

kept his gaze trained on her face.

"But you don't have any proof, do you?" Her voice betrayed her as the tone shrank to more of a whine. "Just want to place blame?"

Nausea hit hard, making her throat burn and her mouth fill with saliva. She could run for the outhouse or at least hope to get in the back door, if only her legs hadn't gone soft. She swiped fingertips across her forehead, her hand coming away slimy with sweat. Before she could even clamp her hand over her lips, she turned and threw up into the sink next to the stove. Not much but enough to make her immobile as she leaned over the sink, staring at the yellowish substance puddle close to the drain. She gagged again, but nothing else came up.

"Almighty Lord," Money exclaimed. "What is wrong with you child?"

"Pa," she wiped her mouth with a tea cloth, the closest thing at hand, "I'm surprised you hadn't figured out Johnny and I are going to have a baby."

Chapter 18

A Month Later

"Johnny, come home." Tilly silently chanted. "Please come home. I can't do this alone."

She was sitting in Dr. Glenn's examination room, after talking extensively with his nurse and wife, Nellie, and was getting more upset by the minute. Tilly had enough trouble talking about the changes happening to her own body without some snooty woman mentioning her husband's name over and over again. Johnny this, and Johnny that, Johnny should be here, why wasn't he with her? Was this woman the only person in town not aware he hadn't been seen since the last snowfall, the day after Valentine's Day?

Only Tilly knew there was a card on her nightstand hinting they should start a family. She was the only one in this whole town who knew the levels of their intimacy. How he was a good man. How he wouldn't up and desert her. Only she knew they'd been together as man and wife the night before he disappeared.

Nellie and Mrs. Osborne were friends so, no doubt, her troubles must have made for some lively discussion over tea and cookies. This woman probably hoped for some new little tidbit to pass along. To beat out Rita Mae's ma with something deliciously juicy. Were their lives so empty? Or, was Tilly's imagination simply running rampant?

A thin line of sweat trickled down Tilly's back as agitation worked from a flush in her cheeks to shaking legs lacking the strength to hold her up. Yet her tailbone was burning with a million prickles from sitting on the hard examination table as the white walls pressed in closer. Dr. Glenn probably thought he was doing her a favor keeping this small room so warm but he would have been wrong. Her hands and feet tingled endlessly and she wanted to smash moist palms into the face of the ticking wall clock announcing each second Johnny wasn't here. *Tick…tock…tick…tock…tick, I don't want to be sick; tick…tock…tick…tock…*

Nothing was fair right now and, oh, how she'd love to spit at the nurse's retreating back. A glob of spittle running down the seam of the starched white uniform would serve her right but, instead, Tilly gulped down another wad of bile.

Thad was right. Anything she did now was up for scrutiny, scalpel-like dissection, and eventually exaggerated rumors. The women of this town loved to weave a story to make their dull little lives seem so much more interesting. Mrs. Osborne and another friend, Mrs. Barnerd, had been stirring up trouble for weeks now, after some temperance woman, a Mrs. Wise, had come to town and riled up those attending a gathering at the opera house to argue the ills of drinking. Someone had actually thrown tomatoes at the lectern, bits of red streaming down some of the ladies' coats and the front of the podium, and now those two were talking up the ruination of the village's youth. Of how this had all come to pass because of those reprobates serving hooch, giggle juice, booze in speakeasies, behind locked doors, and running blind pigs while the law looked the other way.

Tilly believed these women used gossip and rumors to besmirch her Johnny but, even if the truth came out, would they stop? Hadn't they ever been taught *because whispered tales seldom are true*?

Tears began coursing down Tilly's cheeks. Why, oh why, did she have to be fodder for their gossip mill? And, on top of everything going wrong in her life, she and her pa had barely spoken two words to each other since she told him about the pregnancy. Money acted like she brought shame to their family; he didn't even try to help her feel better.

"Dear Tilly," Dr. Glenn greeted her, as he strolled into the room.

How he ever found Nellie to be a suitable wife was beyond Tilly. For each snooty comment coming out of Nellie's mouth, a kind, fatherly word of advice was passed along by this man. His whole presence calmed the tornado of thoughts swirling around in her head.

He frowned a bit in her direction. "We ran the tests and you are with child. But you already knew, I'm sure."

A week earlier, she'd had enough uncertainty. Strange, fluttering sensations woke her at night, first seeming like an upset stomach, but then more. Tiny bumps would push out below her navel then recede. Or, a big belch would unexpectedly rise up through her and release before she was quick enough to clamp a hand over her mouth.

So she made an appointment. Nellie drew blood from Tilly's rail thin left arm, had her drain her bladder into a cup but then been told to expect to wait at least a week to find out if the *rabbit died*. How crass, and the nurse had actually said those two words with a slight smirk on her face.

Tilly had wanted to slap the look off the nurse's face. An innocent animal would die to prove a new life was about to come into this world. A world where Johnny was still missing.

If Nurse Nellie had any integrity, she never discussed patients and their problem outside this office but somehow this information might have been wildly too spicy to keep under wraps. Would there be whispers behind closed doors, promises of keeping a secret, or tantalizing Rita Mae's ma with a mystery of guess who this or guess what? Tilly was glad she'd confided in her friend but could Rita Mae have been tricked into saying more than she should?

"All right, young lady," Dr. Glenn continued, his voice as calming as sipping warmed milk late at night. "Let's dry those tears and talk about what we are going to do for the next few months."

****

Dr. Glenn had all sorts of precautions for Tilly to think about—eat more, sleep at least eight hours each night, try not to work as hard, release unsolvable worries, ignore those people whose only purpose served to upset her.

He told her to pack away her corsets, which she'd acquiesced to immediately. She'd put them so far away, those wildly constricting forms of torture might never see the light of day again.

In the doctor's opinion, reading was the best way to relax. To get a little exercise by walking to the ladies library a few blocks away and find something to take her mind off her troubles. Or, listen to the Victor phonograph player, even if she only had one record. Funny thing, he told her to trim her long hair so she wasn't carrying so much weight. She couldn't. Johnny needed to come home to the same Tilly he'd left behind.

The list went on and on, but she couldn't remember most of what Dr. Glenn said. She'd basked in the quiet of the examination room and let his words drench her like a warm waterfall, assurances all would eventually work out.

The glow of his words lasted up to the moment she walked in the back door of the house to find a mess in the kitchen. Her father had helped himself to whatever he felt like having for breakfast but left the clean up to her. So typical of him.

The house was otherwise quiet. She stood surveying the mess then headed to the parlor and cranked up the Victor…*I've Got a Crush on You*…

Tilly did remember one thing Dr. Glenn mentioned. She was to put up her feet once in a while and so she would. Since Johnny had disappeared, she'd taken to piling copies of the newspaper—at least the ones not torn to shreds—on the table next to the sofa. An hour of prescribed reading wasn't going to hurt anyone and might actually do some good.

An advertisement caught her attention for some beef and pork specials. The pork immediately reminded her of last Christmas with the pig snout, eyeballs, and intestines. A shudder ran down her spine. But Dr. Glenn had mentioned the importance of eating for the baby and right now a beef stew, filled with potatoes and carrots actually made her mouth water. Stew beef was running at fifteen cents a pound at Mr. Navarro's. Maybe after a little more reading she would take a walk back downtown and pick up a little something.

Fortunately, she had a few successes with selling purses and hats lately, so maybe a little bit of splurging was in order. Working with fabric and beads was her only salvation while waiting for Johnny to return. And, thank goodness for the generosity of Mr. Hamilton to display her wares in his dry goods store. Those tall glass panes at the front of his building turned out to be the perfect place for the women of the village to discover her handiwork.

The rabbit died. What an awful way to confirm being with child. Tilly gently smoothed her dress covering a now bulging stomach. The lightweight fabric was perfect for soft flowing ruffles to cover the mound and helped to keep her condition away from prying eyes.

A few months back, she'd rummaged through a closet in the sitting room off their bedroom and found a number of simple yet elegant dresses, some adorned with subtle beading at the neckline or cuffs. Her mother must have worn these at some point, but they were in nearly-new condition. Rather puzzling to Tilly.

All the same, time to put these dresses to better use than be dust collectors. With the Singer sewing machine now permanently set up in the sitting room, Tilly easily redesigned two of the dresses into one. The shift, styled in the shape of a giant wrap designed to hang loose from her shoulders and gather at one hip, became her going-out dress for any shopping or errands. When she was home, a robe covered her condition.

Even with all the precautions from Dr. Glenn to be restive, calm, and to put aside worries, if she allowed herself to think too much about her husband missing, panic swelled in her chest of how she'd handle a baby alone.

Oh, Johnny, please come home.

Chapter 19

A Few Hours Later

"What'ya doin' here," Johnny's ma asked. Her voice was as rough as wooden wheels scraping over cobblestone. She coughed hard before continuing. "Been long time since you came knockin'. Not sure you're welcome at my door."

"Wait, Mrs. Miner." Tilly slammed her hand hard against the door as the old woman pushed back. "I need to find Johnny."

"He…ain't…here. Ain't seen him goin' on long weeks. Left me high 'n dry."

Tilly wedged her foot between the frame and the door, keeping it from closing. She was taking a chance of the old woman pinching her toes if she chose to but, more importantly, a mystery needed to be solved. After realizing her own father wasn't going to be of any help finding Johnny—sitting at the kitchen table with a blank expression after she'd blurted out the news about the baby—she had to take action.

Early on, a few weeks after she and Johnny got married, Johnny's mother, Clarine, had made her thoughts explicitly clear no one was good enough for her boy, especially the likes of *a mere wisp of a girl with no gumption*. Tilly heard these derogatory comments in a roundabout way from Rita Mae through her mother's gossip. She'd laughed but those few words stung. She made an effort numerous times to have her mother-in-law over to their house, but there was always some excuse. Tilly finally gave up. No doubt, this too became a point of sorry contention.

Today, all earlier nonsense and hurt feelings had to be put aside. Tilly had racked her brain on where to look, who to talk with, where to find someone who might offer a clue or suggestion, and to stop sitting long hours in the sheriff's dusty, smoke-filled office. A man does not up and disappear. Nor does a man, after slaving long hours turning a rusty, beaten-up motorcycle into a pristine machine, disregard all he's said and ride in snowy weather.

This was a small town, after all, and vanishing into thin air like Houdini was not normal. A few had the temerity to suggest he jumped the train, heading west in search of gold. One too many times, she heard how he was guilty of stealing, of running a blind pig, and the town was better off without the likes of him. But no one had an explanation for the missing motorcycle.

Oh, how they all turned on him and chided her for not accepting he was gone. All because of rumors and gossip, and *because whispered tales seldom are true*. Oh, how could a childhood poem keep running through her head whenever she wavered, possibly believing the worst?

"Please," Tilly begged. "Please, I need to find my husband."

"You talkin' nonsense girl," the old woman muttered barely above a whisper, her feverish gaze dimmed by confusion. "Figured you were stoppin' him from seein' his old ma."

"He's gone missing and hasn't been home since the middle of February." Tilly spelled out her words slowly to the woman.

"And you think I'm hidin' him here?" Mrs. Miner let go of the handle, letting the door slowly swing open. The woman forced a smile on her face, showing off a gaping hole where there used to be two front teeth. "If you aim to accuse me of somethin'…say so…or get on your way, missy."

"I'm not accusing you of anything," Tilly replied, her courage breaking down from an hour earlier when she'd been certain confronting the old woman was the only way Johnny would be found. "I don't understand what has happened."

Tilly peeked into the gloomy living room. She'd only been to this house one other time in the last six months and, after a quick look, nothing had changed. Well, maybe a little more filth. How this woman held Tilly in such bad judgment was beyond her. At least the home she kept for her father and husband was clean, organized, and brighter by far.

"Look around." Clarine fanned her hand out like a *grande dame* showing off a palace. "Go ahead, you ain't gonna make a liar out of me. Johnny ain't here."

Tilly shuffled a couple steps backward, positive in her desire never to cross the worn threshold. But her eye caught sight of something to turn her stomach upside down. What looked like a scarf was draped over the handrail for the stairs to the second floor, matching the description Johnny had given her when he complained about being blamed for stealing. Were there two in town made of this beautiful brown and black glen plaid? Its colors blending into a luxurious blur of squares. Or, was this the one reported stolen? And, if so, how in the devil did it end up in this old woman's wreck of a house?

She grabbed hold of the railing around the porch, a splinter immediately catching on her ungloved hand, digging deep into her middle finger. Tilly winced but didn't dare say anything. Her legs had gone wobbly.

"Girl, you as white as my best set of sheets," Clarine commented, a look of concern actually replacing the usual scowl. "Are you sure you don't want to come in an' set a spell?"

Bile threatened to work its way up Tilly's throat, but she swallowed hard a couple of times, not wanting to show weakness. But, white as a sheet? Sheets in this old broken-down house would be more like an oily-gray rag.

"Mrs. Miner," she said, finally finding her voice. "If Johnny shows up, tell him I need him."

Tilly turned and bolted down the steps, beginning to lose faith Johnny was safe but praying her legs carried her down the sidewalk and eastward back home. Showing weakness in front of her mother-in-law would have only fanned the flames of her contempt.

"What…did he get tired of always havin' to tell ya where'er he went? Did he figure out you ain't half the woman he thought?" Hate bubbled out of the old hag's mouth like a seething volcano.

"No…" Tilly's legs were moving but each step felt like suctioning her feet out of muck. She turned back toward the porch. "And, I'm not a girl with no guts, as you told someone. Something about being a mere wisp."

The look of shock at hearing the gossip making full

circle back to Tilly, told her the entire story. Finally, she'd surprised the old woman. Mrs. Miner could call her a *mere wisp* all the old hag wanted to, Tilly'd never be bothered again.

"So you heard," the old woman finally found her voice, no rasp nor choking sound. "Am I wrong?"

"Yes, you are. I'm the only one fighting for my husband. I'm the only one with the strength of faith he'll return, including you and every single person in this village." Tilly had never before spoken her mind and, for once, her actions actually felt right. She stepped a bit livelier, the imaginary muck falling away.

"Hey, if Johnny ever decides to come home, tho," Clarine loudly cackled, "tell him he needs to come see his ol' ma." The woman's witchy laughter echoed down the street, caught by the wind, swirling overhead like a threatening thunderstorm.

Tilly ran across the street, barely missing a pile of fresh horse dung, still steaming. Alas, the rancid odor was the last thing she could take causing her to bend forward and add a lumpy stream of yellowish-orange bile alongside the pile. She gagged again but was void of anything else in her stomach. She staggered backward a couple of steps, temporarily losing her balance.

A street vendor had hot popcorn bouncing inside a bright red handcart, with hand-lettered glass, keeping the kernels trapped. Unfortunately, the sweet, tantalizing smell wafted her way, co-mingling with the manure in the road.

She clamped the glove she'd been strangling in her hand over her mouth and staggered to a bench in front of the druggist's building.

Tilly slumped forward, forcing her panicked breathing to slow down. Luckily, there weren't many people, and so far no one she knew, walking along the plank sidewalk. So much hate filling one body. How Johnny came into this world and survived being raised surrounded by such bitterness was beyond Tilly's comprehension.

Her new mother-in-law appeared to like her at first, even offering up intimate details of why Johnny was the way he was. Clarine had talked at length of stubbornness and how being so bull-headed would *serve him well*. Not her words—more like *gits the man what he wants*. How a woman like Tilly could help a man like Johnny. At least all of this was face to face; behind her back, a different tale came her way. *A mere wisp of a girl with no gumption, no guts*. As hard as Tilly had persevered by learning how to cook and being the perfect mate in bed to make Johnny happy, these hurtful words still stung.

Well, Tilly would show the old woman. Her husband hadn't left of his own free will and she would look for the answer until her dying breath. And now, little did her mother-in-law know, but she'd lost any right to being a part of this child growing up.

"You are as white as my best set of sheets."

Tilly nearly jumped up off the bench. Was she hearing voices? Had an echo of her mother-in-law's cackle carried over the trees and houses to the center of town? She looked upward. Oh, God. There stood Mrs. Osborne, her eyebrows arched in question, a smirk puckering her face. Tilly looked around but, regrettably, Rita Mae, was nowhere to be seen. She'd have to deal with this gossipy woman on her own, without the soft tempering of her best friend.

"Good morning, Mrs. Osborne," she said, barely above a whisper. A sour odor assailed her senses, making her swallow hard a couple times to prevent anything else from heaving upward.

"Are you okay, dear?"

"Oh yes, I'm fine," Tilly lied but, at the same time, wondered if Dr. Glenn's wife, Nellie, might have said something to Mrs. Osborne.

"Must be so very difficult, what, with your husband gone missing." Mrs. Osborne said in a syrupy sweet voice, bending down so they were eye-to-eye.

She would not cave. Tilly pressed her lips together and sucked in deep breaths through her nose, willing nothing would accidentally be blurted out that this woman could turn into something hurtful.

"He'll be back," she finally replied.

"Oh, I've heard talk," the old woman continued as if Tilly had never spoken. "The Klan's rounding up no-goods and cleaning up this town."

Tilly chose not to reply.

"Heard your husband's maybe gotten himself in too deep."

You nasty old woman. There was no way she was going to say those words out loud but, oh, how she wanted to. Instead, Tilly stood, her legs unstable but strong enough. "If you will excuse me, Mrs. Osborne," she managed. "I have some shopping to do."

"Mark my words, young lady. I won't rest until this town is rid of the likes of those running blind pigs, drinking behind locked doors, and frolicking with wanton women."

Tilly couldn't take any more of this woman's self-righteous attitude. She turned back toward Rita Mae's mother and stepped right up to the woman, nose-to-nose.

"Now you listen to me," she began. "You mind your own business, stay out of mine, and if I hear one more rumor or bit of gossip about my husband, I will…I will…"

What? What could she do? Nothing. Maybe some of what her mother-in-law had said was true; she's *a wisp of a girl with no gumption*. No, no, no, she was different. No need to treat a person poorly, even if that someone was a nasty, mean gossip. She turned on her heels and headed into Dr. Spencer's store, spotting the first opened door for her escape. Anything to get away from yet another unpleasant encounter.

She barely stepped inside the store, the bell jingling overhead, when she about ran into the backside of a rather large man.

"Oh, dear," she exclaimed. "Mr. Navarro, I didn't see you there."

"Ah, Mrs. Miner. Not sure how you could miss me." He straightened up to his full height.

Tilly's mind flashed back to the loud pounding at the back door, someone yelling for her husband to get outside, and him saying he'd take care of the ruckus. Him arguing with someone in the dark, not far from the shed. Then, the Victor being presented as a belated Christmas gift.

Had she unwittingly spotted Mr. Navarro? The shape of the man seemed familiar at the time but far enough away and being so dark, she'd never figured out whose stance reflected defeat. And, as was the usual, Johnny would not discuss what happened; she was to forget hearing or seeing anything. But, why now, did she have the strangest feeling Mr. Navarro had stood in their backyard and he was the one handing over the Victor. Possibly, under protest.

Shelves of food spun in front of her, the sunlight coming through the front windows caused sparks at the edges of her eyes, and the floor tilted. Her thoughts spun wildly like the spoked-wheel round-about they played on as children…round and around, hanging on tight for fear of being flung aside. Tilly clutched at her stomach, the roiling threatening to explode again. She had to get home.

"I'm sorry, Mr. Navarro," she apologized. "I'm really most sorry."

"No need to apologize. No harm done, my dear."

She escaped as quickly as she'd done from Mrs. Osborne. The fresh air hit her in the face, allowing for a couple deep breaths. She willed her stomach to settle down. Keeping her eyes trained on the sidewalk, Tilly walked home as quickly as possible, maneuvering around nails popping up from the plank sidewalk, and making sure to avoid manure in the road. The couple of blocks seemed more like two miles.

She paused briefly on the sidewalk in front of their house, the couple of porch steps looking more like a hill to be struggled up. Once through the front door, she fell onto the couch, visions of fainting out on the dusty road having her in such a panic.

****

Well, life certainly happened in threes, after all. Didn't hardly matter if they were good or bad. Unfortunately, this time wasn't like Rita Mae's luck a few months back. This was all bad. Her mother-in-law's spite, Mrs. Osborne and her initial care turning into such snide remarks, and then running into Mr. Navarro's back. Well, Mr. Navarro's back wasn't the problem; realizing there was something awfully wrong about her receiving the Victor from Johnny as a Christmas gift became too real.

Granted, she'd wondered about the gift. How he walked in the back door carrying a large box moments after having an argument with someone. But, she had put all her concerns aside.

Now, the thought made her sick. Had Johnny come into the Victor through devious means? Was her beautiful phonograph player tainted with deceit and corruption? Had Johnny actually been stealing when he was so adamant otherwise?

Tilly sat at the kitchen table, a cup of tea going cold between her hands, as she mulled over the day's disaster. As soon as she felt well enough to stand up from the couch, she made her way up to their bedroom, changed out of her street clothes, and slipped into the oversized robe she'd hastily draped over a chair earlier.

She stood long enough in front of the mirror beside the armoire, pondering over how her stomach was now bulging out. She was five months with child, from what Dr. Glenn calculated and of the date she'd never forget. Especially when she was dressed in only her slip. She probably wouldn't be able to hide this fact much longer and then more than her pa and Rita Mae would know the truth.

Chapter 20

Six Months with Child

Ten photographs splayed out over the bedcovers. Ill-gotten coins would have been more welcomed. But then, Johnny would've returned and life might have resumed as before. Instead, one picture was already ruined from two teardrops landing directly on top of faces frozen in time. The heavy paper had immediately absorbed the salty water, tiny puckers damaging the smooth surface. As the water evaporated, white residue outlined the blurry circles, obscuring the smiling expressions once so prominent.

Tilly couldn't take her gaze off the couple staring back at her from so many different poses. She was almost back in the mirrored fun house at the fair. Oh, how she and Johnny would spend their waking hours, once a year for a whole week after the last harvest in the fall, located at the outskirts of town. The fairgrounds would be filled with circus animals, odd and interesting travelers, carnie food, rides, and all sorts of displays by local farmers.

Her favorite was stepping into the hall of mirrors where a hundred images would come and go, twist and turn, depending on which way she moved, and then Johnny would sneak up on her, sometimes tugging on her braid. How he loved to make her squeal.

Tilly's legs trembled with weakness at the memories of those heady fall days when they were growing up. The innocence, those carefree times, the moments of not being an adult.

A lifetime had passed, or only a blink of an eye. A tick of a second off the clock since a breathtaking and exhaustingly-glorious couple of hours posing for Mr. Jensen. She could still conjure up the sulfur smell surrounding them with each startling flash of a bulb. Johnny's enthusiasm had left her breathless.

"Till? You here?" Rita Mae's voice—without the normal *yoo-hoo*—echoed up the stairs from the kitchen.

"In our bedroom," she called out. Tilly swiped at her wet cheeks, then gathered up the photographs, placing the spoiled one at the bottom of the pile.

"Oh, oh, let me see," her friend enthused, as she came through the door archway. "I love lookin' at these pictures Mr. Jensen took at Christmas time."

Tilly nodded and handed the pile to Rita Mae.

"I can't believe you haven't done anything with these yet," her friend continued to rattle on. "Showing them off and all, especially with Johnny gone."

"Missing, not gone."

"These are beautiful. Just gorgeous. Oh, this one of the two of you looking off in the distance. You need to frame this one." Rita Mae was either so intrigued by the collection or being stubbornly oblivious to the fact Tilly wasn't saying much.

Either way, Tilly composed herself. A month ago, after the debacle with her mother-in-law, she pretty much figured staying inside, away from prying eyes and salacious comments, gave her peace.

Kindly enough, Mr. Navarro delivered groceries,

Thad became her best informant of what was happening in the village, and even Mr. Jensen stopped by one afternoon for a short chat. Her pa became a bit gossipy while they sat at the kitchen table for their evening meal. Rita Mae was a lifeline to what movies were playing at the Vaudette, and Mr. Peek stayed true to his word, ushering her in while he waved off any payment. Tilly spent some days creating more purses, matching hats, and even a shawl or two but, more often than not, staring out a window instead.

"I bet Mr. Hamilton has the perfect frame for this one," Rita Mae said. "How about you and me go shopping today?"

"No, I'm fine staying here," Tilly replied.

"Aw, come on. Do you good to take a walk, you know. Plus, we could deliver more of your beautiful creations."

"I get enough walking for all my trips to the outhouse. And, my visits to see Dr. Glenn, too."

The doctor's office was located a couple doors down the street and her last visit happened a week ago. She'd complained how often her day was interrupted by nature calling but he'd merely chuckled. "All part of being with child," he assured her.

"Could you take care of this? Take these to Mr. Hamilton and see if he has a frame. Maybe he'd give me one in trade." The coins in the canning jar were dwindling.

"I can," Rita Mae replied, "but I'd rather we go together."

Tilly wandered over to the single window in the bedroom, the one overlooking the back yard. She spotted the same cat, nonchalantly licking away at a paw, after having found a sunny spot by the outhouse. Seems she'd been adopted by the animal, as it was usually close at hand whenever a trip to the outhouse was necessary. The cat would even follow Tilly's circuitous route away from the shed.

She turned to see her friend placing finished gloves, hats, and a couple of scarves into a box. Rita Mae worked diligently, her head bent in concentration, her face set in stone as if to prevent her mouth from working. She was so opinionated but knew the limits of what to say, and this was one time not to push.

"I'll take them this time, but will you think about going to a movie? It's been a couple of weeks."

Tilly didn't have the energy to answer.

"*Syncopation* is playing at the Vaudette," Rita Mae continued. "Barbara Bennett isn't nearly as pretty as Delores Costello but she and Bert Glennon sing in this one. Can you believe what's happening in movies? Not only talking but singing, too."

"Singing, you say." Did sound like fun and, oh, how Tilly would love to sit in the dark theater, living in a fantasy world for a couple hours. "Maybe…"

Rita Mae twirled around, dropping the last hat into the box, squealed, and gave her a quick hug. "Maybe means yes! I'll be back in a bit and see what time the movie starts." She tossed the last scarf over the items to keep any dust from the road off them, hoisted up the box, and headed out the bedroom before Tilly could change her mind.

Maybe he'll come home when I'm not here. The sound of his voice is fading. Tilly slipped the photographs into the armoire with her discarded corsets and slowly pushed the drawer closed on Johnny's smiling face.

****

Tilly had so enjoyed the movie with Rita Mae last night. As she thumbed through a copy of last week's newspaper—one Mrs. Harbinger had been so kind to leave on the front porch to be found once she and Rita Mae returned from the show—she searched for an advertisement for the next movie Mr. Peek might be offering at the Vaudette. Hopefully, a comedy or musical.

Felt as delicious as a piece of fresh apple pie to forget her troubles, if even for a short time. But, unfortunately, the editor of the newspaper seemed bent on reminding her.

When the lion and the lamb lie down together, the camel and the blind pig will do the same thing.

Not even ten in the morning and, with a single, short sentence, exhaustion slithered through her body and weighed down Tilly's shoulders. She let the newspaper fall to her lap while at the same time closing her eyes. A slow motion movie began traveling through her thoughts…intestines, bits and pieces of a pig, and ribbons of blood then, like in the Vaudette, lights, action, camera…

…A spotlight shone down on a man having a tug of war with a pig, a glen plaid scarf being used as the rope. The man lost his footing and disappeared from the cone of light into the darkness. The pig danced a jig while the scarf floated upward, taken away by a rush of wind…

Her eyelids fluttered opened enough to see the wallpaper at the other side of the room, the cabbage roses wavering to and fro as if a breeze had caught their petals.

...Another spotlight appeared to the left of the first. A motorcycle, reclining on the ground as if napping, lovely yellow daffodils sprouting up between the wheel spokes. The petals grew so fast, they disappeared from the bright, white light leaving only gently swaying over-sized green leaves creating an umbrella above the fallen bike. Within seconds, the motorcycle was blanketed. The breeze sighed...

A musky, somewhat sour odor tweaked her olfactory, reminding her of those long lost days of exploring old cellars. Descending into the darkness, holding Johnny's hand as her lifeline to safety, their fingers intertwined so nothing would separate them.

...A third spotlight grew brighter as the first two faded away. Pairs of deerskin gloves, cloche hats with peacock feathers, and furry muffs marched as stiff as soldiers two by two across ice-coated spikes of grass. Crunch and crackle...the grass cried as blades were crushed to the hard ground...

She shivered.

...Fingers squished deep into the dough, then expertly folded the rubbery substance in half, both palms sinking deep into the ball. Repeat, then repeat again, over and over...

"Till."

No, the bread needs to be finished. He will be home soon and he loves pan bread, no, biscuits. He wants biscuits, nothing else. Oh dear, I should be making those, not kneading this. What am I to do?

"Till, wake up."

"Huh?" She jerked aside from the hand grabbing her shoulder. "No, no, I have to finish."

"What are you mumbling about?" Rita Mae asked, continuing to push Tilly's shoulder. "And when did you get a cat?"

Tilly opened her eyes, a fretful expression on her friend's face coming into focus.

"What?"

"A cat, a yellow, kind of orange-ish, scruffy thing," Rita Mae replied. "I called when I came in the back door but you didn't answer. I came in here and there's this cat on your stomach, pushing and pawing at you. Jus' like kneading bread."

She sat up, rubbed the sleep from her eyes, and worked to make sense of what her friend was saying. She gazed around the room, taking in the newspaper which had fallen to the floor, the dying embers in the fireplace, and the gramophone making a scratchy sound since the record had long since finished. No cat, though.

"The mangy thing ran off," Rita Mae offered up. "I'm sure my gasp scared it." She walked over to the phonograph player and gently picked up the arm and needle from the slowly-spinning record. The room was too quiet and, so typical of her friend, she had to fill in the hushed spaces. "You okay?"

"Tired, I guess," Tilly finally replied. "Do you ever dream?"

"Sometimes, but I don't usually remember much. Why?"

"Ever since *you know what* happened," Tilly slowly circled her fingers over her ever-growing mound, "I've been having the strangest dreams."

"Like what?"

"Maybe of Johnny, definitely his motorcycle. But the motorbike is always fallen over, and, oh, so many other visions."

"Do you think your dreams are trying to tell you something?" Rita Mae sat down next to Tilly on the horsehair couch. Her friend enveloped Tilly's hands in hers, warm and comforting to her ice-cold ones.

"Yes, he's in trouble," Tilly quickly replied.

"Or, something worse has happened," her friend suggested.

"Johnny is not dead."

"Then, where is he? Why hasn't he come home or, at the very least, let you know where he is?"

"Something or someone is stopping him."

They sat in silence for a long minute. Rita Mae opened her mouth to speak.

Tilly held up a hand. "I want to go talk with a psychic."

"*Dry up.*" Rita Mae gasped. "Tell me you're joking."

"Why would you think I'm not serious? Honestly, no one believes me about Johnny. They all believe he's run off. Saying he's gone west to dig for gold or something." Tilly stood up and started pacing back and forth in front of the couch. Her head was spinning with how and where she could find a psychic. Maybe get answers. Take this on herself, not ask for help from her pa or Johnny's ma or even Sheriff Calkins. Let them all assume the worst.

She had a few coins in the Mason jar. How much could a couple of minutes cost with someone positing a solution? By no fault of her own, she had become the poor abandoned bride of Johnny.

She wasn't.

"Till," her friend pleaded, "you ain't yourself. You

can't take the word of someone making up whatever you want to hear."

"Who says?"

"All this talk is making you sound like some crazy person. You're supposed to be the normal one." Rita Mae attempted a laugh, but failed as a nervous twitter escaped her lips. "The townspeople will talk even more if you go through with this."

"Not if we go to Howell," Tilly suggested. "We could take the train there and no one will be the wiser."

"We could tell anyone asking we're going shopping," her friend said, perking up. "Howell has the latest fashions, especially since Detroit is so far away, so why not say that's our reason?"

Tilly grabbed the newspaper up from the floor and started leafing through the pages, running her fingers down the columns. The train schedule was posted weekly. Of course, the notice showed up when she didn't care one way or the other. But, now she cared and couldn't find it.

"Aha!" Her fingers—smudged with ink from the newsprint—landed on a small framed advertisement at the lower corner of page eight. "Wednesday morning, 10:00, to Howell, heading onto Detroit. I'm going to be on that train. How about you?"

"Tomorrow?"

"Yes, why wait?" She stuck one finger into her mouth, cleansing off the black mark from the newspaper. She noticed the small scar from the splinter wedged into her skin from her mother-in-law's porch railing. The old cut still hurt once in a while, a nasty reminder of an ugly morning and of the infection Dr. Glenn finally had to treat. She'd actually drained the little bottle of Listerine she'd bought to sterilize her split lip, trying to take the sting out of the offending sliver.

"We don't even know if there's a psychic reader in Howell. Maybe we should reconsider this."

"I'm tired of the whole town saying I'm the reason Johnny's not here." Tilly scanned the newspaper. Maybe there'd actually be an advertisement for one.

"Aha," she repeated, spotting three lines of typeset in the Howell business directory. *Madame Bonavaire, Psychic and Medium, readings every day except Sunday, between the hours of high noon and sunset*, listed below *Dr. Bennett, D.D.S.*, and directly above *Mr. Cruickshank, Attorney-at-Law*. Madame Bonavaire was in good company, squeezed between a dentist and a lawyer. She must be reputable. "We'll get on the ten o'clock train, have an hour to find her, then be back here by dinner."

"You're serious, aren't you?" her friend commented, a look of resignation spreading across her features.

"You bet your sweet Aunt Bessie." Tilly giggled, even if there wasn't such a person.

No one, especially Clarine, would ever again say she was but *a mere wisp of a girl with no gumption* after this. She was going to find out what happened and all of this would bring him back. He'd find out they were going to have a darling little baby and no more would she go to bed with the fireplace poker her only protector and companion.

Chapter 21

Wednesday, Nine Thirty in the morning

Tilly stood beside Rita Mae off to the left side of the platform. The train pulled up alongside the station portico, slowing to a stop with a bluster of squeaking brakes and a column of acrid smoke puffing from the stack above the engine. The spinning of the huge metal rail wheels acted like a vacuum, sucking air off the platform and pulling them a step closer to the tracks.

Goosebumps pocked her arms as excitement and anticipation worked through her. Both the train ride and what they might unearth in Howell bounced back and forth in her thoughts.

Although the day had started out a little cool, especially when Tilly made her early morning trip to the outhouse, no doubt this August day would heat up. But, no matter. She still chose to wear a lightweight coat to cover her expanding condition.

Rita Mae gave her best effort to talk Tilly out of the train ride, saying the jostling and bouncing of the cars would surely do more harm than good. Tilly was not to be dissuaded from her mission. The sooner she found out what happened to Johnny, the faster he'd get home to meet their baby.

"The trainmaster said nearly an hour to get to Howell. Where are you lovely ladies off to this summer morning?" They turned to the familiar voice while he tipped a deep brown felt fedora, instead of his usual tam, toward them.

"Why, Mr. Andrews, how nice to see you." Tilly realized she was being unusually formal in front of Rita Mae. The next time Thad was at Tilly's back stoop, she'd remember to call him by his first name. "And, you look so different."

He wore a natty brown suit, so unlike his usual summer uniform of navy work pants and a white shirt with a patch over the left breast, *Milkman Thad*, so he'd never be mistaken as anything but the local deliveryman. He looked slightly uncomfortable as beads of sweat set upon his forehead. Overdressed for the weather, same as Tilly.

"Are you heading to Howell also?" Rita Mae showed her usual curiosity, getting right to the point.

"I'll accompany you ladies there, if ye'd allow me to come along, but then I'm off to Detroit to visit with me da," he replied.

"Your what?"

"Me Father," Thad answered. "Sorry."

Both Tilly and Rita Mae nodded in unison.

Just then, the train whistle blasted so loud, conversation would have been pointless. The porter descended the two steps from the train to the platform and held out his hand to assist them into the car. Tilly led the way to matching bench seats facing toward each other. They sat down side by side with Thad across from them. Other passengers moved on to other seats, passing by, nodding quick hellos.

A few minutes later, Tilly's stomach heaved slightly as the train car lurched to and fro. Before too much longer, the ride smoothed out and she was able to find some comfort. She pulled her loose-fitting coat a little tighter around her stomach and placed her handbag on top. A warming breeze swirled above their heads since the windows had been lowered from the top and not the bottom, although a rush of cool air might have helped settle her stomach sooner.

Streaks of green whisked by as soon as they'd left the clusters of homes making up Cedartown. For the remainder of the ride, all they'd see were the blue-green haze of pine trees, or the massive trunks of oak trees. The branches and leaves creating a canopy over the train tracks, or an occasional dirt road. Sometimes a cloud of dust, created by an automobile or wagon waiting by the tracks, would linger in the still air.

Tilly failed to notice her surroundings. She was lost in her thoughts of what a psychic reader might conjure. She didn't dare mention anything of their mission to Thad. Not because he would tell anyone but more because she was starting to have a few doubts. What if she and Rita Mae couldn't find this Madame Bonavaire? What if she didn't like what she heard? What if everyone was right all along about Johnny?

The hour dragged on slower than an evening meal with her pa—rarely much conversation, mostly chewing, an occasional burp from him, then going their separate ways.

As soon as the train came to a halt—not a complete stop as the cars kept ever-so-slightly bouncing back and forth like an impatient child eager to be on the move—the two of them disembarked, bidding farewell to Thad.

The station platform was at least twice the size as the one they'd left an hour earlier. A building towered above them and stretched nearly a block long, double doors pulled wide open all along the trackside. The day had heated up in the time they'd been traveling and those in the station must have been hoping for a breath of air. Tilly was also feeling the warmth but truly hoped she could continue to wear her coat until they found Madame Bonavaire.

"Now where did I put the slip of paper?" Tilly rummaged through her purse. She'd memorized every word regarding this psychic but, in her nervousness, her mind had gone blank. "Oh, good, here it is."

Rita Mae looked over her shoulder at the slip of paper, *114 Walnut Street, Howell*, in the smallest typeset.

"This way." Rita Mae took Tilly's arm so they were heading north from the train station.

They had about half an hour before the meeting and, while on the train, they'd decided purchasing a small gift for Madame Bonavaire might be a nice gesture. Especially, if this woman told her something, anything, positive.

The downtown came into view after they'd walked but a city block. And, oh, how grand this town looked compared to Cedartown. Tilly spotted at least three dry good stores, five meat markets, separate clothiers for both men and women, shoe stores, lunchrooms advertising oysters would be coming in September but for now "enjoy canned salmon at its best," and a delightful looking candy store within a few steps from where they stood.

And, so many shoppers. Ladies, dressed in bright summer dresses, and men, so handsome in their seersucker suits, strolling along the main street, pausing to admire a window dressing or two, or hurrying into and out of stores. Street vendors were hawking a myriad of wares, their voices carrying above the din of automobiles and impatient horses. The courthouse loomed off to the right where townsfolk were enjoying the summer day by lounging on the few benches scattered throughout the front lawn, while others strolled along appearing to be in deep conversation. There were children squatting a step down from the cement sidewalk to play marbles in the dirt, strong concentration on their faces as they aimed a marble in hopes of knocking an opponent's glassy prize outside an etched circle.

Tilly marveled at the carnival-like atmosphere swirling around them.

"There." She pointed toward the storefront with a sign above the door. Sweet Sensations must surely have the perfect little gift. "Let's get her a small box of chocolate."

A few minutes later, they left the store with the present carefully secured in a small bag tied with a festive red and white ribbon.

The time inside—hovering over so many different selections—gave Tilly a chance to calm her nerves. Between the excitement of seeing the downtown and their impending visit with Madame Bonavaire, she felt a bit light-headed. Was she intimidated by the prospect of meeting this psychic? No! Need to stay strong in her decision. They'd come this far, no turning back. So, they forged ahead.

At midday, noon to be exact, she and Rita Mae stood in front of what they hoped to be 114 Walnut Street, their intended destination. Tilly rapped her knuckles on the tall, narrow door squeezed between a barbershop and a clock repair store. A small sign above the door dangled by a single nail, looking like any second the next unsuspecting customer might be conked on the head. The rancid smell of burned hair coming from the barbershop had, no doubt, turned away a client or two. Why barbers thought singeing the ends of newly-trimmed hair would stunt quick growth was beyond Tilly. But it was the latest craze.

No answer. She looked side to side. They were the only two people on this alley-like side street. The hustle and bustle of the city faded away once they turned the corner. The sun beat down on them, the brick and stone reflecting additional heat. A stream of sweat slithered a slimy worm trail down her spine.

Rita Mae knocked this time—harder.

"Maybe she's not open yet," Tilly said, debating between relief and disappointment.

Before another word could be muttered, someone cracked open the door, ever so slightly inward. They leaned forward but there was only darkness.

"Who's knocking?"

If Tilly didn't know better, the woman's witchy voice was not unlike her mother-in-law's tone. She took a step back, positive mistakes had been made. She was wrong to leave the house this morning, putting her unborn child in danger by getting on a train, and definitely mistaken to believe someone in Howell had answers.

Whoever was on the other side pulled the door open a bit wider and reached out a gloved hand, crooking one finger, inviting them to step forward. Tilly's legs were going wobbly so she grabbed at Rita

Mae's arm for support. As if they had no choice, she and her friend crossed over the threshold. Almost immediately, a cool air surrounded them, sending a shiver up Tilly's back. Probably for Rita Mae also, as they both shook in unison.

"Madame Bonavaire?" Tilly finally asked, a quiver in her voice similar to when tears were threatening. "My name is Tuesday. This is my friend, Miss Osborne."

"Tilly and Rita Mae," the old woman said, her voice no longer witchy but heavily accented. Old country, maybe German, perhaps Russian.

Tilly was aghast. She'd purposely used her given name, wanting some anonymity but that certainly wasn't working. How could this shriveled up, bent over, woman possibly know their names?

"How do you know our names?" Rita Mae asked, not bothering to hold back.

"Oh my dears, too trivial," Madame Bonavaire replied, a look of impatience matching the dismissive wave of her hand. Her words were clipped and comments shortened. A bit hard to understand. "Important thing is you here now. Come in, come farther in."

Tilly's eyes had somewhat adjusted to the shadowy room since a small lamp off to one corner cast enough light to see where to step. Cluttered would be too kind of a word to use for this small parlor. A table, the top oddly clear of anything, took up the middle portion of the room, two chairs opposite each other. A stuffed chair was next to the table with the lamp. Other than a path wide enough to get to each chair, vases and statues of varying sizes, shapes, and heights covered the floor, rugs stacked as if for sale by a carpet salesman, and trinkets dangling everywhere like there'd been a rainstorm of jewelry. Tilly didn't dare bump into anything for fear of causing an avalanche.

"Tilly, you sit there." The woman indicated the chair between the door and table. "I sit here. You," she pointed simultaneously at Rita Mae and a chair in the corner, "sit there. No speaking. We start now."

Madame Bonavaire settled into the chair, adjusting her flowing dress and numerous scarves until the fabrics fell into place like a gentle waterfall. She went silent, held her head high, and remained as still as a statue while Tilly settled into the chair, placing her purse on her lap.

"First, we talk about money. Save gift for later, if you like what I say."

"Oh yes," Tilly replied, startled by the woman's comment about the present they'd brought. Was she showing off for them? Tilly opened her purse to take out a few coins. "How much?"

"How much you want to give?"

Tilly looked over at Rita Mae to see her friend shrug both shoulders noncommittally. Between what she'd pulled from the Mason jar, then spent on the round-trip train ticket and chocolate, she had about five dollars left in coins. Hopefully the woman didn't ask for more. Tilly offered the coins in her open palms.

Madame Bonavaire indicated with a nod of her head to let the money shower down from Tilly's to the psychic's waiting hands below.

"We begin now," the woman said, once the transaction was complete. Her words slightly muffled by the scarf covering her face; only dark brown eyes visible. She quickly deposited the coins into a pocket hidden away by all of the folds of fabric in her dress. She then reached her hands across the table, indicating Tilly should place her fingertips onto the woman's palms. The gloves from earlier had been removed and Madame's hands were surprisingly smooth, as if they'd never seen rough work.

Rita Mae sneezed, startling all three of them. She held her hands up in apology and promptly sneezed again, dust particles floating in front of the dim lamp.

The woman sat still, waiting until Rita Mae settled back down. She never moved her hands, only shifting her eyes slightly leftward patiently waiting for calm to descend on the room again. Tilly's fingers were shaking, not horribly but enough she was starting to wonder how long she'd have to hold this pose.

"We begin again." Madame bowed her head and began a low, monotone hum. Curiously, Tilly relaxed. Her fingers settled and once again rested slightly on palms rubbed smooth from a thousand or more other nervous fingers. "Tell me why you show up at my door."

"You know our names," Tilly said, ruffled by the statement. "Shouldn't you know why we are here?"

"Oh, I know why, my dear," she replied. "I want to know your reason."

Tilly was confused. She'd always thought talking with a psychic or medium would be simple, not a puzzle to solve. Those she and Johnny had seen at the fairs and circus always seemed loud, aggressive, and a little too eager to get greedy hands on their nickels. Johnny would scoff at the ridiculousness of how someone could know a person's deepest secrets. But, she'd always been intrigued.

So, what was her reason? To find Johnny or to know what happened to him? All of the sudden, Tilly wasn't sure. If this woman told her he ran away, would she want him back? If the answer was he was gone forever, could she cope?

"You have been loved," the woman continued, as if answers weren't necessary. "You are with child?"

Tilly swallowed hard, her stomach threatening, once again, to betray her.

"You will have your child the day of the first frost this fall."

"Madame Bonavaire," Tilly interrupted. "What about Johnny? Will he be with me?"

The woman bowed her head closer to the table, the top of her head visible where a crown had been created with numerous strands of pearls, glittering stones, and silver chains. She remained motionless for a few minutes. She finally looked up, stared hard into Tilly's eyes, neither blinking nor breaking their locked gaze. The woman's eyes beckoned Tilly forward while, at the same time, unnerving her down to shaking toes.

Another minute passed by.

And then, surprisingly, the woman threw her head back and cackled. Not necessarily with glee but something near exuberance. Tilly's heart surged with hope, at first.

"My child," Madame Bonavaire finally said. "I see so much I cannot talk about. We must meet again before I tell you anything."

Tilly's shoulders slumped involuntarily and tears threatened to fall. This trip had cost her too many coins, nearly emptying out the jar. And, for what? To be scammed for more coins? She couldn't afford to pay more nor could she stand to leave without something.

"Can't you tell me anything?" she pleaded. "I paid you all I could."

"Oh, dear, we meet again soon. You have given me enough. I need something else. I need something of your husband's," Madame rattled on. "But, leave your friend home."

"But I can't come by myself."

"Oh, my dear, I come to your house." And, without hesitation, she rose with more energy than exhibited in the last fifteen minutes. "Now, go home. I come to your house in two days, at sunset. We hold a séance."

"A séance? I thought those were to raise the dead. No, no, no, Johnny is not dead."

"You misjudge me. We reach across time and space to find husband."

"Hogwash," Rita Mae coughed the word into her handkerchief, loud enough for Tilly to hear, but hopefully not Madame Bonavaire.

"Isn't there anything you can tell me now?"

"No, my dear, must wait. I prepare myself, you must also. Now, go, go."

****

"What happened?" Rita Mae's voice was muffled by the piece of chocolate she'd stuffed in her mouth, not bothering to swallow before asking the question on both their minds.

Tilly and Rita Mae had been ushered out of the small, cluttered room, past the narrow door, and a loud bang came as the door slammed shut before they turned back around. They were now seated on a bench in the town square a block away, the bag of chocolate pieces between them.

Fortunately, they'd found some shade and an empty bench under one of the tall elm trees scattered around the courthouse lawn.

Tilly let her coat fall open at the front, a blessed breeze cooling her. At this point, she didn't care if anyone noticed her mound. Madame Bonavaire obviously could tell by looking at Tilly, some puffiness in her fingers, and the shade of green she constantly wore like a mask over her face. No psychic training necessary.

"I'm not sure," Tilly replied. She also nibbled on some of the chocolate, a bit more delicately than her friend, though. In their rush to get out of the cloying parlor, she forgot Rita Mae was holding the bag filled with sweets, which now seemed rather fortuitous. They hadn't offered their thank you gift and, since their usual lunch hour had long ago passed, this would be their snack. Anyway, this so-called psychic hadn't been of any help so she didn't deserve a gift. "How does she even know where I live? Or know our names? And, why did she say she knew why I was there but I had to tell her? Why all the mystery?"

"She's an act, belongs in a circus. The only difference is she happens to use her home instead of a tent at the fair," her friend answered. "Ma says they are all as wicked as saloonkeepers. All turning people into something they ain't."

"Hardly explains how she knew our names and about Johnny missing before we even said anything."

"You know news of Johnny's been in the newspapers."

"But, months have gone by," Tilly answered. "Oh,

I'm so confused. I'm not even sure I want her coming to Cedartown."

"But all the money you gave her..." Rita Mae began.

They sat in silence, both having grabbed another piece of chocolate. The clock tower resounded with three strikes of the bell, startling Tilly out of her thoughts. With the last train heading westward to Cedartown leaving Howell half-past the hour, she stood and smoothed down her dress and coat. They had just over fifteen minutes to walk back to the station and board the train.

"You're right, you know," Tilly finally answered. "I need to see this through."

Chapter 22

Two Days Later

"Pa, you can't be here," Tilly exclaimed as her father stepped into the kitchen from the back stoop. "I thought you were going to be late, heading north out of town to shoe a horse at some woman's farmhouse."

"House was empty, no horse." He hardly acknowledged her. He headed upstairs grumbling a few more unintelligible words.

Tilly leaned hard against the sink willing her heart to slow down, her knuckles turning white as she twisted a towel she'd been using to dry some dishes. Wasn't she already nervous enough knowing Madame Bonavaire was going to enter her home within the hour? And now, her pa had shown up unexpectedly, and with such a curt explanation. He'd been out of the house so much lately, she'd taken to eating alone.

Now, he was home and probably wanted attention. If she had any kind of luck—other than bad—maybe he'd stay upstairs for a while. Maybe stretch out for a late afternoon nap. Just in case, she pulled out a pot of split pea soup from the refrigerator she'd made earlier in the day. Only a few minutes to put a flame under the pot and have soup and fresh bread for dinner. Now to prepare herself for Madame's visit.

She paced back and forth, taking notice of the

framed picture of her and Johnny secured to the wall by the back door. Was a photograph the "something" she needed to offer up to Madame Bonavaire for the séance? She looked out the back door.

What? They'd been told *at dusk.* How, or better yet, why had she arrived so early?

The psychic was lurking in the backyard by the shed, with the persistent feral cat following close enough to the woman's long skirt they looked attached like marionettes. The animal was quite curious, winding around the fabrics enveloping Madame Bonavaire, while pushing its stubby nose against a bag being dragged along by the woman. She shoved it with her foot, enough so the animal eventually lost interest and slunk away. Tilly hurriedly stripped off her apron and headed outside.

"Good evening, my dear." Madame Bonavaire greeted Tilly like a friendly neighbor instead of a garishly dressed psychic wandering around in the backyard. "Ready for answers?"

More puzzles.

Tilly needed to find out where, what happened, and how Johnny was, but did this bizarre woman even want to listen? If the questions weren't voiced, how could answers be found? *Patience, yes, yes, patience is a virtue.* Goodness, how her own mother's preaching came back at the oddest moments. But Tilly was far beyond having any patience—Johnny seven months missing and her the same number of months with child, while her own father and, well to be utterly honest, the whole town having distanced themselves. Even her only loyal friend was becoming ever more cynical.

Madame Bonavaire headed into the shed, nary a

backward glance. Tilly assumed she should follow the woman, although she hadn't been inside the building since late winter. She hesitantly stepped closer to the archway and let her eyes adjust, which didn't take long since both outside and inside were close to the same ambient light.

The woman was quick, having already pulled the only table in the shed to the center and was positioning two candles on the rough surface. One tilted precariously while she kept moving the base around, trying to find a flat part. Once satisfied they were stable, she lit them with white phosphorous matches struck against the coarse wooden slab.

"We begin," she said. "Quickly, before we are bothered further by cats."

Two mirrors, about the size of the framed picture of her and Johnny, had been braced upright at each end of the bench. The candles multiplied, reflecting back and forth between the mirrors. Tilly was back in the funhouse with all of the full-sized mirrors fooling her and Johnny.

The woman placed two long tubes on the table, one on each side of the lit candles. The mirrors reflected those as well. Tilly stepped forward and fingered one of them.

"Spirit trumpets," Madame Bonavaire said, causing Tilly to pull back her hand. "Don't be afraid. We speak then wait for voices. If there are any."

"But then you are saying Johnny is a spirit?"

"Let us ask questions. Maybe someone else will answer," she replied, somewhat dismissively.

"My husband is not dead so we will not hear his voice," Tilly spoke emphatically. She had to continue to believe.

"We'll see," the woman responded.

"What about those mirrors?"

"Oh, so exciting. If we hear voices, we put mirrors together and maybe see image."

The temperature dipped from the usual hot and humid. Not completely surprising for the end of August but enough to give Tilly pause. The weather was always unpredictable, but usually the heat would last long into the wee hours before any relief would come. A soft breeze, working its way through the shed, lifted tendrils of loose hair and offered additional respite. The flames atop the candles flickered but didn't go out. Sounds faded as she concentrated on how Madame Bonavaire whispered into one of the tubes.

Nothing made sense at the moment but she didn't dare move. She'd become much like one of the many statues in the narrow little parlor they'd been in two days earlier. Tilly kept her gaze trained on the spirit trumpets, yet intermittently looking from one mirror to the other to see if anything new appeared. And, hoping she wouldn't sneeze.

After a minute, maybe two, the woman slowly stepped back from the table, letting the tube fall from her hands. Her expression was unreadable—good, bad, scared? She shook her head as if to clear cobwebs.

"Nothing," she finally said, moving quickly, laying the mirrors down so they no longer reflected. She snuffed out the candles by wetting her fingertips and pinching the flame, making a sign toward the sky. She couldn't gather up her items fast enough. "I hear nothing but chatter from my dear family. Oh, if they would only let me help you. But they say you need to be strong. Not to worry what anyone thinks of you. Not to worry about your dear mama, she is fine, and not to let anyone change your mind."

"But, but…" Tilly stammered. "Nothing about Johnny? Does silence mean he's not dead? He'll be coming back to me? My mother? How do…?"

The woman shook her head, causing her jeweled crown to clink and ping like a wind chime.

"I cannot help you," she finally said, walking toward the road. But then she stopped and turned back. "Have you had any dreams?"

"I don't understand."

"Dreams. Anything since your husband left."

Tilly looked deep into the woman's face, wondering if she was truly bothered by something or if she was fishing for information. More likely than not, Madame Bonavaire was a fraud and had read about Tilly and Johnny in the local newspaper and now hoped to make more money off of her grief. Probably knew her mother had died in 1918 during the flu epidemic.

As doubts resurfaced, she kept those strange dreams sealed away.

If anyone had witnessed his last living moment, they would have marveled how a lock of shiny brown hair gracefully brushed his forehead. How his blue eyes remained open, the light extinguishing by each second, yet still catching a slight glint from the moonlight above. How his body folded in on itself like a marionette having its strings snipped all at once. Or, how the motorcycle had been leaning against his hip, toppling in slow motion and coming to rest over his now-still form.

What did these dreams mean? But she wasn't

offering this up and she wished for this woman to leave now, never to come back. She had her hopes raised once too often. Think, think, what to do now. Tell the woman to leave. Seems if she was any kind of expert psychic, there'd be no question of Tilly's wishes.

"I go," the woman mumbled, as a ghost of a breeze moved through the shed causing a few leaves to rustle across the dirt floor.

"What is all this twaddle?"

Money's booming voice echoed throughout the shed, bringing both Tilly and Madame Bonavaire to attention like soldiers. He stood in the doorway, his face shadowed as the evening light faded to a dusky hue. No one moved. Even the brown leaves stopped their erratic dance across the floor as the cooling candles settled down, releasing single columns of smoke toward the roof.

Not a word was spoken as he looked from the table with candles and odd-looking tubes, to a woman dressed in the darker colors of the rainbow now hunching over as if to defend off a strike, to Tilly frozen in place. He finally turned toward her with his hands raised in question but she still couldn't move.

"Get out," he finally said, turning toward Madame Bonavaire. He straightened up taller than Tilly had ever seen him, his cane shaking as he held it like a sword, moving it from pointing directly at the woman then out the shed door.

"Pa, wait," Tilly tried but failed. "She's only trying to help."

The woman began stuffing the spirit trumpets into a large bag she'd placed under the bench upon first arriving. She reached for one of the mirrors but must have caught her toe on the rutted, dirt floor and tripped as Money poked the bench with his cane. The mirror slid off the table.

"Curse on you, old man," she screamed, as the mirror broke into a thousand splinters. She quickly scooped up as many of the pieces as possible, even some dirt, into the bag with the tubes. She pulled the ties closed as if to stop a wild animal from escaping.

"Now look what you've done," Money yelled, his face ashen and his breathing coming in ragged fits. "Get your cockamamie voodoo junk out of here."

Not even worrying about retrieving the second mirror, Madame Bonavaire swung the heavy bag over her shoulder, then slunk down like a troll from the weight of it, and struggled eastward toward Howell.

Tilly's voice was useless and her legs gave way. She collapsed to the floor. The old man moved quickly, placing his hands on her shoulders as if absolving her of all her sins. Her tears fell unrestrained and unabashedly to the dirt floor, puddling to reflect her failure.

Chapter 23
Time to Heal

Tilly took to her bed. For over a week, she didn't see anyone, not even Rita Mae. Money left her alone. She come down to the kitchen, made a cup of tea or coffee then retreated back upstairs, without a word.

The only time she spent any time away from her—their—bedroom was to drag her swollen body to the outhouse, checking first that the incessant cat was nowhere in sight or the shed door was closed, not able to ominously bang against the building frame, reminding her of the emptiness inside. She cursed her father and finally Johnny for never installing an indoor toilet. Once done, she hurried back into the house and up the staircase. Even deliveries from Thad Andrews were ignored, barely appreciated, yet coins left so he and Brown Molly would still come with the much-needed milk.

Once there were no more tears to be shed, her strength began its slow return. Her thoughts solidified and grew. She'd be giving birth to Johnny's child in less than two months. She'd lost so much faith so toughening up was the only option. He needed to return to a healthy wife and a bouncing, bubbly baby.

No longer would she seek out comfort from anyone spewing false hope, nor would horrible words about her husband be given credence, nor would she fail their child. She believed *because whispered tales seldom are true* and would no longer be swayed.

Tilly built a shield of anger to hide insecurities and fears. She had to hang on and survive, even if that meant without Johnny. But, she would. For this baby and even for and because of her husband.

Chapter 24

October 29, 1929

A *thwack, smack, thwack* invaded Tilly's daydream like a persistent woodpecker searching for bugs in a hollowed-out tree. She ignored the intrusion.

Knock…knock…pound…stomp…stomp…knock, knock.

She dragged her swollen body from the bed she and Johnny used to occupy together. Her once lustrous hair hung limp past slumped shoulders. She'd been forbidden to fill their claw-foot bathtub with warm water in order to soak away—unsafe for the baby, according to Dr. Glenn. No reason to take chances. His calm assurances were tempered when she spotted a slight wrinkle of his nose as he examined her. She cringed ever so slightly of having gotten to this point but didn't care enough to take even a *birdbath*, as her mother used to call those quick clean-ups with a warm washcloth.

If given a choice, she'd never leave their bedroom. Night after night, her dreams would arouse primal senses to the point of imagining Johnny's fingertips caressing her. Her tears would wet the pillowcase as the morning light invaded the bedroom.

But this was no dream. Someone was making a great deal of noise at the front door and it appeared they weren't going away until she answered their pounding.

She pulled on the robe hanging at the foot of the bed, toed the fireplace poker out from under the bed and grabbed hold of the familiar weapon, then slowly waddled down the chilly treads to the parlor. Whoever stood on the other side of the door could wait. Or leave. Made no difference.

Oh, it must have gotten frightfully cold last night. Before she made her way to the door, she caught sight out the front window of how a light frost covered the bushes and grass. *You will have your child the day of the first frost this fall*. Strange how those few words entered her mind as she rested a hand on the doorknob. Prickly spikes burned from her fingertips up her arm.

"Good morning, my dear." The woman beamed as if she were Father Christmas, moments earlier arriving with a most splendid gift. "Today is a special day, you agree?"

Tilly took a step backward. Never had she seen a woman going door-to-door but, with large leather bags hanging from each arm, who knows what wares she had to sell. Tilly half-expected Mrs. Osborne to darken her doorstep, reminding her of the sins of the faithless. Not some stranger.

"You will hold your child today."

And then she knew.

Madame Bonavaire stood before her, minus trinkets, scarves, and flowing fabric. No gloves covering her smooth hands and fingers. And, no wonder, she didn't have to hide them. This woman before her was young, maybe only a few years older than Tilly.

So she and Rita Mae had been fooled by a grafter,

after all. Disguising herself as an old woman and making out to be a psychic. A fraud, pure and simple.

Without a word to this charlatan, Tilly slammed the door closed. She turned and headed toward the kitchen, only to find her pa settled in at the table, working away at a once-full bottle of milk. All of this set her teeth on edge. He could have as easily answered the knocking but no, he acted like a deaf, old man. And so much milk being delivered for only the two of them. She'd paid precious coins from the Mason jar for this milk Thad faithfully provided and most of which her father drank, never offering to help pay.

"Morning, child," he acknowledged her. "Sleep well?"

"No." She waited for his response.

Nothing came. Tilly seethed. Madame Bonavaire— or whatever she called herself—was probably still standing on their front porch. Pa sat at the kitchen table as if this was any other day while frost covered the ground outside and her thoughts burned inside. Injustice was crashing down around her like a thunderstorm.

She still held the fireplace poker in her right hand. Her grip tightened with the fury of the last nine months of disappointment and now hope being chipped away by a miner's chisel. Too many people telling her to believe their truth, pressure coming and going…her fingertips burned.

"Are you going to make me breakfast?"

Oh, the gall of the old man. Granted, he stood up to Madame Bonavaire in defense of her but, since then, nothing. Left her alone when maybe a little compassion would have been a salve. She hadn't asked for any of this. Not her absent husband, nor dwindling money, to be the subject of rumors and gossip, maybe even a laughing stock by her persistence Johnny hadn't left on his own free will, none of the last year and all of the troubles. She'd wanted to be the necessary wife she read about months ago, helpful, loving, happy.

Yet, here she stood, helpless, unloved and unappreciated, and as unhappy as any woman could be.

Money rose from the table, having finished off his glass of milk. He took hold of his cane and turned toward her. Her stomach churned and her head pounded so loud inside she was sure her pa could hear the drumbeat. He could have scowled or said he'd lasso the moon and all her wishes would come true; none of it mattered. Her arm took on a life of its own. She swung the poker around her swollen belly and made contact with her father's cane. All of her anger and frustration channeled from her through the cold, metal weapon. A splintering crack resounded throughout the room, louder than a tree finally giving up and crashing to the ground, its branches and leaves coated with ice from the first winter storm.

Time froze as well. A slow motion movie played as she gazed down at the poker, then releasing it as if her flesh had been singed. The metal clattered as it hit the wood floor and rolled over a time or two, finally coming to rest up against one leg of the kitchen table. Then, all was silent.

"What the devil has gotten hold of you?" Pa looked down at the cane, now lying on the floor bent at a forty-five degree angle in the middle, sharp pieces sticking out at the break. "Have you gone plum crazy?"

"Maybe I have," she screeched loud as a hoot owl, bending at her long-gone waist, her stomach clenching worse than being put in a vise and squeezed to bursting like a ripe lemon. "Maybe I can't take this…you…anything…everything anymore."

"Calm down."

"No, I will not calm down. You're the reason Johnny's not here." She grunted, cradling her arms farther around her stomach. The baby was pushing down hard on her hips. "I read. I've seen articles about the Klan cleaning up blind pigs and you think he's involved. Am I right?"

Money moved closer, raising his hand toward Tilly's shoulder, but she batted at him like swatting a fly.

"You're the reason this table was covered in blood, guts, and awful bits and pieces of pig." Tilly continued to growl, the words barely distinguishable through gritted teeth. "You telling me something about a warning, as if you were helping. Well, you're not. You are the reason no one is looking for Johnny."

"Now, now, child."

"I am not your child," she shrieked, then started coughing. Her throat was raw. She bent forward, her breath caught in her lungs as if the wind had been knocked out of her body.

Spilled milk puddled like a series of little lakes on the tabletop but was now curdling with something oily, a grayish-green tint feathering the edges of the liquid. Tilly's legs wobbled as sparkly flashes of light gathered in her vision. Her breathing came in short bursts and something warm trickled down one leg.

She crumpled to the floor, clutching her stomach, an odd "arrrrr" releasing from her lips. And then, blessedly, all faded to dark.

Chapter 25
Advancing Years

February 15, 1931

Friends traveled through Tilly's life—some to stay and others never to return. Those absent usually were the ones she found boorish or rude and no longer needed in her intimate circle. Because of this attitude, her number of friends had diminished in recent years.

But Rita Mae would always be her best friend. Hadn't they secretly pricked their pinkies and then interlocked their fingers in a blood oath to be friends forever, no matter what? Even though they were nearly the same age, just months apart in their birthdays, Tilly stood as if the weight of the world rested on her shoulders and a few frown lines had crept in her expression, giving her the appearance of being older.

"Yoo-hoo."

Tilly jerked at her friend's greeting, the back door banging hard against the frame. A picture—a fading photograph of her and Johnny a few months after their wedding—rattled on the wall, finally slipping off the nail and crashing to the floor.

"Oh, God," Rita Mae exclaimed. She grabbed at thin air as the frame barely grazed her fingertips and landed hard on the linoleum, shards of glass jitterbugging in every direction, while the picture fluttered to a rest under the table. She was gulping in mouthfuls of air like she'd run from one end of their village to the other.

Tilly sighed, rose from where she was sitting, and retrieved the picture. She knew the photograph so well.

A little over two years ago, Mr. Jensen, the photographer, had fussed and hovered about them like a moth to a light, telling them how beautiful they were, all the while her husband's tentative smile directed toward her. Tilly stared straight into the camera defying anyone to tell them this wasn't their happily ever after. But now, looking back, maybe a single flash of the bulb was their last happy moment.

At least, in this picture, he was a living, breathing man. She shuddered at the tradition of photographing someone already dead, posing them as if alive, to help preserve the last image of a loved one before lost to fading memories. A chill raced through her—someone walking over her own grave—at the ugly turn her thoughts were taking. Johnny was alive, as alive today as in the picture two years earlier. She had to keep believing.

"Hey," Rita Mae said, obviously interrupting her friend's thoughts. "Did you hear the news?"

She looked up. "News?"

"Delores Costello just married John Barrymore. He's older than her own mother by six months! Six months—can you believe the scandal?"

The photograph slid from her fingers to the floor, fluttering down to the upturned frame as if the two were inseparable.

"*Dry up*, stop talking. Where and when?"

"Don't know yet," Rita Mae replied. "Been trying

to listen on the radio. Ma kept talking over the announcer so I didn't hear much."

"Johnny's gonna be devastated," Tilly commented. "He loves Delores—pretty sure he'd rather have married her than me!"

"Oh, oh, she was so good in *Noah's Ark*," Rita Mae spoke up, stopping any momentary silence to come between them.

"I'd rather watch the one where she was so glamorous," Tilly continued, hardly missing a beat. "You know the movie. Where she's like a princess; never any drudgery like housework."

"Johnny hated that one, didn't he? Wouldn't want you to forget the dishes and ironing, right?"

"Hates." Tilly corrected her friend, lost for a moment in thoughts of swirling gowns, swaying in a man's arms to the dulcet tones of *I've Got a Crush on You*. "Calls what I do *woman's work* and always emphasizes the woman part like he'd go soft if he did anything inside the house."

"Johnny wouldn't ever've gone soft," Rita Mae confirmed. "He was a lot of man for you, Tilly."

"Is." She corrected her friend once again, her own thoughts heading down a dark path all too familiar. Had she maybe been too much woman for him? Maybe why now two years later with no sign of Johnny? He'd been given up for dead but not by her. She wouldn't, couldn't. Otherwise, she truly was a widow and their nearly two-year old daughter, Tiz, was fatherless. But, if he was truly dead, then he'd not run away from her, which might possibly be worse, finding out she'd been deserted.

Something was different only a few months into

their marriage. Or, he'd changed. Tilly puzzled over all the clues she dismissed, but never came up with a solution. Sure, she knew he was getting his hands on tiger milk, hooch, booze, giggle juice, rye mash doctored up with berries and herbs, but was there another reason he'd disappeared?

Back then, Johnny had worked an odd job or two. Sometimes working for Money, which he hated, while she took in sewing and mending for the neighbors. He'd even had a job with clothier Mr. Straws, such a nice man even if the pay hardly added up to buy groceries. Wasn't the *man of the house* supposed to bring in the money and the *lady of the house* doing all else? Tilly began to feel she'd gotten the wrong end of the deal, making money for the two of them and keeping order to the rest of their lives.

Two years since he disappeared, and now she truly was doing it all. Being the necessary wife when nothing was needed of her except to wait.

"Nothing started yet for dinner? Ma's making a chicken. If ya want, the two of you can come over." Rita Mae was obviously surveying the rest of the kitchen, looking for the makings of dinner. "By the way, where is sweet little Tiz, anyhow?"

"*Glorious Betsy*," Tilly muttered.

"You say something?"

"Oh, no, finally remembered the name of the movie. Can't believe she's married. Probably won't do any more movies. Same as Maude Adams won't. So unfair."

"Time for dinner?" A voice pierced through the room like the blaring of the noon siren, causing Tilly to cringe. Janeska, Money's wife of a little over a year, walked into the room. The former Madame Bonavaire, now Janeska Monroe and minus all the glittering affectations of a psychic and reader, had made herself perfectly comfortable in the house and home built by Money and Theodory. The only home Tilly had known and the only dwelling she and Johnny knew as newlyweds.

This interloper had become the matriarch, after helping to birth baby Tiz nearly sixteen months earlier and then wheedling her way into Money's heart. Or, maybe she'd actually conjured up some magic potion. Tilly still wasn't sure of which.

Two babies had been born, but only one survived. Tiz's little sister, Wendy, all of a day old, was buried beside her long-gone grandmother. Such a sad little headstone tucked into the ground next to the other one worn down by age, wind, rain, and snow. Tilly rarely walked the ten blocks any longer, making a point to go in different directions.

Tuesday, October 29, 1929, the first frost of fall as well as the day the stock market plunged, taking fortunes and lives, saw the arrival of Janeska. She arrived no longer dressed as Madame Bonavaire but as a midwife to help Tilly.

That was also the day Money's cane was nearly destroyed by one swift swipe of the fireplace poker as Tilly doubled over in labor. A few hours later, Tuesday "Tiz" Miner arrived. But labor lasted another twenty-four hours.

The next day, a warm October Wednesday, the day before Hallowe'en, "Wendy" came into the world, but her lungs were smaller than kidney beans and incapable of gulping in much-needed oxygen. She only lasted a couple hours on the day of her birth, taking her last breath while tucked away in a deerskin-lined drawer acting as a makeshift crib.

Tilly couldn't have cared less what those babies were called. Johnny had not come home so Janeska and Money finally named the newborns. Being as original as her own folks were in naming their only daughter, Tilly was not surprised the days of the week were used, once again. Let people be confused between Tiz and Tilly, it was of no consequence. Maybe the townsfolk would talk about strange names instead of how the babies were born without their father around.

Sixteen months later, even though the rest of the country suffered from the deep economic depression, their oddly-assorted family was surviving. Actually, better than Tilly expected and she suspected mostly in part due to Janeska. Tilly'd given up adding coins to the canning jar from the sale of deerskin gloves, matching purses, and cloche hats made from wool.

Janeska returned to Howell two days after baby Wendy had been laid to rest, sold the little storefront home before the effects of the downturn hit Michigan, unloaded trinkets and jewels bringing in a small fortune as part of her contribution, and settled in the Cedartown house as a nursemaid to both Tilly and baby Tiz. Before long, a strong bond grew between Money and Janeska, especially after the woman saved at least his daughter and one granddaughter, if not both babies. They'd finally married ignoring the fact twenty years separated their own birthdays.

If there'd been any discussion of the woman living in the house, Tilly hadn't been included. To her credit, Janeska became indispensable, both to Money, because she loved taking care of a man, and finally to Tilly since taking care of a baby was the woman's other love.

The newborn would be swaddled and cooed over while Tilly slept, read, sometimes never having another person enter her bedroom except for those times the baby needed to suckle at her breast. Once done, Janeska took the child and Tilly could go back to private thoughts and dreams of Johnny strolling through the doorway. It was better than any romantic movie she and Rita Mae had seen. Tilly was Maude Adams—beautiful yet wasting away with worry and anxiety—only to be saved mere moments before succumbing to death. Glorious, famous, and a magnificent ending. Happy ever after.

Somehow, Tiz was a happy child. Love was lavished on the child by both Janeska and Money, more as if they were the parents and she was some odd-duck of an aunt. Gossip died down, people went back to tending their own worries, and months piled one upon another, villagers finding other gossip to rip into like ants on a piece of bread.

And, for Tilly? She simply didn't care what anyone thought anymore. Let Janeska and Money care for her and the child while she spent days on end dreaming of her and Johnny's short few months together. Occasionally, she'd tussle the curly blonde hair atop Tiz's head, the young gal's smile and twinkle in her eyes making her look more like her father day after day. Most oftentimes, Tilly preferred the solitude of reading the newspapers, searching out the latest local gossip and information of the movie stars she used to love to watch.

"Sometimes I wish I had a picture of Wendy,"

Tilly muttered, still holding the graying picture of her and Johnny. "I can't hardly remember what she looked like."

"Ah, child," Janeska answered, as Rita Mae opened her mouth to speak, "best to let the babe go. Never have understood wanting a photograph of a dead baby."

Tilly truly wanted to scream at the woman but instead she slid her arm through Rita Mae's crooked elbow and dragged her toward the back door. Better to walk with her friend than to say words which couldn't be unspoken.

Chapter 26

December, 1933

"I'm dying."

No *hello, how have you been*; nothing even close to anything resembling manners, a harsh *I'm dying* from Tilly's mother-in-law, not-so-dear Mrs. Miner.

Well, you look more like death, hardly warmed over. Tilly nodded in greeting, thankful she didn't blurt out the first nasty thought entering her mind. The woman always looked rough, but this visit she appeared to have climbed out of the bottom of a coal pit and walked to the house without getting cleaned up. She was dirty, carried a haggardness of hard years piled one on top of another, and Clarine's eyes were hollow and rimmed in a sickly yellow shade.

"Hello, Mrs. Miner," she finally said, keeping the door hugged close to her shoulder so the old woman could neither enter nor snoop. "Can I help you?"

Tilly had not seen Clarine a little over four years. The old woman hadn't the decency to come meet Johnny's daughter and Tilly heard the gossip. Clarine had been spreading vicious lies and rumors how Johnny probably wasn't even the father. Tilly, *a mere wisp of a girl with no gumption*, no doubt, must have been taken in by some grafter—a drifter—coming through town.

Tilly was tired, exhausted from standing there for

two minutes trying to figure out what to do next, even how hard to slam the door in the old woman's face. The couch beckoned her where she would gladly sit all day and read. Instead, she'd made the mistake of answering the knock at the front door.

"Did you hear me?" Clarine's voice still resonated with the same witchy scratch, but now an underlying whine had crept in. "I said, I'm dying."

"I heard you," Tilly answered. "What do you want from me?"

"I want to see the child."

Tilly's hand twitched, causing the doorknob to rattle. Her spine responded like hackles on a dog's back as anger escalated. This filthy, mean, disgusting excuse for a mother-in-law had no right to meet Tiz, nor any claim on a daughter-in-law she'd long ignored and derided the last time they'd been face to face.

The slamming of the back door made them both look beyond the parlor toward the kitchen. A child's laughter reached their ears. Clarine raised up on her toes and tried again to look over Tilly's shoulder.

"I have a right, you know," the old woman spoke.

"Right? You think you have a right to see my daughter?"

"Johnny's daughter, too. My granddaughter."

"So now, you're singing a different tune?" Tilly wasn't backing down. She was on edge, ready to fight, especially so she could put to rest their last encounter. When she'd stumbled backward, getting a splinter in her finger from the porch railing. Oh, how the wound had festered and became horribly infected before Dr. Glenn could remove the offending piece of wood. The woman's cackling was the final straw as Tilly threw up in the street. Those five minutes left her drained and humiliated. "I've heard you didn't think she was Johnny's daughter."

Finally, the old woman was surprised. Her eyebrows shot up, she took a similar step backward, and never took her glare from Tilly's face. But not for long. A raspy cough, and then many more, took a toll on Clarine. There was even a splotch of blood on the dirty handkerchief she'd held close to her lips.

Tilly's stomach turned at the sight.

"I…I…"

"Don't worry," Tilly said. "I know the truth, believe what you want."

"Mommy?"

The sweet, high-pitched voice startled both of them. Tiz had made her way from the kitchen into the parlor and was standing close to the door.

"Oh, baby," Clarine screeched, her arms outstretched. "Come here, come give your grandmother a great big hug."

The child had gone still. She remained half hidden inside the folds of her mother's dress. She frowned up at Clarine and then looked back toward the kitchen where Janeska stood in the doorway. "Grandma," she called out, and ran back toward Janeska's open arms.

Clarine's shoulders slumped even further down, as if she were melting wax from a burning candle. Before long, there'd be nothing but a blob on the front porch.

"You are not her grandmother," Tilly said, and then her twitching hand pushed the door closed. She turned on her heels and went back to the book she'd been reading in the parlor before the unfortunate interruption. She toed at the fireplace poker she now wished she'd greeted Mrs. Miner with, and her hands shook ever so slightly making the words on the pages blur.

Without another word from anyone, Janeska carried Tiz back to the kitchen.

****

A couple days later, Prohibition was repealed, and a month later, Clarine was dead. Some suggested tuberculosis, but Dr. Glenn remained mum. Tilly was positive the old woman's shriveled-up heart finally stopped beating. *Nothing can survive in a drought* was the way she thought of Mrs. Miner.

But then, a week later something very odd was discovered by Tilly on the very last page of the newspaper. If she hadn't been so bored one afternoon and couldn't think of anything else to do but read every single article in the latest issue, she'd probably have missed the few sentences. The entire little note looked more like an advertisement, printed inside a border surrounding it like a gift.

Dear Mere Wisp:

I am gone now so the truth can be told. I don't know where he went or what happened to him. He was only trying to protect me and keep me from jail. I was the one running the games; I took presents from the men and told them I'd keep their secret safe. Then they called it stealing.

It's my fault he's gone. I'm sorry.

Mere Wisp? Clarine's voice echoed in Tilly's head. She'd only heard the old woman say those words once, although others had been more than willing to pass along rumors and gossip, but the screeching, witchy tone would forever reverberate. This apology, of sorts, had been given to the editor of the newspaper to publish upon Clarine's death. Coward, to the end. She couldn't have said those words, instead of in some cryptic letter, the last time the woman stood on the front porch of this house?

After Johnny disappeared, talk of blind pigs operating in town, of the Klan having to clean up these ways of serving alcohol, and of stealing had died down. Blame had been placed on her husband and, with him gone, Clarine must have ceased her illegal operation. All too coincidental.

Maybe this was the reason Sheriff Calkins ignored Tilly's pleas to find Johnny and the townsfolk had shunned her. The man knew all along what was going on. She thought back to the morning of discovering the pig guts, entrails, and eyeballs and then sitting across from the deputy sheriff after Johnny and his motorcycle vanished. He'd been worthless. Mr Peek was the only person standing in her corner.

Mrs. Miner giving her a gift? Tilly traced the printed box around the letter. The pig guts were most certainly not a gift—more a warning as her pa had said—so what was she to make of the old woman's ramblings?

Tilly looked up from the newspaper and gazed straight toward the silent Victor. Even the music she'd loved so much no longer held interest. A movie played through Tilly's mind of a night when an insistent banging came at the back door as the wind whipped the tree branches and leaves, and a moonless sky plunged the backyard into darkness. Someone yelled, "Miner, open up, I know you're in there," and then Johnny heading outside to talk with a shrouded figure after saying, *doll-face, wait here*, coming back inside moments later with the phonograph player. Was this what Clarine wrote about? Gifts for silence?

Was the scarf draped over a handrail in her mother-in-law's house the same one Johnny had been blamed for taking? Someone must have given it to Johnny or Clarine in payment for silence but then claimed it had been stolen to save face. Who, she wondered, claimed it stolen by Johnny instead of given away?

Were all these bits and pieces reasons why Johnny had been gone nearly four years?

The truth had been right in front of her all this time and she'd failed to believe it. Johnny had been involved in running a blind pig, even if only to help his own mother. He'd taken the brunt of the blame. All of the rumors and gossip had been close to the truth; she'd naively turned a deaf ear. And, he never was able to confide in her.

The newspaper slid off her lap, fluttering to the floor like a giant butterfly. She'd spent years waiting for word from him, to have him walk through the door, yelling *hey, doll-face*. Or, to have him climb into their bed after tossing a handful of coins on the spread, smelling like he'd bathed in rye mash. Only to have them forget the money in their moments of passion and tenderness. Maybe all she had left of him were a few fading photographs taken by Mr. Jensen. And their daughter.

Maybe she finally had to admit she was widowed. And, to accept the only gift the old woman offered; truth in death. But, most importantly, the time had come to mourn a life she knew in her heart no longer existed. Maybe.

But first, she needed to make something right. Especially, if what she was thinking was true. Tilly grabbed her sweater and left the house without a word to anyone. She headed toward the downtown rehearsing what to say to a man who'd been so kind, after all this time. She quickly ducked into Mr. Navarro's grocery store, looked around to see how many customers were shopping, and headed straight back to the meat counter. Fortunately, before she could lose her nerve, she waved at her German friend and beckoned him over.

"Mr. Navarro," she said, barely above a whisper. "I need to talk with you."

"My dear," he replied, "but don't you look flustered. Is everything good?"

"Yes, maybe, I don't know, but I need a favor." She pushed aside his concern. How he could be pleasant when all these years she'd housed his stolen Victrola, was beyond her. "I don't know how to ask this."

"Calm down, don't be nervous. Please ask away." He gently placed his grizzled hand on her arm.

"Do I have your phonograph player? I mean, did you give your Victrola to Johnny?"

He pulled back his hand, paused, then rubbed his scratchy looking beard, ran fingers over his eyes, and stared long enough, she was fairly certain he wasn't going to answer. Her knees wobbled and she would have preferred to be any place else, but she waited.

"My dear," he repeated, slowly shaking his head back and forth. "Yes, I'm afraid the Victor used to be mine."

"But, why, oh why, haven't you asked for it back after all these years my husband has been missing?

And, especially now his ma doesn't run her pig thing?"

"Pig thing? Oh, you mean playing cards?"

"Yes, didn't you give the player to Johnny so she would stay quiet?"

"I did," he bowed his head, "at first, but then the time came you needed the music more than I ever did."

"I don't know what to say, Mr. Navarro. So, so sorry, I never knew anything about how Johnny came to have the player." Her words coming out in fits and starts. Tears were threatening, either from shame or the grocer's kindness, she couldn't be certain.

"My dear, go home, enjoy the music I never had time to listen to," he said with a smile, placing his hand, once again, on her arm. "Think of the player as my gift to you, child."

Chapter 27

Summer of 1935

Brown Molly chewed a bit of apple instead of snorting at the milkman as he tiptoed over the dewy grass to deliver six containers onto the back stoop of the house at the corner of East Grand River and Collins Street.

But, no matter how quiet his footfalls hit the ground, it made no difference. Tiz was already lying in wait. She jumped out from behind the cornflower-blue blossoms of the hydrangea and giggled at his mock surprise.

"Well, top o' the mornin', little lady," he greeted. "What brings you out so early this bright sunny day?"

Tiz immediately looked down toward the wire carrier, as she did most mornings. Thad pulled out one of the glass bottles, gently released its cap, and offered up the half-full container. She gulped down the milk in a few quick seconds.

His reward was a smile made twice as wide from the ring of milk around her lips. Tiz handed back the bottle and took off toward the hydrangea bush, turning once to give a quick wave with her pudgy little hand. Another twitter from her, more like the sound of a bird up in the tree, drifted his way.

"Good morning, Thad," Tiz's mother said. She was

standing behind the screen door just inside the house.

"And a fine mornin' to you, Tilly."

"I see you've already served up my little girl. She was out there nearly half an hour waiting for you."

"Such a patient little thing, she is," he replied. "How is she?"

"Oh," Tilly began, her smile fading. "About the same. Still no words, but she's always happy to see you, I'm sure."

Silence stretched between them, lost in thoughts of the little girl. Inexplicably, the child had stopped talking about a month ago. There had been no bump on the head, no traumatic event to make the words disappear, nothing anyone could figure out. Dear, grandfatherly, Dr. Glenn said, "Oh, give her time. She's playing a game. She'll soon get bored and then you'll be wishing for some quiet."

But, all these days later, and the little girl was still mute, except for contagious giggles. Even Tilly was not immune to the laughter.

Days and weeks flew by, half-full bottles of cold milk were consumed, and sometimes Thad would be greeted with louder chortles. Always, Tilly stood on the other side of the screen door and soon Thad looked forward to having longer conversations with her. Sometimes, their talk would last long enough he worried about his other customers missing their milk. But, no matter, this was his favorite stop on his route through the sleepy, little village.

Fall would soon be upon them and Thad worried about Tiz hiding behind the now leafy-green hydrangea bush. The morning frost would be cold upon her bare feet and the chill in the air could invade her lungs.

"How are you this cool morning?"

Tilly's beauty had intensified over the years, soulful eyes grown larger and bottomless as sorrow changed her, but a smile to make the sun shine a little brighter when she chose to release her loveliness upon the world. She'd had her hair cropped to a bob, wore dresses she'd restyled—so she told him—from a closetful of her mother's dresses, and carried herself like a starlet freshly discovered in Hollywoodland. She was a hidden treasure in this village.

He cared immensely for Tiz but feelings for her mother had grown even larger than he ever imagined. Goose bumps ran up his arm at her innocent question.

"I am fine, and you?" Thad took a step up on the porch as Tiz ran back to the bush to hide, and her mother opened the screen door to accept the bottles of milk.

"Would you like to come in for a few minutes? Janeska has made some fresh coffee and crispies to ward off the cold."

"Won't the rest of your family be wanting those treats?"

"Oh, Thad, you must know, there's always room for one more here. It is little Tiz, her grandpa and Janeska, and myself, and Mr. Miner will never be coming home."

He looked at her lovely smile and entered the back of the house, having waited all these years to hear her say those words of her long-lost husband. His heart swelled, not caring if his other customers had to wait. He was finally home and, somewhere off in the distance, close to the hydrangea bush, he heard, "Thank you, mister milkman."

Chapter 28
Thad Loves Tilly

A few months later, Thad and Tilly became husband and wife.

"You may now kiss the bride," the minister said. He moved off to the side, leaving the newly-wedded couple standing together in front of the Victrola. Thad moved closer to Tilly, still holding both of her hands. First he kissed the back of each hand then met his lips to hers. The kiss was short and chaste. A brief smile between them and then they turned to scan the attendees populating their parlor.

Six-year-old Tiz wore a red velvet dress, long enough to brush the tops of her shiny black boots bought special for the occasion. Tilly's saintly patience faltered to get her daughter out of soiled dungarees and a smocked top and into suitable attire for the occasion. If the young girl lasted all of about thirty minutes before kicking off the boots and running around in her stocking feet, Tilly would be satisfied. Tiz found her voice, rattling on about everything from bugs to the moon, making up for lost time during the months Thad and Tilly had grown closer. Going silent by the little mischievous imp was a ploy pulled off to perfection.

Grandpa Money stood off to the side during the ceremony, stiff and uncomfortable in a black wool suit and stiff leather-soled black shoes, all newly purchased from Mr. Hamilton, while Janeska wore a loose, flowing dress, a melded-wool cape covering her ever-growing mound. She was with child and there would soon be a baby in the house, filling up the spaces with nighttime feedings and daytime chortles and fussing. Rita Mae never held still; she flitted from one person to the next, short bursts of conversation so there was never any silence in the parlor.

Johnny's presence hovered off in a corner, never far from Tilly's thoughts. As much as she railed against admitting he was gone, he'd now become one of the ghosts in this three-story house.

The Valentine's card with the word *thee* made to look like *three* was buried deep in the armoire. Fading photographs and the card were wrapped up in the button-down nightgown she could never wear again. The Russian nesting dolls lay alongside the package of memories, all crammed in a round hatbox she'd used for delivering her latest designs to the dry good store. She'd notice the box once in a while, at the back of the closet where two pairs of footwear stood as sentinels as shields, but she never pulled it out from the day, almost a year ago now, when she packed away her previous life.

*Neglect to provide…*wording on the annulment papers. Within seconds of Tilly intimating to her pa she now believed her husband would not return, Money walked the couple of blocks to Judge Cole's house. There, the two of them hatched a plan to help Tilly move forward. The next week, the Judge presented papers for her to sign officially dissolving the union. "Based on the fact he abandoned you," was the way he'd termed the reason.

Secretly, she would always believe he was prevented from coming home, but now she kept those thoughts tucked away. If she'd been told only once her obsession to find out what happened to him made her sound a little crazy—especially after so many years—she might not have wavered. Too many times, she'd been shushed to stop talking, to accept the fact he'd left. No one wanted to listen so she stopped bringing up his name.

But, as time moved forward, Johnny was no longer in her thoughts every minute of each day. Maybe he was the one she wanted to talk to, tell him about something interesting or exciting in her day, or how Tiz was growing up so quickly, looking more and more like him. How she'd come running into a room excited to tell a story, show a discovery, or wrap her arms around the backs of someone's legs. Her version of a hug. How the sunlight bounced off her chestnut hair the same way it used to off his, how the deep blue of her eyes twinkled with mischief, how her slenderness mirrored his lankiness, how she'd leave the house letting the door slam hard. But, he wasn't around, not even to sit across from each other, sharing warm pan bread fresh out of the oven.

One frosty morning, not too far off from her daughter's sixth birthday, the house was silent. The hour was early, as the rest of the family slept, no one creaking the wooden floors or treads, no wind battering at the shakes and shingles, not even a stray dog's barking heard off in the distance. Tilly had been awake for a couple of hours, lying in bed wishing the clock could be turned back to a morning full of Johnny in the fall of 1928. The echo of *hey, doll-face*, whispered in the soft breeze coming through the open window. He'd barreled into the bedroom—after being out all night—and tossed coins onto the bedcovers. Oh, how her anger had turned to passion as she paced his needs.

She now saw that morning as their turning point—the beginning of the end. After all these long years of lonely nights, she finally had to box him up and tuck away a life which no longer existed. No one could ever persuade her he was dead, but she'd finally been convinced of him never coming home. So, she stacked up the photographs taken by Mr. Jenson and wrapped them in the nightgown she wore the morning their daughter was conceived, a single coin left over from the bounty he offered her, along with the dolls reminding her of the morning she discovered the motorbike missing.

Tilly had finally pushed him to her most private and treasured thoughts. She could no longer be Mrs. Miner, but maybe Mrs. Thad Andrews, the wife of a milkman. And, she might find a small measure of happiness so elusive all these years since a cold night in February, 1929, when Johnny did not come home.

Chapter 29
When Tiz Was Nearly Ten

Oh, how fast the years rushed like a river tumbling down a mountainside.

The household—filled with Tilly and Thad "Papa" Andrews, Tiz Miner, Money and Janeska, along with baby boy Silas—was always in a state of flux, someone coming and another person leaving. Their home was almost a happy place.

The Great Depression, as it was now being referred to since Herbert Hoover's concession the economy truly was a train wreck, had finally found its way to Cedartown. Jobs were lost and dinner plates held smaller portions. Less meat was available for sale by Mr. Navarro, there were reduced selections for the ladies at Mr. Hamilton's, and fewer coins were available for buying extras.

Their family had not gone without, though. Not like others Tilly knew of. They'd been lucky. Residents found ways to afford milk and her husband was there to deliver. And horses always needed new shoes so work was steady for Money. She was the only one who never contributed coins, having lost interest in her sewing.

Eat it up, wear it out, and make it do, or do without.

Tilly pondered the quote she'd read in the local newspaper. Food never went to waste. Not in this house. Leftovers—if there were any—were always made into a new and different meal for the next day. The children's clothes were constantly being mended and resized. Only necessities—coal, for instance—were purchased. Mr. Gillam, now hunched over but nary an ounce of flab on the old man, would arrive, like clockwork once a month before sun-up, to dump coal down the chute. Some mornings she'd brood over years earlier carrying the fireplace poker and, in particular, the morning her pa warned her of ill will toward Johnny by some of the townspeople. Rumors—*don't be in a hurry to tell it, the tale that was whispered to you, for here is one thing to remember, because whispered tales seldom are true*—and gossip never proven but still hurt to this day. Johnny's mother was to blame, right?

Mr. Adams, the editor of the newspaper, died a few years earlier. Some said a heart attack, but she always wondered if the Crash of '29 had been too much for him to bear. His unwavering faith in humans doing the right thing may have been tested too severely by the greed found in Wall Street. Some upstart from New York City had bought the paper from Widow Adams and nothing ever seemed the same. Tilly only rarely picked up a copy of the weekly, especially since her former teacher, Mrs. Harbinger, had also passed away. So many gone. Instead, she and Tiz spent hours at the new Ladies Library located in the same building as the lock-up, both lost in their own imaginary worlds.

They were doing well enough, they even were able to help others, including Mrs. Osborne.

Rita Mae had been hesitant to mention their dilemma, but she and her mother were doing poorly. Mr. Osborne had also died a couple years earlier, leaving the two of them with nothing but the house they lived in. Rita Mae's younger brother, Del, left for Detroit to work in one of the factories about the same time as their father's passing. He was good about sending money once in a while but there was never enough.

"Yoo-hoo," came the always familiar greeting through the back door.

"Rita Mae," Tilly called out. "I'm in the parlor." She stood up from the couch, setting aside her musings. Safer to give thanks for good fortune in the face of others' sufferings. Especially, seeing as she was almost content on most occasions. She quickly tapped her knuckles on the edge of the Victor. She didn't have the heart or desire to be reminded of Johnny so the phonograph sat silent, although Mr. Navarro came to mind more often than not. His kindness and understanding the day she approached him, a few years earlier, had never left her.

"Here's your mail from Mr. Dunn," her friend said, handing her a single envelope. "He asked if I could bring it in."

Tilly flipped the small package from the front, over, then back again. Their address showed under Thad's name giving her pause of how seldom a letter or package actually ended up in their mailbox. The letter looked more official than anything previously placed in their mailbox. Odd, too, since he rarely received mail.

Her husband sold his small dwelling located close to the creamery and moved his meager belongings the day after they married. Because she was adamant about not using the second-floor bedroom, Pa and Janeska were uprooted from the third floor and the newlyweds settled in.

Brown Molly spent her afternoons and evenings nestled in one of the many stalls close to the creamery, happily biding her time munching on grasses and oats. The first time Tiz had gone missing, a mere month after the ceremony, they found her sound asleep in a corner of the horse's stall. Anytime afterward, whenever anyone realized the young girl had not been seen around, someone would wander the two blocks to the creamery, peek over the half wall, and expect to see her and the old horse either having some grand conversation of nays and giggles or of Brown Molly offering warmth and bulk to slight, little Tiz.

Toddler Silas had a small room adjoining his parents' room through a pocket door and at night, now ten-year-old Tiz slept in what used to be a sitting room on the second floor. Tilly had tucked away her sewing machine and ambition to make high-fashion styles for the ladies in town, although she did think often how much she loved making those deerskin gloves for Johnny. How they fit so perfect, like a second skin.

"Oh dear." Rita Mae interrupted Tilly from her thoughts. "What do you suppose this is all about?"

"We won't find out until Thad comes home." She stared hard at the words *Selective Service System* stamped in the upper left hand corner. There were rumblings of war reported on a weekly basis in the newspaper. Nazi troops, under the force of Adolf Hitler, were invading Austria, Poland, Czechoslovakia, marching across Europe; killing, maiming, and imprisoning innocent citizens. But the fighting was over there. Serving in the military was voluntary so why was he getting a letter from the local draft registration office in Howell?

"Can I talk with you about something?" Rita Mae's voice had slumped to a whisper.

"You know you can," she responded, setting the letter on top of the Victor. Thad and Tiz wouldn't be home for a while longer. Her daughter had decided she wanted to be the first milklady in town, so the two of them were testing the waters. They left the house at three in the morning—long before the dawn—and headed to the creamery for the day's orders. Tiz was still rubbing the sleep from her eyes as old Brown Molly, still able to do her job, pulled the wagon onto Collins Street after delivering milk to the Andrews' household. "You always can, you're my best friend."

"Something has come up." Her friend sat down in the threadbare chair by the fireplace. "You know how we've always said we would be together—friends forever? Blood sisters?"

A hollow pounding in Tilly's ears matched the heavy beat of her heart. No, she didn't want to hear what might be coming next. Nothing good ever came from such solemnity. She backed her knees to the edge of the couch and sat down where earlier she'd been looking at the paper. The springs protested with a similar groan building within her chest.

"I'm sure I don't want to hear." She sighed, but ultimately resigned to whatever was about to land in her lap.

"Ma and I are moving to Ypsilanti so I can teach at the normal college," Rita Mae blurted out as quickly as tears began coursing down her cheeks. Choking sobs made   her words...*moving...in...with...ma's...brother...*nearly impossible to be understood.

Oh, God, this was the last thing Tilly ever considered. Yes, maybe her friend had accepted a job in Howell or they were going to sell and move into a smaller house or there was even an engagement on the horizon. But deserting her? Going so far away, a two-hour train ride, a continent away.

"No," Tilly cried out. "You cannot leave. What will I…who will I…the movies…Oh, Rita Mae, this can't be happening."

"Mommy, mommy!" Her daughter's voice broke the moment, echoing throughout the whole first floor. "Papa let me deliver all of the milk." Tiz came barreling into the parlor, oblivious to anything other than what she'd accomplished in a few short hours.

Thad strode into the room a few seconds later, beaming from the enthusiasm of their newest *little milklady*. He even had a patch made—*Milklady Tiz*—to sew onto a shirt or jacket.

Tilly slunk farther into the couch and didn't respond, not caring to acknowledge what was good right in front of her but choosing to wallow in the next bad thing to worm through her life. Oh, how she wanted to keep her daughter's smile front and center, but the drop of her eyelids and the down turn of the young girl's mouth spoke volumes. Another failure.

Her papa placed a hand on Tiz's shoulder and steered her out of the parlor, but he remained in the room. Disappointment hung in the air like gathering clouds. But, nothing else mattered. All Tilly could think about was her best friend—her blood sister—no longer living down the street, nearly within shouting distance. She gazed over at her tear-stained friend and sent over a shaky grin.

Rita Mae stood as if to leave. Tilly grabbed at her friend but only served to run arched, tense fingers down her arm, losing touch at their fingertips like falling from a cliff's edge. *Please, please, let's go back five minutes before a single tenuous strand of happiness was pulled taut again, close to breaking.*

"I've gotta go." Her friend sniffled, pulling Tilly into a hug and squeezing the breath out of both of them. They choked out a crying last gasp before separating. "Ma's waiting."

****

The house was dead quiet. No stealthy creaks as if a ghost was heading up past the third floor having been welcomed into Heaven. No sugar pops to make the coal flame a little brighter. No music. No conversation.

Thad may have retreated to the kitchen or might have even taken her daughter somewhere. Tilly didn't care. She needed to be alone. Thad liked to hang out at the grocer's once finished with all of the milk deliveries and Tiz loved to tag along. Of course, she usually benefitted from the walk to the downtown by getting a peppermint stick from one of the many jars lined up by the cash register. She'd come home smacking sticky, bright pink lips, showing off how she could stay atop his shoulders waving her arms, chanting, *no hands, see no hands, but hard I won't lands.*

Just as well. Tilly needed time alone. Yes, she'd been wrapped up in her grief over Rita Mae's leaving but she couldn't miss how her daughter's smile faded or how Thad grimaced. Wasn't the first time. She tried so hard to be a good wife to him but he wasn't Johnny. Though she would try to hide her feelings, this wasn't the marriage of her dreams. Johnny's ghost lived in this house, a constant reminder of what they had for such a short time. She was crazy to live in the past but found solace for surviving in the present.

Once again, she disappointed him. Thad tried so hard, at least for the first few years, occasionally bringing a smile to her face. Of course, the indoor plumbing he installed a little after they were married had done the trick for a bit. The old outhouse had been torn down, the ground reclaimed, and now a vegetable garden rivaled any other one within the village providing them with succulent melons, emerald green and sunshine yellow wax beans, strawberries as large as plums, and peas as round as marbles.

But, lately he'd changed. He was distant, distracted, seeming to have taken a step away from her and this house. Nothing she could pinpoint specifically, but he started lavishing more attention on Tiz. Someone who clearly loved him back.

"Till, ye done crying?"

She startled at his deep Irish brogue. From the look on his face, he may have been standing there for a while, as he twisted his tam between browned, rough hands. Years outside had weathered his skin, the backs of his hands freckled with dark brown age spots growing larger any time she bothered to look close enough.

Tilly stood and retrieved the envelope she'd placed at the top of the Victor. She handed over the package without a word. He actually flinched once he saw the return address. She waited while he read the letter, her hands firmly clasped behind her back so he wouldn't see how they shook.

"Pursuant to your request to serve in the United States Military," Thad read with a monotone voice, as if the words were tightly strung on a wire, "you have been accepted to assist in the formation of an adjunct office to be located in Paris, France. You are to report for duty, at the Howell Draft Registration office, Monday, August 28, 1939. Be prepared to ship out same day." He looked up from the yellow sheet of paper he slipped out of the envelope.

"So…"

"Ye know I have to go," Thad interrupted her before she could utter another word. "This is me country."

She merely stared toward him. In a split second, he'd become yet another ghost in this house, gone within the next two weeks to a foreign land she couldn't even fathom. Another person was leaving her and there was nothing to be done. Two weeks from today, he was leaving and none of this made sense. Damn the flag he'd so proudly displayed on Brown Molly's bridle.

Tilly had no words for him, at least not any of kindness or support. Not even offering him a smile, she turned on her heels and headed out the front door.

****

The next morning, as Thad entered the kitchen looking for something in the way of breakfast, he instead found his wife sitting across the table from Money. Neither Janeska nor young Tiz were anywhere in sight. He dug deep into his pants pocket to retrieve the letter and placed it in front of Money without a word, and then moved over to the sink to pour a cup of coffee.

"Damn-it, Thad," Money railed. "What the devil

have you done?" He didn't wait around for an answer. The scraping of his well-worn and mended cane could be heard long after any other mutterings by him. "Tetched in the head, boy...crazy..."

"I need to do this," Thad whispered.

Money left, but Tilly heard her husband's answer, her sour thoughts spinning. First Rita Mae's news, now this. Was there anyone else in her life readying to leave? Eventually they all left—her mother, Theodory, when she needed her the most; her husband, Johnny, now forever a ghost living in her head; baby angel Wendy, only one day old before leaving forever; Rita Mae, the friend she'd always thought would be there to keep her sane, leaving tomorrow; and now, Thad, gone in two weeks.

Served her right for ever having a thought about being almost happy.

Chapter 30

Twelve Months Later in 1940

Tiz could only be described as miraculous. If there was laughter in the house, she was the reason. If little Silas needed some distraction, she was at the ready. At eleven years old, she was the one working alongside Janeska to put together the evening meal.

A year had passed since Thad deserted their family. Tilly always explained his leaving in a bitter way to whoever would stand around long enough to listen. No reason to hold back this time. Years earlier, everyone was convinced Johnny had deserted her but she wouldn't accept it. When she finally admitted her lot in life, even if she didn't completely believe he would never show up again, something called happiness or at least contentment seemed within her reach. But now a year had passed with her, once again, waiting, waiting.

A letter might find its way through the post but those were few and far between, and Thad never said much. He couldn't disclose his location, what he was doing, who he spoke with; he could only ask questions she had no interest answering. The small pile of unanswered letters resided atop the box containing old memories she'd tucked away.

Thad was becoming her history, not her present.

Townspeople were so proud of Thad for serving

his country, but Tilly saw the whole sorry story differently. If asked, she'd set them straight. He didn't have to go to Europe to fight someone else's war; he didn't have to go to Howell to find a new direction, and for all she felt, he never had to leave their village. There was plenty enough for a milkman to keep busy with. But, he no longer took care of the business.

Thank the good Lord for Tiz. As soon as Thad left for Europe, the young gal had marched into her mother's bedroom and announced she was the new milklady. She was intent on convincing her mother she could take care of Brown Molly, was strong enough to load up the milk containers into the wagon, and no one was going to stop her from spending her mornings delivering cream and butter to those her papa had taken care of.

Tilly'd been so astounded at her young daughter's confidence she was left speechless. And, since then, a day had not passed she even hinted at shirking the commitment. Each morning, long before the sun rose, Tiz climbed out of her warm bed on the second floor of the aging house. She slipped into long johns and layers of clothing to then walk the two blocks to feed Brown Molly a few extra-special oats before bridling the horse to the old milk wagon. Thad taught Tiz all she needed to know for continuing his tradition. She'd fill the wagon with bottles of fresh milk, buttermilk, and sweet cream butter, making her own home the first stop.

Money and Janeska had their own opinions, but Tilly had no time for them. She often retreated to the bedroom on the third floor not particularly expecting anything from anyone. In many ways, her daughter now acted more like the grown-up while Tilly, the needy.

"Ma," Tiz called, barreling through the back door, long after the sun had reached far above them.

The dog days of summer were upon them. Such an evil time, with the air thick and languid, barely a sluggish breeze to lift loose tendrils of hair from her neck. Tilly was sour and lethargic. She didn't even have the energy to answer her daughter. She looked up from her noon meal of lukewarm tea and stale biscuit, watched as the young gal stripped off her knee-high boots and then headed to the sink to wash her hands.

The girl's hands had started to darken from so many mornings holding the reins, weathering from the sun, cold, wind, and rain, and getting calloused from toting containers day after day. Maybe Tilly would look for a piece of deerskin to put together a pair of gloves, possibly a little big, what with the child growing so fast and all. It was the least she could do.

The best she'd done lately was to start adding Tiz to the wall where Tilly and Johnny had measured each other years ago. Without fail, on the anniversary of her husband's disappearance, she'd note her weight and height—writing this on the inside of the cupboard door where the old Mason jar still resided. By the time Tiz was measured and recorded on the wall, the girl's head reached as high as Tilly's shoulders, and was less than a dozen inches below the hatch mark for Tilly in 1929. Tiz was growing so fast her skin could hardly keep up, stretching taut and firm over such thin legs and arms, with gangly knees and elbows she hadn't grown into yet.

"Ma," Tiz repeated, her voice quavering slightly, "Grandpa said we need to let Brown Molly rest. She's too tired anymore to pull the wagon."

Brown Molly…funny how many times the horse seemed to know exactly what she and Thad had been talking about all those years earlier. Their incidental meetings at the back door of the house sometimes were long and full of fun banter, other times short. Brown Molly would snort, nay, or splutter, shaking her bottom jaw like it had come unhinged. Tilly closed her eyes, letting memories drift forward from the far reaches buried below hurt.

Oh, the time Thad had misplaced his new coat; Brown Molly recognized what had happened. If one memory could go untarnished, she'd savor that conversation with relish. Except, unfortunately, for Johnny's reaction to her laughing with the milkman. He'd started to change day by day and then a few months later, disappeared. Tilly could see so clearly now. Thad had been there the whole time. Johnny had been her first love, but Thad had been the constant in her life. She never appreciated him; oh, how he must have endlessly sensed her indifference. No wonder he had to find an honorable way to leave instead of carelessly walking away.

"You listening to me, Ma?" Her daughter's voice was edging toward frustration. "What am I gonna do?"

"Well," Tilly finally answered, tucking her memories deeper away, "let's have a talk with your Grandpa. If he suggested a change, he better have a solution."

"You never help," the young gal continued to complain. "Grandpa said I should talk with you, but you hardly say anything."

"Now, Tiz…"

"I'll figure out what to do myself, like I always

do." Her daughter shrugged her shoulders. "You know, Ma, I might as well be on my own, for all you care."

"Don't say…"

"No, really. When I'm old enough…"

"Now, you listen here, Tiz. Don't you go threatening to do something you aren't going to follow through with."

"You ever know me to not do something I said I'd do?"

Tilly didn't answer so Tiz continued.

"Do you remember when I quit talking? You don't need to answer. Of course, you remember. You finally started caring. I finally felt happy and wanted. You put me first. And you started talking to papa more."

"I couldn't hardly stand you not talking."

"It worked," Tiz confirmed with a smile.

"Worked?"

"I had to be the one to make you notice me, papa, and to pay attention to what's right in front of you. If I stopped talking, you'd have to think about something else. Don't tell me you never saw how quickly I went back to singing and nattering on once you invited him in."

"Thad's not your father," Tilly said, deflecting her anger in a different direction.

"But he's my papa. He's been the only father I've ever known," Tiz said defensively. "He loves me."

"Don't forget, he also left." Tilly sighed and rested her hands on the kitchen table. They were ever-so-slightly shaking. Tiz was right. Her daughter had always been strong, not fragile, not allowing the world to squash her. Her girl would be leaving soon enough, probably much earlier than anyone was ready.

"I'm goin' to talk with Grandpa," Tiz continued. "You sit there and let me take care of everything. Like I always do, like papa taught me." Not waiting for a reply, she slipped back into her boots and left before getting anything to eat.

Chapter 31
Busy Work

"No, you need to put a check next to those needing assistance yet," Deo told Tilly, his forefinger running down the chart, as he leaned in close over her shoulder. His warm breath brushed her cheek like a kiss.

She moved slightly away. Not because she wanted to but because putting distance between him and her was the proper thing to do. A month after taking a job at a branch of the Office of Price Administration, Deo was the only one willing to talk with her. Two other women in the office maintained a wide berth as if she bore a white stripe down her back and was armed with stink glands.

"I knew your husband," Deo continued, after taking a chair next to her desk.

"You know Thad?"

"No, no, I mean Johnny. I knew him."

Silence stretched between them as Deo stared hard at Tilly, she maintaining the blank expression perfected over the last dozen years. People either divulged knowing and hating her first husband or quietly admitted they liked the man. But, nothing ever changed. No one offered up answers or even bothered to help in her search.

"How did you know Johnny?" Might as well get this conversation over with so they could move onto the work at hand.

"Can't say I knew him well."

"But you knew him." Tilly's hands began to shake. Years had passed without his name being mentioned, as if he never existed. Her female co-workers wandered by, then exchanged knowing glances. "How?"

Deo was slick; dressed in a gray pinstripe slim-fitting suit, no doubt obtained through his father's storefront, Minto and Blackmer. In the intervening years, Mr. Straws had sold out with the new owners bringing fashionable Detroit and New York stylings for men to the small village. But, it wasn't just his clothing; he moved with an air of authority, never a hair out of place, a jaunty attitude.

She liked he didn't rush into an answer. Even reminded her somewhat of Johnny.

"Would you care to have dinner with me?"

Her eyebrows shot up, dissolving any nonchalance. Deo's lips curled slightly upward into a sweet smile, giving her cause to remember how Johnny's gaze made her stomach flutter years earlier.

"Oh, you must think I'm forward," he continued. "I've thought of asking you many times but didn't want you to take my suggestion wrong. Thought we could catch a meal at the Twin-Q Inn before you walk home. I've no plans."

Tilly nodded before she came up with ten reasons not to, the first and foremost she was married to Thad. But, he'd left to go fight someone else's war a couple of years earlier instead of battling at home to keep their family whole. Now, the question was never being asked when he'd come home, especially since the bombing of Pearl Harbor.

"I'd love to," she responded. It was just a meal, after all, and no one at home would take note of her absence. Even when she was there, she was more a ghost than a presence.

Tilly gathered up the papers spread across the desk, resolving to finish the project of helping others with rationing books for sugar, fuel, oil, and meat. The Office of Price Administration's brochure of rules only served to puzzle users, and she was there to help sort through each family's rationed amounts and how to record their portions. After retrieving her coat from the closet, Deo, being such a gentleman, helped her slip it on.

They were out the door and across the main street before questions or comments transpired. Gave Tilly a smidgen of satisfaction they'd be gossiping since she'd reached the point of not caring what others thought or said these days.

****

"Before we order," Tilly began, "tell me how you knew Johnny."

"First off," Deo said, "I did go to Sheriff Calkins with my theory as soon as I saw the news article in the paper."

"Theory?"

"He was murdered."

"By?"

"Klansmen."

Tilly's head was spinning like cotton candy in the sugar bowl. For years, she believed her husband was still alive but prevented from returning. Deo was the first person, other than her father's protestations, to bring blame on the Ku Klux Klan. The investigation had gone nowhere, and now the presence or power of the group had diminished over the years. Especially, with Prohibition having been repealed. It was as if they'd gone into hiding.

She could have railed at her dinner partner but, by now, acceptance had worn her down. Instead, finding out how Deo knew Johnny, not his suppositions, was more important.

"Met him at a couple card games."

There it was. He was going to tell Tilly how Johnny ran a blind pig, his disappearance was inevitable or he got what was deserved for breaking the law. Her hands began to shake so she slid them down to her lap. But, then on second thought, why avoid the obvious?

"I can see I'm upsetting you," Deo commented.

She casually waved him off, swatting his words away like an annoying fly on a hot summer day.

"All right. Heard tell of one game where he got sucker-punched but I wasn't there. Played a few card games, when it was only him and a couple other men from the village. Usually late afternoon and just for a few pennies. Never amounted to much. But, before long, he'd have to leave, making some excuse of helping his ma. Always thought that was decent of him but felt bad for him at the same time. It was real obvious he didn't want to leave and, eventually, I found out he was helping her with the gambling and some drinking. I got the impression he was pressed into it."

Deo's soliloquy was long and drawn out, interrupted once when the waiter refilled their water glasses. He hardly paused even then, acting like the speech had been rehearsed, and the time had come for him to offer his words before forgetting.

A sand castle wall slowly crumbled within as each word he spoke chipped away at exhausted defenses. Tilly found herself relaxing and accepting what she always knew to be true. Spoken words meant more than reading a little boxed-in letter of apology from her former and, by then, dead mother-in-law.

Their dinners arrived and they ate in silence through most of the meal, but Tilly was comfortable for the first time in a very long time. She'd sneak a glance in Deo's direction and catch his eyes gazing upon her face.

"When's your husband returning from Europe?"

She startled at the change in conversation, first having to shake off the notion he wasn't asking of Johnny but Thad instead. Yes, her husband, the one she hardly thought of as the months piled up since his escape. But she wasn't interested in moving to a different subject quite yet.

"You suspect the Klansmen." She set down her fork to then blot her lips with a napkin.

"Only rumors."

"But, what did you hear?"

"They called him out and then he'd ridden his motorbike somewhere to meet them. He was being blamed for running a blind pig and the Klan was cleaning up the area."

"So, my pa was right when he said Johnny was dead."

"Not sure your father ever knew for sure. What I heard later was he tried to talk the Klan out of whatever they were planning. I don't know if he was ever a part of that group, but heard he had some sway with a few members. I believe he was trying to protect you and Johnny."

Tilly's undigested dinner was threatening to reappear and spill all over the white tablecloth as her mind played the old scene of entrails, a snout, eyeballs, and blood everywhere. So, the Klan was to blame all along, and her own father had prevented further investigation. Would he have gotten into trouble, or worse, made to disappear? Had he feared she'd been left completely alone? Was he ultimately protecting her knowing Johnny would never return?

But none of these questions were answerable. Money's memory had become so erratic, asking him would only serve to upset. Tilly long ago put Johnny to rest and now the same action was necessary to these questions.

Working in the rationing office gave her quiet satisfaction and stilled the parts of her life never to be resolved.

Chapter 32

1942

August, 1942
The Department of the Army deeply regrets to
inform you of your husband's, Thaddeus R. Andrews
United States Army Reserve, death as a result of an air
raid bombing on July twentieth in the year of the Lord
1942 in the performance of his duty and the service of
his country. The Department extends to you its sincerest
sympathy in your great loss. To prevent possible aid to
our enemies please do not divulge the name of his
station or location. Return of body if recovered
impossible at this time. If further details are received
you will be properly informed.
                    Rear Admiral Johnson Jones
                    Chief of Army Personnel

The two officers, dressed in the deepest navy—
nearly black—Tilly'd ever seen, stood at attention
while she read the telegram. No words were spoken by
either man; they merely waited for a reaction and
possibly any questions. None came to mind. Long
before this date, she knew in her mind's eye—in her
heart—this would happen. The only emotion to strike
now was disgust from what he wrought down on their
family.

Thad didn't have to enlist in a war the country was

not involved in at the time. Now, the war raged on and he was gone. He'd left them, left them all to fend for themselves.

"Oh, dear," she finally said, her hands fluttering up toward her face. All she could think about was how Maude Adams would have acted. She'd have reclined on the settee, waiting for someone to bring her good news to counter-balance the bad. Would she faint dead away? Would the "vapors" take over? Should she be the perfect hostess, the necessary wife? Oh, what did she do with the helpful newspaper article reminding her to be… "Oh, where are my manners. Would you gentlemen like to come in?"

"Ma'am, we are sorry to give you this news, but we cannot stay," the taller of the two men said, both of them shaking their heads. "Is there someone here with you?"

Tilly turned to scan the parlor. Indeed, was there anyone she could lean on? Her pa was never around when she needed him the most, Janeska usually steered clear, Tiz and that boy, oh, yes, Silas, the toddler always under foot. They were forever off somewhere far away. From her. Left alone.

"Mrs. Andrews?" One of the officers stepped forward. "Are you okay?"

"Oh, oh," Tilly repeated for the tenth time. Nothing but simple words were beyond her ability. "Oh, yes, I'll be fine. I always am. No one, but I'll be fine." Yes, Maude would have responded with manners. Put on a smile and never let the world see her vulnerable. Without even offering a proper farewell to the two officers, she let the front door swing shut and made her way over to the parlor couch.

Well, this time for sure, she was most definitely a widow, and no doubt, soon to be considered the widow of a war hero. Fawned over, not pitied, but alone again. The rumors would cease to exist.

An hour ticked by, silence surrounding her and thoughts of how she was a May pole and everyone in her life circled around her, some coming close then others letting go of the ribbon and disappearing out of sight. Thoughts of heading to her work and having a chance to talk with Deo stabilized her.

But then, the back door slammed against the kitchen wall frame and her life would now begin as a widow once the words were spoken to her family.

Chapter 33
Healing

"No one home?"

"I'm here." Tilly bantered, as she admitted Deo in from the front porch. She turned on her heels and led the way toward the parlor, assuming he would follow. When she turned back, he was still standing, his back up against the closed door. "You can come in."

"I just don't want to intrude. I know it's been a couple of months since you got the news." He slowly took a couple steps closer.

"No thin ice here." She laughed.

Three more steps and they were in each other's arms and her long-held breath slowly emptied from her lungs with great satisfaction. His arms were like a blanket warming and protecting her from outside distractions. Their lips came together in a soft kiss that soon turned urgent. She took his hand and they climbed the worn staircase up two flights to the third floor.

If she ever gave thought to these afternoons of their clandestine times together, rationale had been on her side. She'd been left alone and widowed. Deo's willingness to hold her helped that ever-elusive happiness—or at least some contentment—to enter her life. After all these years, it was no one's business but her own.

They sat down hip-to-hip on the bed, the old

springs groaning a heavy sigh. He held her left hand in his right, their fingers intertwined.

"I don't suppose we should be all that long," she finally said. "Did you see the latest rationing for rubber tires?"

"No shop talk," he scolded, raising her hand to his lips then brushing her knuckles against his cheek.

"Deo," she began, but paused. He'd helped so much over the last several weeks but she couldn't continue like this forever. Maybe her conscience was preying on how Tiz might view this, or Money's judgmental look, or Janeska's silence. Or possibly, it was because, when they were between the covers, she closed her eyes and imagined it was Johnny lying next to her, his hands on her waist before moving upward, his legs tangling between her warm thighs.

"Don't say it."

"I have to." She slowly moved her head back and forth. "You have been lovely and what I needed so bad but we can't keep doing this."

Deo released his grip on her so he could cover his face with his hands.

"Will you marry me?" He begged the question, with desperation edging it like a worn doily. It wasn't the first time he'd asked.

"I can't."

How many times she declined probably equaled the number of times they'd sat on this bed together. In her heart, she would always be married to Johnny. She no longer felt anger, a drive to find out what happened to him, or even sadness. In these moments with another man, she found serenity. But she'd forever be married to her first love.

Chapter 34
Sunny Adores James

Sixty-two years later—June 2, 2004

"Hey, you two," shouted a gruff voice. "What the hell you doing over there?"

Sunny turned quickly away from her husband, James, to see an old—more like ancient—man leaning heavily on a crooked cane while bracing himself against the doorframe of the three-story house they'd been admiring. At one time, the old house may have been elegantly groomed, but now, ivy was slowly swallowing the front up, obscuring windows and doors, even creeping onto the roof. From Sunny's perspective, if the old man stood still for long, he'd soon be engulfed in green leaves.

James moved over in front of Sunny and quickly waved. So like him to appear oblivious to another's anger, what with his outgoing greeting and all. She cringed.

"Good morning, sir," James called out. "Just admiring your beautiful place."

"Get on your way."

While Sunny remained standing behind her husband, she quickly snapped a couple pictures with her pocketsize digital camera. They'd been examining a name carved into a plank of stone attached to the soffit of an outbuilding close to the street at the east side of the house. She took pictures of the shed and then a few of the house, after balancing the camera in the crook of James' arm, hoping the old man wouldn't notice.

"Sorry," James continued, undeterred. "You own this place?"

"Are you deaf?"

"Not particularly, curious though."

"Move along," the man pointed his cane in their direction, and then waved it back and forth like a pole that had lost its flag, "or I'll call the police."

"No need to call in the authorities. I come in peace," James called out. "But, can I ask you one thing?"

"You just did." The man's voice was a low growl.

"No, no, a real question."

"Then will you leave?"

"Can we come back again? I'd like to ask you a couple of questions. Unless, of course, you'd be willing to talk now." James was speaking fast, something he did when he was pleading for a *yes* answer.

How often he started to sound like a sped-up recording when he was working to convince her of something she probably wasn't going to buy into. Like the time he got the wild idea they should have a sky-diving adventure together. He could talk as fast or as long as he wanted, she wasn't having any part of his plans. James finally gave up and jumped out a little twin-engine plane almost solo, plunging toward the ground on the back of an experienced diver. She took loads of pictures while her own feet were firmly planted on the ground. Of course, she didn't record his screaming even if she was so inclined.

Sunny freely admitted she was pretty much chicken of trying anything new and different, afraid of rocking the boat and drawing attention to herself, and was the most happy when she could fade into the background. And, right now? With the two of them being in the limelight, she was a nervous wreck. She was sure the old man had found some way to call the cops while they stood across the front lawn from each other and they'd come careening around the corner, lights flashing and sirens blaring, to haul her and James away, throw them in jail, and toss the key away.

As if her thoughts conjured up this scenario, sirens wailed off in the distance. The whine pulsated as it seared through the trees, around the downtown buildings, and was gathered up by the wind, eventually dying away.

Of course, at this point, her legs were imitating gelatin; weak and shaking to the point she'd better find somewhere to sit down soon before she landed face first on the ground. She grabbed at the back of James' shirt to pull him away from the house, but he wasn't having any of her reticence.

"I mostly want to find out if you know anything about the name on this building," James called out, pointing to the carving over the shed doorway.

"Why?"

"Like I said, curious."

"Curiosity killed the cat," the man whispered just loud enough for the words to float across the lawn to them. "But, hey, it's your funeral."

Such an odd comment. Still, James took a step toward the front of the house while Sunny continued tugging his shirt, willing her legs to operate in some semblance of normalcy. On second thought, she would have preferred the cops' arrival as opposed to the old man's turn of phrase.

"Okay, first off, my name's James and this is my lovely wife, Sunny," James began, pulling her up alongside him, as they took more steps closer toward the shriveled-up man who was leaning evermore heavy on the cane. "Sunny is short for Sunday; her being born on the first day of the week and her parents taking an easy route. Don't you agree?"

The old man appeared transfixed by James' quickening chatter.

"Must say, you talk a lot," the man commented. In the span of only a few minutes, he'd deflated like a leaky balloon, exhaustion evident in the slump of his shoulders. The fight had gone out of him. "You got your question ready or you gonna talk my head off?"

With each comment, Sunny started sensing a loneliness in the old man. At first menacing and blustery, he was now transfixed. He became a bit engaged, even if conversation might not have been an art form he practiced much in the last few years. His stare remained on her and James, never wavering. Sunny felt a connection to the old man—a shyness or a wariness of what life was going to throw at them next.

Half a dozen steps and they were within a few feet of the old man. A fat, black cat with white mittens slithered out the front door and around the man's cane, then wandered over to James and Sunny. She bent down to nuzzle its head and was rewarded with a push against her fingers and a loud purr.

"Go on, get out of here," the old man admonished the cat. "Damn cat won't leave me alone. Kind of like you people."

"Sir, we do hate to intrude," James began, "but I'd like to ask you about the name on the building."

"What about it?"

"Yours?"

"Was my father's. What's your interest?"

"So Silas Monroe is your father…"

"Was. Still deaf?"

"No, curious. Remember?"

James was getting impatient. Sunny had seen this side of him before. The time had come to intervene, seeing as they were the ones intruding. Nothing was going to be served by them demanding information when the old man seemed reluctant to begin with.

And, most importantly, James needed some answers.

He was pacing the floor more often than not, late at night, long after both should have been getting a good night's sleep. He described what was happening but could never fully remember the sequence or, as he had taken to calling them his movie-like dreams, of a man falling to the ground, hands being stripped of gloves, and laughter off in the distance. The scene replayed continuously some nights. They were both hoping for some answers once he stumbled on the thought of doing his genealogy to get to know long-gone relatives.

"So you've lived here a long time?"

"You've asked two questions, both of which I'm sure isn't any of your damn business." The old man turned slightly as if to head into the house. But he looked back. "Got a question for you. What's this all to you?"

"My last name's Miner, full name James Money

Miner. Monroe is also a family name." James waited while Sunny jittered away next to him.

"So? Monroe's a common enough name. You saying we might be related?"

"Yea, guess I'm thinking we are," James answered. "Been looking a long time for any family and you might be all I've got."

"Mr. Monroe," Sunny finally spoke up. "Can we possibly sit down somewhere? James has a few more questions and we've come a long way."

****

For a man with the welcoming elegance of a spiny toad, Mr. Monroe turned out to be both gracious and rather talkative. As hard as Sunny worked to overcome her shyness, she stepped up her game and gave him a smile to melt the earlier icy moments, and they were now seated on the long front porch. The cat curled up close behind the old man's chair but far enough away from the crooked cane as if maybe pokes were a normal occurrence. Up close, she could see why the cane was bent, having been patched with screws holding a couple small wedges of wood like a splint mending a broken leg. The screws were rusty and the wood pieces worn smooth, indicating the repair work had probably been done long ago.

Sunny and James sat across from the old man, all in wicker furniture in need of some high-powered spraying attention. The chairs were so caked in dust she was sure they'd have crosshatch imprints on their denims when they stood up.

From her vantage point, she could see through a massive window into the living room—probably more well-known in its day as a parlor. The room was more like a museum where velvet cording needed to be strung at the doorway preventing entrance. A Victrola commanded the west wall, situated between two other floor-to-ceiling windows, and a couple of high-backed stuffed chairs book ending a rather large and uncomfortable-looking couch. The room was small by today's standards with only a few scant items filling up the space.

Mr. Monroe leaned his chin on bent and gnarled fingers, as his eyes glazed over, thoughtful.

"So, you're telling me my father, Money, and your Grandpa Johnny, you say, were in-laws. Let me get this straight. Johnny was your grandpa, married to Money's daughter, my half-sister. Bet all your research never told you she was a strange one."

"No, sir," James replied. "Research only gives you the names, not much else. But I figured with nearly thirty years between you and her birthdates, something interesting must have happened."

"Oh, it did."

Chapter 35
Elena Fancies Alex

Same Day but in Another Part of Town

They were married in the spring of 1976.

Such a quiet year otherwise—well, maybe celebrating the United States' two hundredth birthday proved to be a bit exciting, but what about NBC retooling their peacock? Like their branding wasn't recognizable enough?

George Foreman was all over the boxing news and Sonny and Cher could sing together on stage, even if they were divorced, and, oh my, her favorite, Olivia Newton-John. She was everywhere, in the movies and song after hit song.

Most curious, by fall, Jimmy Carter—a damn peanut farmer—had become the President of the United States. A Democrat shocking the nation by defeating Gerald Ford. At least Alex saw that election as the downfall of the country, if anyone asked. Secretly, she and Alex had cancelled out each other's votes.

But, for Alex and Elena Tripp, 1976 was their beginning and, now look at them, nearly thirty years later. The struggles they'd been through and survived as a couple. And, maybe, just maybe, found themselves a little bit happy.

This last year had probably been one with the most

adjustment, but she'd ponder those worries another day. Right now, time to do something new.

Elena's fingers danced over the keyboard, typing away at her first-ever blog post for the newly-born *Tripping through Life*. She loved the internet and how her creative juices worked overtime. She labored long and hard on what to call this blog of hers and then inspiration struck one morning, sometime around two o'clock. She'd lain awake next to her snoring husband, contemplating the years ahead.

Thirty years together had been full of love, drama and disappointment, amusement, maybe boring once in a while, but always with stumbles along the way, making up their lives as they went along. Then a thought hit her. The next thirty years would no doubt have a few more trip-ups. And so, *Tripping through Life* was born.

June 2, 2004—Let Us Begin

Not sure if anyone out there in this big, wide world will find my blog, take the time to read and come back for more visits, or even care enough to comment, but here goes something.

My name is Elena, been married 30 years, we have two grown children and a grandchild on the way, and I am not an alcoholic. Although, we do enjoy our glass (or bottle) of wine with dinner. Retirement is looming on the horizon for my husband, Alex, and we recently decided our settled, simple lifestyle needed a major shake-up before the real change happens of spending all of our days and nights together.

What this means is we recently moved into a turn-of-the-20th century, two-story Victorian house a mile north of our little village. And, as a master of understatement, I can assure you this house, built before 1900, needs some work.

Well, some renovation won't be necessary. We purchased the house from an elderly gentleman who had lived in the house over 50 years. He'd modernized the kitchen so we, at least, can cook! I'll save more of the history for another post but, as an enticement, think about tales you've heard of rye mash and bathtub gin, the smell of herbs and spices, and rumrunners sneaking around in the dead of night.

As my husband likes to refer to pretty much everything he owns, this house is now one of his works in progress. As we learn more, you will too.

After raising our family in the big city way, we decided to try out small town living. To say the least, this new life has been an adventure...

Elena's fingers paused in mid-air. Or should she say *change*? But one word was too simple of an explanation for what was happening; adjustment, alteration, modification, needing fine-tuning, loads of tweaking. The list could go on forever.

To say the least, this new life has been an adventure...nay, a major adjustment.

This blog is going to be my way of journaling the renovations to the house, life changes as we discover them in a small town, and our marriage and its survival.

I hope.

I truly hope, she thought.

Elena stood up from her desk in the third floor attic room. The house had been listed by the real estate company as a two-story farmhouse, but they discovered an attic accessible by way of a pull-down wooden staircase. Turned out to be more than sufficient space for an office. She could stand, without stooping, in the center of the room and placed her desk at the west wall facing the north-south road. For all of her books, journals, and magazines, they lined the sloping roof with shelves.

This was the first room made more livable after purchasing the farmhouse. Being more than an office, the attic would prove to be a sanctuary once Alex retired. With cozy and quiet topping her list for an office, Elena was happy with the end results.

She was content, and yet, restlessness had become her devil lately. Pacing back and forth in front of the desk became a routine when concentration was at a premium. She and Alex were six months out from his retirement, and she was worried. Granted, this house had become a great distraction and, no doubt, they'd fill their days with work yet to be done. But, then what?

Buying this house had been Alex's idea but she certainly hadn't been *agin it*—a phrase he'd picked up and started using since their transition into country living.

Living a mile from the main four corners certainly gave her reasons for more exercise, biking into town to pick up groceries for their evening meals. Her morning routine quickly settled into a bike ride—weather permitting—to town, shopping for a few essentials and taking care of any other errands, ending up at Café Steamy for a coffee and quick conversation with the owner, Toni, then back home to organize her day. Some days she worked on a project inside the house; sanding or staining or replacing bits of broken hardware. Actually, she became proficient with a hammer, brush, screwdriver, most any tool. Other days, she'd retreat to the office and write, hoping to complete a manuscript she began when they were first married.

But, even her creativity had stalled, until stumbling upon the idea of writing a blog. She was fairly certain there were others out there in the same situation as she and Alex. Maybe this would be a way to connect and commiserate.

"Damn it all to hell!"

"Alex, is that you?"

The back screen door slammed hard against the doorframe and the rattling reverberated the walls throughout the entire house. Elena paused to save her work before heading downstairs to see what had upset her husband.

"Hey, baby, sorry about the interruption," Alex apologized as Elena walked into the kitchen, located down the hall from the living room, at the back of the first floor. "Thought I'd get all sorts of chores done this weekend, but I've run into a bit of a hitch in those plans." He held up one half of a rusty hasp, minus the screws where the latch had been secured to something and flicked the metal piece through the air.

Elena wasn't quick enough and the metal clattered to the floor, coming to rest by her stocking-feet. She bent down to pick up the item and had the absolute, most crazy sensation as her fingers touched the surface. She quickly drew back her hand and looked up at her husband.

"Where'd you find this?"

Alex retrieved the metal plate from the floor.

"You won't believe this," he began. "Oh, God, come on. You gotta come see this."

Before Elena could say another word, Alex turned around and was out the door, down the steps, and was jogging across the back yard toward an old, partially-standing, mostly rotting barn which stood at the back of the property. He left the barn door open and disappeared through the dark opening before she was down the back stoop.

Elena was getting insight to what retirement could possibly be like. Her at his beck and call—what he was doing more important than what she was involved in. She shook her head, trying to clear any ill self-prophesizing thoughts.

"Coming," she replied. Elena stepped over the threshold and waited a moment, allowing her eyes to adjust from the bright sunshine outside to the inky black inside the barn. Time and other projects had gotten in the way of tackling this oversized shed and she never paid much attention to what needed to be done. If the walls had fallen down, she wouldn't have been bothered. She looked around unable to spot her husband who, as it turned out, had exited out the large back opening anyhow.

"Stay right where you are," Alex warned her as he stepped back into the doorway. "Let me get some light on this."

She followed him to the back of the barn and then out the door, heading in the direction of a granary lean-to she'd hardly noticed before this. Alex held the door open and, as she crossed over the threshold, the situation became quite apparent. He'd lost a battle prying open a trapdoor. Bits of splintered wood were scattered all over the dirt floor as if he'd been creating a bed for a horse. The trapdoor, sized about the same width and half the height of a bedroom door, with a couple of hinges at one end closest to the common wall of the barn, was still firmly embedded in the floor. The remaining half of a hasp was still secured to the other side of the trapdoor. Whatever had kept the hasp securely locked had been beaten apart by the crowbar Alex had obviously dropped to the floor.

"What in the world did you find?" Elena asked, taking a step closer. "And, why haven't we noticed any of this before?"

"The best I can figure is the previous owner never came out here," Alex replied, stepping over to a large table. "I started moving this old bench and the legs hung up on something. Turns out those two hinges were the problem. Once I moved the table, I pushed aside most of the grain dust and dirt."

"Someone went to a lot of trouble to hide this." She looked over at some burlap piled off in the corner. "Have you pulled the hatch open?"

"No, waited for you. Thought you might be interested."

They stood over the planks of wood like attendees at the cemetery waiting for the casket to be lowered into the ground. Although this time, the opposite was the case. They were both momentarily frozen in their own thoughts of what might be lifted out. An exhumation of sorts?

Alex ran a hand through his salt-and-pepper hair then squatted down, took hold of the staple loop the metal hasp had been hooked to and pulled. A small plume of dust arose but he couldn't get a firm hold of the small ring and his hand slipped. He sprawled backward, creating a larger cloud of dust as he landed solidly on his rear end. He righted himself, grabbed the crowbar, crammed the forked end into the loop, and pushed upward. Still nothing. Not a squeak, not a budge, only a bit more dirt or grain bouncing on top of the wood planks.

Elena looked around, spotting a smaller piece of wood leaning in the corner. She was able to wedge an edge in a small space between the floor and an edge of the split trapdoor. As Alex cranked again and she leaned hard on the plank, the trapdoor groaned in protest and then gave way.

****

June 3, 2004—Mind-Boggled

The most unbelievable find has happened to my husband and me. I can't write about it yet, but I had to say something here so you will come back.

Who knew old houses had such treasures buried deep inside. And, who knew what heyday would ensue.

Elena's fingers were twitching with excitement. Oh, when those three police cars and a fire rescue truck came speeding up to the farmhouse—within minutes of Alex's call—their sirens so loud to scare off birds within a mile radius, she'd still get the shivers remembering what they found. The officers had swerved into the driveway, careened around to the back of the house, and circled the building like wagon trains back in Old West times, guarding the house from intrusion.

And now she could write what she knew so far.

The police finally called to report the brief investigation into the body buried on their property was completed, case closed. A missing person had finally been found after so many years and a family member had been contacted and informed. Arrangements were being made. Johnny Miner—as the skeleton had been identified—would be placed in a proper plot next to a daughter named Wendy he never met since she was born nine months after he went missing. If possible, Elena hoped she and Alex could gather with any family and a minister around the new grave while a few words were spoken.

Such a short story for a life-changing event. How some lives must have dragged on for years without resolution.

June 15, 2004—Letter Found with Body

I can now talk about what we found. A body—more like only the skeleton—was found by my husband in a granary building at the back of our property. Inside the granary is a cellar where the body was found. A trapdoor had been locked and covered by dirt, burlap, and a big table.

We now know, both from the police and newspaper articles, the body was placed there sometime in 1929. A box, containing a few interesting items—gloves, a pistol, and a letter—was added to the cellar long after that time.

The person who wrote the note may have had only a few years of schooling and the teacher in me so wants to correct spelling errors, but here is the letter as found. It does ramble on but, at the same time, tells so much:

August, 1939

Tilly, I love you, but canna keep this to meself any longer. I have done something very bad. You may never learn the truth but I canna leave without writing.

Johnny's dead because of me. Not only because of

me but by my own hand. I shot him. In this box, you will find the pistel—me Da's he gave me years ago. It is the one and only time I ever shot.

I have lived with guilt from the day I took a man's life, but I can no longer live with you after learning the truth. 'Til you told me it weren't him running the blind pig, but his own ma, I thought I was protecting you from such a scoundrel. He was getting in trouble with the KKK, your own pa being a member, and they were going after him.

When I heard you had a Victor, I knew it was Navarro's. Heard tell he lost it because of blackmail. I thought Johnny was the one. The scarf found in his ma's house belonged to me own Da. He said he'd visited the blind pig a few times and used it to keep Clarine quiet. I thought Johnny done stole it.

All I wanted to do was warn him. I'd heard talk the Klan was going to meet him at the tamarack swamp north of town. I followed him, hid in the woods, waited while he and three others argued. Then, when they left, I begged him to stop what he was doing for your sake but he wouldna listen. I walked away but he kept yelling at me. Words all too true, I cared too much. In anger, I turned and shot. Only meant to scare him.

But I shot him through the heart. I thought about putting him in the shed for your pa to find. Instead, I hid him and hoped to forget this ever happened. I knew a woman north of town making hooch and Johnny was getting some from her. And I knew she had an old barn but nothing in it except a horse.

I buried the motorbike under branches and hoped it'd never be found. I stripped the gloves off his hands and you will find them in this box. I wore them for a brief moment but couldna keep them. If only you made a pair for me.

Now, since you told me what you found out 'bout Clarine running the blind pig, I canna live with what I've done. I have joined the Armed Services and will fight for our country. I don't believe I'll return.

But, before I could leave, I wrote this letter, and am going back to the barn. I canna bear to look at the body but I wanted to put this letter, the pistel, and the gloves in a box for safe-keeping. Maybe someday you can understand, maybe someday you will forgive me, but I canna forgive myself. Me guilt is killing me more than I can bear, knowing you have suffered because of me.

I will miss Tiz and how she calls me Papa. Me little milklady.

I am sorry,
Thad Andrews

So, there you have it. Did Mr. Andrews return from the war? Has anyone found the motorcycle? Whatever happened to the house where the blind pig was held? And do any of those people—Thad, Tilly, Tiz, Clarine, Johnny—have family who can answer my questions?

As I learn more, you will, too.

Chapter 36
Tilly Still Loves Johnny

A Few Days later, 2004

"Johnny? Is that you?"

James looked down at the shriveled-up woman in the hospital bed, her body barely making a mound under the covers. The bed had been cranked up so she was partially sitting up. Even though the sheet somewhat covered her chin, a pale-blue silk ruffled collar still peeked out, framing her face. She looked overdressed for where she was, but at the same time almost like an old-time actress awaiting her loyal fans.

The covers over her were as straight and tightly tucked in as if only moments ago a nurse had been in the room. He didn't know how to respond to the question and looked around, hoping for some inspiration. Here lay his grandmother, someone he'd never met, and hardly knew anything about. But he had a story to tell her.

"No, ma'am," he replied with some hesitation. "My name is James. I'm Tuesday's—Tiz's—son. Do you remember me?"

"Tiz? Where is my daughter? Has anyone seen her?" Her eyelids rapidly blinked while she twisted her head side to side.

"Ma'am, she died."

"Gone? She's gone, but tell me, Johnny, it's really you, right? You came back. I always knew you would." Tilly rattled on, not making sense. Hands so white but with thick ropes of blue veins tracing up her wrists shook in agitation.

James had been warned about her confusion long before he stepped into the room, causing him to hesitate repeating his name. Best to let her believe what she wanted to for now. Instead he would keep talking about his own mother, Tiz.

"She's been gone going on twenty years now. Don't you remember?"

Tilly muttered something he didn't catch as she kept raising up one hand then pressing down hard into the sheet. He couldn't imagine what she was doing except, if he were a Charades-playing man, he'd have thought maybe she was trying to push a needle through fabric. Sewing something only she could see.

"Tell pa to get me some more deerskin." She continued to speak nonsense to him but she appeared to calm the longer he let her talk. "I have two more gloves to make. Johnny, I know you lost your pair and your fingers must be so cold. Tiz needs a pair, too. So cold in the morning when she delivers milk. Don't you agree?"

James looked down at the couple of photographs he held. One showed the contents of the metal box—a pistol, a couple sheets of yellowed, crinkled paper containing a letter he'd read over and over again having nearly memorized every word, and a pair of brittle, dried out deerskin gloves. Another picture showed a fallen motorcycle, rusted beyond any other color than a deep reddish-brown, old weeds having sprouted and died numerous times between the spokes of the cracked tires. After the letter had been examined, a search of a long-ago dried-up swamp close to the farmhouse had yielded the bike.

He was at a loss of how to proceed.

"Tilly, you okay?"

James turned toward the door to spot another equally shriveled-up old woman, but at least she seemed a bit more clear-eyed and was sitting as if at attention. She was trying to maneuver her wheelchair through the archway. "Thought I heard voices."

"Pa?"

"No, Rita Mae," the woman in the wheelchair answered. "Remember me?"

"Oh, honey, you're not Rita Mae. Why do you try to fool me, Delores?" Tilly's voice quavered with confusion. "You can go tell pa I need more deerskin for these gloves."

Rita Mae, as James now had figured out, tilted her head toward the corner and the woman in the wheelchair began backing up to accommodate him.

"Maybe we should let her rest for a minute," he suggested.

"And, you are?"

"James, James Money Miner, her grandson," he replied, inclining his head back toward the room.

"Tiz's son? Oh, I should have known you anywhere. Been stuck inside these walls for so long, I've half-forgotten all I ever knew. Dear girl's been gone for so long, I near forgot what she looked like but you are the spittin' image of your Grandpa Johnny. He wasn't nigh on as handsome as you, even if he was one fine lookin' man."

James had not seen any pictures of his Grandpa

Johnny but had been told there were some in a closet belonging to his grandmother. Once Silas mentioned the bedroom on the third floor had been locked as long as he could remember, James figured that's where he'd like to search.

"You're Rita Mae, right?"

She nodded.

"Why did she call you Delores?"

"It's a long story." She sighed, then giggled like a young girl. The twinkle in her eyes told him those two had a friendship spanning from the best to the worst, and everything in between. "Do you have a lifetime?"

"I have as long as you want to talk," he replied.

"She believes she's a long-gone actress named Maude Adams and I'm Delores Costello. Till and I used to go to the movies as often as we could. Oh, back in the day, talkies were brand new. Coins was tight, but we always found some to go to the Vaudette. I don't cotton to the movies now, would rather watch old ones, mind you." She paused to cough a couple times, clear her throat, and take a sip of water. "Till ain't right in the head anymore. I hate to talk about her in a bad way, but she's not the same no more."

"I didn't even know I had a grandmother until a few weeks ago," James interjected. "My mom didn't talk about family."

"Not surprised," Rita Mae answered. "But, I've wondered over the years what happened. After Money died in '49 from cancer and then Janeska dying a couple years later, leaving Silas with their big, old house, I hoped Tiz would come back. You know, she left home after Thad died during the war. She was only thirteen, I think, when she moved into some boarding house where she could stay as long as she had money to pay and didn't cause trouble. She was a milklady back in them days. Used to call Thad her papa, only father she knew. Broke Tiz's heart when those two officers came to the house to tell Till he was gone. Tiz never forgave her mother for making him leave, the way I heard. My memory's a little fuzzy but I know Till couldn't take anything more. Last straw, you know? She broke and's never been the same since."

"Silas made some comment about her being strange. The way he was talking, does he even know she's still alive?"

"Not sure, all I remember is Till didn't like when her pa and Janeska got hitched and then having a baby boy making young Tiz an aunt to someone so close to the same age. Sometimes I even have trouble keepin' it all straight."

"Did my grandmother know about me?"

"Don't know, she's been here so long," Rita Mae said, her voice a bit hoarse. "Lord, I haven't spoken this much in a long time. No one around here wants a couple of old biddies talking about the old days all the time."

"I'm glad you're here with her," James said, questions now building one on top of another he wanted to ask her.

"I can't get over how much you look like Johnny." She turned slightly to reach back to a nightstand and picked up a framed photograph James hadn't noticed. His grandfather was looking off into the distance with his grandmother staring straight into the camera.

"You know they found him?"

"Heard tell from the news they found some old

bones in a barn north of town. Is it him?" Rita Mae asked.

"Would you like to go outside?" James asked as he nodded yes to the question. He stood and walked around to the back of the wheelchair and then slowly worked their way down the corridor of the nursing home. "It's sunny and the right temp."

"Never would've believed it if the nurses here hadn't shown me the letter. Looked at it with my own two eyes right there on some screen they was showin' me. Thad Andrews a murderer. It just ain't right. But, ya know, Till always believed Johnny hadn't left her. They kept tellin' her to get over it. But she fought hard. Maybe she lives in her head now because the battle was too hard of a fight. You know win the battles and then maybe the war? She never won nothing."

A bench was situated along one of the walkways and she indicated for him to stop.

"Ah, feels good to get out of this chair." Rita Mae sighed as she slowly stood and then inched over to the bench. "Can't understand why this ol' body don't move like it used to. Till and I used to walk all over the place, neither one of us wanting to get into those *autymobiles*, back in the day. Now I can't hardly take two steps without having to sit down." She paused, caught her breath, and continued. "So, tell me something maybe the news didn't say."

"Well…" James began, then pulled out one of the photographs he'd been carrying.

Rita Mae stared hard at the picture. "This the gun he used? That the letter? Oh, God," she exclaimed, clasping a hand over her mouth, tears immediately springing into her eyes. "The gloves Till made for

Johnny. They were the prettiest things she ever did make, poured love into each finger."

He handed over the second picture; the one showing the rusted motorcycle.

All she could do was shake her head back and forth. A tear finally traced down her cheek, following the path of one particularly deep wrinkle tracing from the corner of one eye almost to the point of her chin.

"Maybe it's better Till never knows any of this," Rita Mae finally said. "What good would come of it now? Let me ask you a question. How old are you?"

"Born in '69," he answered. "Mom was forty when she had me."

"Who's your father?"

"Don't know," James replied. "He never stuck around long enough once he found out she was pregnant with me, and she didn't ever want to talk about him. She died when I was 21, off to college, and I never had a chance to ask."

"Guess the Monroe women weren't supposed to keep their men in their lives."

"The most I heard once when she was talking to someone on the phone and didn't know I was listening, was he'd gone off to Vietnam. Never know, maybe someday I'll solve his mystery after this one."

They both sat quietly for a few minutes. A few other residents from the home had visitors, pairs of people sitting on benches scattered throughout the lawn. A soft breeze lifted a few strands of white hair from Rita Mae's forehead.

"Remind me sometime to tell you about a train ride, meetin' a physic, and eating the kind of chocolate no one bothers to make anymore," she said, the twinkle back in her eyes. "I have so many stories to tell you. At least I can pass along as much as I know about your grandmother and mother."

Chapter 37

A Few Days Later

"Let go, Till," Rita Mae whispered, shaking her head ever so slightly. "She's hung on so long."

"She's nearly a hundred," James agreed.

"Oh, I don't mean age. She hung onto Johnny, never believing he'd up and leave," Rita Mae said, her gaze turning toward the window and her voice getting even softer. "You know, she always said the *heart wants what it wants* and her heart never truly found another."

"How'd you two end up here?"

"Simple enough. I came back here after ma died. Found Tilly living with Silas. Money and Janeska were gone. She'd barely leave her bedroom, and he didn't hardly do anythin' to help her. I couldn't stand seeing her so lonely, so's with the little bit of money left from ma and Till gettin' some pension from Thad dying during the war, we put our money together and lived for a long while here in an apartment. For a time she got along good, but last year she fell and been in that dang bed nearly ever since."

They both sat silently absorbed in thought.

"Till might have been happy for a short time after Thad was gone. No, no," she shook her head, "I ain't speakin' ill of the dead. Before she got bad, she'd talk about working for the OPA—they were the rationing folks during the war. Always helping make sure no one went without. She'd talk once in a while about a Deo Minto, too. I never knew him but she always spoke so high of him. By the time I got back here, he wasn't around and rationing was only a memory. Always got the feeling, working in that office gave her purpose."

James tried to imagine this woman lying in a hospital bed with hardly the strength to lift a hand now, had been a part of a war effort he'd only read about in history books. He mostly just wanted to lay his head down next to hers and have all her memories transferred to him so he could truly know her life, smooth out struggles and revel in happiness, and learn from how she coped with each day.

"Del…" Rita Mae continued, bringing James back to the storytelling. "I used to have a whole family; now I'm the only one left. Lost a brother to the flu in 1918, then my brother, Delbert—Del—helped out until ma died. Before he died, he told me something from long ago. He knew Johnny—oh, they played as kids but your grandpa changed once we was all grown up. I never thought he was much of an honest man but, you know, Del told me a thing or two. He'd been there the night Johnny got a black eye. Sucker punched by some old man nearly twice his size."

James' eyebrows arched.

"But that ain't the story I'm wantin' to tell you. Turns out from what my brother said, Johnny wasn't the one runnin' the blind pig, he was protectin' his own kin. Mrs. Miner was mean as a rattler and Johnny was makin' sure no one harmed Tilly and Money."

Rita Mae stopped talking to catch her breath and

take a sip of water. They both focused on Tilly's chest rising and falling ever so slowly. Tilly'd been dressed first thing in the morning in a lovely bed jacket of navy wool-blend ruffles and off-white lace, made from one of the many fancy dresses formerly worn by her mother. Years earlier, Tilly had transformed two of those dresses into a single maternity dress of similar ruffles, while the remainder of the dresses had stayed tucked away. Rita Mae had known of the outfits and brought some along as well as a few other memories when Tilly moved from the only home she'd ever known.

Finally, at Rita Mae's insistence, a seamstress had been employed to make numerous frilly and fancy tops for their famous patient—*Maude Adams*—to wear when receiving guests. Even if there never were any visitors crossing the threshold into the hospital room.

"Whether she understood or not where those bed jackets came from, don't matter, because something special happens. She takes on the hand flutters, arching eyebrows, and sweet smile of her favorite actress and claims she'd be happy to talk unless, of course, the cameras started to roll. No "talkies" same as Maude Adams." Rita Mae paused to take a couple deep breaths.

"Can you continue?" James was getting concerned Rita Mae was exhausting all of her energies between talking and their constant vigil.

"Got to say my words before I can't remember," she replied, then set the glass of water back on the bedside stand. She cleared her throat and continued. "Turns out there was a man from Detroit had a whole slew of these blind pigs from there to here, convincing old women they'd make lots of money and never have another care in the world. Once he'd get them set up with all of the hooch connections and how best to run the pig, he'd ransom more and more money off of them and keep them quiet with threats of being thrown in the lock-up or hurtin' their families. Del told me Mrs. Miner got in too deep and Johnny was trying to free her. Instead, he was blamed for running the blind pig."

"But he had to have known he could get into trouble with the law."

"Guess he hoped Money—your great grandpa—would have kept the law off him. I think the old man even tried. Never knew for sure but I'm thinkin' now he was maybe part of the Klan back in them days. Sometime I'll tell you 'bout the ghosts we thought lived in his bedroom—white robes we was sure were angels waiting to get into Heaven."

"So who was the hot shot from Detroit? Someone part of the Purple Gang? They were running bootleg gin about then, right?"

"Nah, he wasn't from any gang—the Purple Gang were mostly Jewish anyhow. Del told me and I near 'bout fell over in a faint. This guy was Irish. Thad Andrews' father—his da, as Thad would say—ran the business. But, from what Del knew, Thad had no idea what was going on. He was nothing but a simple ol'milkman."

Rita Mae sat up proud as a peacock, as if she'd finally wrestled a secret out of its hiding place. But to James, the room was like a vacuum. The air had stilled yet his mind raced with flashes of nightmares and bits of dreams he'd never figured out. But now, pieces were falling into place and the weight on his shoulders was lessening.

"From what Del told me, he only saw the man once," Rita Mae said, interrupting James' thoughts. "The night Johnny was knocked out cold, this big man showed up right at the end of the fight. Johnny never owned up to Till how he bruised half his face but I figured, at the time, it came from what he was gettin' into."

"So this man, Thad's father, ran a bunch of blind pigs, illegal to begin with and then stealing more from the old women. Sounds to me like a real gentleman." James gently took hold of his grandmother's right hand and ran one thumb over the paper-thin skin. Tilly responded by resting her twitching fingers so they relaxed like a chest relieved of a sigh. "Seems Thad came by bad blood honestly."

"The thing I worried about, though," Rita Mae continued, "Tilly never wanted to know. The truth was right in front of her the whole time, but she couldn't see what she'd never believe. I tried a few times but then decided being her friend was more important. Sometimes all a body needs is someone to lean on."

James' thoughts went to his wife, Sunny. They'd laughed more than once how they were "attached at the hip" but now maybe he truly was starting to understand. She never questioned his need for answers, yet was always ready for whatever boondoggle he dreamed up. Like a road trip to a small village so they could stare at the front of a house he hardly knew anything about. She was what his body needed.

Seconds ticked by and, finally, the only sound left in the room was of Tilly exhaling a rattling breath as she grew more still. The longer they talked, her hands slowly quieted and now lay still. No more sewing gloves for someone.

"Folks thought she was weak and Johnny's ma even called her names—*wisp of a girl with no gumption*—but Tilly was the strongest person I've ever known. Wish I'd believed as strongly as her faith he hadn't deserted her. Wish I never believed all those rumors."

James sat at one side of the hospital bed while Rita Mae was in her wheelchair on the other side. They each held one of Tilly's hands. The woman whose whole life was filled with loved ones leaving her was now herself finally leaving. Neither had the heart to tell his grandmother he wasn't her long-lost husband, nor of Thad's letter confessing the murder, especially not of Johnny's bones being found even if they were now at rest next to their infant daughter, Wendy.

"Johnny…" Tilly's lips moved, exhaling her only love's name one last time.

In the last few moments of Tilly's life on earth, she raised her face upward and an ever-so-slightly uptick of her faded lips looked like a long-ago lost smile finally returning. Maybe her subconscious heard the entire story and she could now let go and rest. The deep wrinkles surrounding her eyes smoothed out as her face relaxed while Rita Mae softly hummed the beginning notes of "I've Got a Crush on You."

"I had to leave once. Now she's leaving. Goodnight, sweet Till."

Chapter 38
Back Home

All things thrive in thrice. Rita Mae repeated those five words a few times over the last couple of days, giving James pause to think of his grandmother's life.

In terms of bad, ugliness in the form of animal parts, his Grandpa Johnny gone missing, Thad a murderer. In terms of good, his mother Tiz's existence born out of sadness, a love lasting a lifetime, and his Grandma Tilly not alone at the end of her days.

His own life? He'd have to do a little thinking.

James and Sunny returned to the house of his Uncle Silas, the former home of Tilly and Johnny and then of Tilly and Thad at one time. He now stood by the front porch, taking a moment to gather meandering thoughts. There were still so many questions he had of this family he'd found while the sudden discovery and loss of his grandmother weighed his shoulders with the heft of an anvil.

He set down the box of memories to the porch edge. It was filled with the framed picture, a glass jar with nothing more than a slip of fabric inside, a tattered Valentine's Day card, and nesting dolls with nearly all of the paint worn off. Sunny was waiting in the car. She smiled toward him. He responded with the best he could offer.

The cat from earlier approached the porch, walking

with its stomach nearly dragging to the boards. The animal took a quick sniff of the box James set down. And then, appearing to consider something else more important, the cat walked to the curb, looked both ways like young children are taught, then sauntered across the street.

James looked away as some teenager laid on the horn of a sporty little car, no doubt irritating anyone within a block radius. By the time he turned back to where the cat had been, there was nothing. And yet, everything. The weight of a thousand dreams lifted from his thoughts and a peacefulness came over him. If he were a superstitious man, maybe the cat had carried away what James had no control over.

He'd found his *thrice*—he could get to know Silas better, the only family left; become part of Rita Mae's life so she was never alone since his grandmother was now gone, and he could show Sunny each and every day how *the heart wants what the hearts wants* and his heart wanted her. He would love her as Tilly had loved Johnny.

"Figuring out what to do?" Sunny had stepped out of the car and walked over to the porch. She gave him a curious look.

He was. The man falling had been his grandfather, deerskin gloves being robbed off his hands, and the laughter had to have been a horse snorting, not laughter after all. But he kept those thoughts to himself to mull over a bit longer. For now, James' silent reply was to take her in his arms, dance a little bit of a two-step with her right there on the broken-up sidewalk, and plant a juicy, wet kiss on her lips. He gathered up the box and they stepped up on the porch and knocked on the front door of the house at the corner of Grand River Avenue and South Collins Street.

Maybe over the ensuing years, James occasionally wondered, but as far as he knew, no one ever saw the cat again. Not James nor Sunny when they came for a visit, not Silas, who was most thankful for the cat's absence and for the couple's visits, nor anyone in the village. That is, if a person were to care enough to inquire. And, to tell the truth, it didn't matter in the least.

Chapter 39
Johnny's Story

Late at Night, February 15, 1929

"What the hell?"

Johnny looked down at his chest, wondering how the devil a bee could sting him in the middle of winter and especially through his wool coat. Instead of being able to swat at anything, his gaze blurred over the dark circle spreading as the wool fleece acted like a sponge. He dropped to his knees and fell sideways, one gloved hand grasping at his heart.

Oh, God, Tilly, please, nothing was supposed to be this way.

I was only trying to protect you.

If only I'd told you the truth.

Hey, doll-face…please forgive me.

I love you.

****

He walked over to the fallen body.

Johnny's voice, scratchy and faint and completely unintelligible, still brought a wry smile to Thad's face. Those eyes of a rapscallion told him all he needed to know—who had aimed the pistol at his heart, pulled the trigger to release the ball, and knowing the bullet had found its mark. Maybe he'd finally shut up. Such incessant yelling about how Thad loved another man's wife. Didn't he know Thad was only trying to protect Tilly from the trouble Johnny was getting into while running a blind pig? The Klansmen threatened a tar and feathering or other form of death, if punishment didn't stop him. The lone fact being the man's action could leave a widow behind.

But Thad would watch over Tilly now, keep her safe. He'd ignore this ever happened, simply walk away. Let the world believe Johnny deserted his family. No one would ever find him in this swamp. In a short time, the murky land would swallow Johnny whole and weeds would blanket the motorcycle forever.

Or would it? *Think.* This was the meeting spot for the Klansmen and Johnny. Others might return. *Have to hide any evidence. But where?* He could hide the body in the shed where the motorcycle usually was—no, he'd be found too soon. Thad's thoughts were shooting off like sparks from a bonfire as he worked away at a solution.

Johnny stared up from the ground, not blinking. *Oh God, he's still alive.* Thad squatted down on his haunches, within a couple feet of the man he shot moments earlier. Thickening blood seeped from Johnny's chest, a red oval spreading out as a slick puddle formed on the ground. *Won't be much longer.*

As Johnny closed his eyes, a shabby cat came close to sniff at the deerskin gloves. Thad stood and booted the cat a good five feet, then stripped the gloves from the dying man's hands. He wasn't going to need these any longer.

"Me da might like getting these," Thad spoke aloud, his voice drifting off through the browned sumac. "Make up for the scarf he lost a bit back."

271

Thad turned to walk away, his foot catching on the front tire of the fallen motorbike, nearly tripping him headfirst to the ground. Standing a few feet from the body and bike, he looked back, and then the weight of what he'd done took him down to his knees.

He'd shot a man. He killed someone's husband. He would be found out.

No, he couldn't walk away. Better to properly hide anything and everything associated with the last few minutes and to take care of the widow who would suffer, without her ever learning the truth.

In a flash, a thought, a plan, took shape. There was a woman north of town—*oh damnu' ort*, damn it— what was her name? Didn't matter. She was known for making bootleg gin, hooch, flavoring rye mash, damn woman. She deserved to have a body on her property. Consequences for her actions. None of this would have happened if not for her.

He ran back to where he'd left Brown Molly hitched to a tree. She'd found a patch of browned blades of sedge grass and was enough preoccupied, she startled when Thad burst toward her. The horse neighed in protest, sounding more like a wicked laugh. She skittered back a bit but he caught her reins and pulled her in the direction from where he'd been.

Dusk was fast approaching and he needed to work as quickly as possible. Of course, he'd wait to approach the back of the barn, which was only about a quarter of a mile away, once the skies were completely dark. He looked toward the heavy cloud cover and smiled. Darkness would help—no moon, no stars, to spotlight him. It was so cold, though.

He grabbed Johnny's feet and pulled him away

from the motorcycle. He then broke off numerous branches of dead sumac and covered the bike. He stood back to survey his handiwork. Someone extremely curious might spot something out of the ordinary, but he couldn't worry for now. And, come spring, burgeoning weeds would quickly cover the evidence.

Good, now what to do with the body. "Ol' girl," he said, "I'm needin' your help, if ye will." He pulled the blanket out from under Brown Molly's saddle.

Fortunately, Johnny was slender of build and, with all the milk cartons Thad hoisted each day, the dead man was easier to lift than expected. Once he was draped over Brown Molly's back, Thad covered the body with the blanket. He'd come back later for the saddle. The horse protested having something foreign placed over her, but Thad was able to get her moving by pulling on the reins. "Come on, ol' girl, walk on."

Before long, Thad and the laden horse approached the backside of the barn. The farmhouse was mostly dark, a single bulb burning on what looked like a back porch, giving him pause. But, no movement so he caught his breath, helping his heart to slow down a bit. The barn was his first plan, but then he noticed a door standing wide open to a granary attached to the building. The clouds parted long enough, the moon shone down and illuminated a rectangle the size of the opened door. If ever destiny was not to be ignored, this was the moment.

By all intents and purposes, it looked like no one had stepped a foot inside the granary for years. He pulled the reins downward so Brown Molly would have to duck her head a bit to get through the doorway. She balked again but finally followed.

"Walk on, Brown Molly, let's get in here."

Once inside, Thad pulled Johnny's body off of the horse, not caring how the dead man folded at odd angles, arms splayed out, legs twisted. He grabbed the blanket and spread it back on the horse's back and looped the reins over a beam. Even though this building looked deserted and unused, he couldn't leave the body out in the open. Thad wandered around a bit, rubbing his nicely gloved hands together for extra warmth, and then spotted what looked like a hasp and clasp.

He hurried over to it, undid the latch, and pulled open a trap door. He couldn't see well enough what was below but, at this point, nothing else mattered. He dragged the man's stiffening body over, dumped it in, stripped the gloves from his hands and threw those in. He picked up the cap and ball pistol, the metal hot in his bare hand as if guilt could burn. He threw everything down the hole, closed the plank door and scuffed some dirt back over the whole floor.

From the doorway, he surveyed his handiwork, then pulled on Brown Molly's reins, and man and horse wandered into the open field. Thad brought a hand to his forehead to wipe away sweat and, in the inky darkness, nothing could be seen. In that moment, his life fell into a void of black he could never return from.

His guilt would soon be worn as heavy as an oxen's yoke.

Chapter 40
Better Off Forgotten

"*Maman, Maman, viens vite,*" the young lad called out to his mother to hurry over as he pointed in the direction of a cat pawing at the ground. Son and mother had been traveling back to their farm a few miles outside of Bordeaux, France, after a day of shopping. They'd stopped along the way to enjoy a bit of fruit purchased at the market.

The boy wandered off a little bit while the mother took a few minutes to stretch out on a blanket they'd pulled from the trunk. The sun was warm and the breeze was slight.

"*Maman,*" he called again.

She roused up, leaning on her elbows, shading her eyes against the afternoon sun. He continued pointing at the ground so she finally acquiesced and headed over to where he remained rooted to the spot. They stood together, watching as a feral cat—nearly skin and bones, the animal's fur hanging in ribbed lines across its sides—continued to paw at the dirt, causing a bit of a dust cloud to rise up around the animal.

"Shoo, shoo," she called out, waving her hands.

They walked over to see what had been so interesting to the cat and found a square of something sticking up from the ground; a patch of sorts, dust covered and faded. She reached down and pulled the item free, pounded it against the ground a couple of times, and then held it up so they could both inspect it. They barely made out the words—*Milkman Thad*—sewn, in once was probably a bright red on a light background. Now the colors had faded to pink and the white dirtied to brown.

Son and mother turned around at the same time, looking for the animal, but it had disappeared. The only thing left was the dusty, old patch, one of too many artifacts to count from years earlier. So many American men had died in France, allies during the world war, and most probably *Milkman Thad* was but one more of those men who gave of his life.

"*Venir le long de, allons voir votre Pappa,*" the young woman spoke softly to the boy, placing an arm around his slim shoulders. They were off to see the boy's papa.

She slipped the patch into a pocket of her dress, wondering what this man might have been like, was there family somewhere wondering and never knowing what happened to him, or did they even speak of him to this day? Or, was he long forgotten, never having had much effect on those lives around him?

Author's Note

The early 1900s are rich with inventions, progressive thought bringing women the vote and a higher importance in this modern society, and definitely changes, some considered good while others not so much. Many of these new ways can be found in simple, short articles in local newspapers. All of the articles shown in this story are actual, slightly edited (to change names) or paraphrased news items found in *The Fowlerville Review*, a newspaper founded in 1874 by W.H. Hess and G.L. Adams, and published and edited by Mr. Adams from the beginning until he sold the paper in 1928. He died the following year, but the newspaper continued in publication until 1972.

Real life memories are the most informative. They cut to the chase without any sugar-coating. To that end, this author drew deep from the well of information from Rita Van Amber's four recipe books, published in the late 1980s and early 1990s, where she compiled memories, stories, and recipes, and even a few appropriate quotes, of those alive during the Depression Era of the 1930s. These books were published by Van Amber Publishers, 862 East Cecil Street, Neenah, Wisconsin, and are still in print. Because this author discovered these books, there will be some interesting cooking in the house.

The lyrics I referenced for "I've Got a Crush on You" were taken from a version done by Frank Sinatra, years after the song was composed by George Gershwin. In 1929, the song had only been recently used in the Broadway production, "Treasure Girl," and would not have been available for the Victor/Victrola.

But, the words are perfect for Tilly.

"All things thrive in thrice" became popular during the first world war, also known as "three on a match." From the Wikipedia site, "the belief was that when a first soldier lit his cigarette, the enemy would see the light; when the second soldier lit his cigarette from the same match, the enemy would take aim at the target; and when the third soldier lit his cigarette from the match, the enemy would shoot their weapon and the soldier would be shot." This author translated that good things can come in threes, while sometimes bad things might happen in threes, and other times, a combination of good and bad can come in threes.

"Don't Be In a Hurry to Tell It!" is a poem found in a January, 1930, issue of *The Fowlerville Review*. There was no attribution to the author. So much of this story was surrounded by rumors, lies, and gossip swirling around in a small village, this poem became an anthem I came back to time and time again while composing this manuscript.

As far as the cat goes, I'd like to believe Johnny's spirit lived within each cat mentioned and was a little bit instrumental in putting this murder mystery to rest.

And, don't believe everything you hear *because whispered tales seldom are true.*

A word about the author...

Prior to self-publishing two local history books and my debut novel, *Juniper and Anise*, I raised a family of two lovely daughters; was featured in national magazines, with over 350 designs published in the area of handiwork; wrote motorcycle racing articles for magazines and newspapers; spent years working behind the scenes and modeling in live fashion show productions; and have owned my own commercial embroidery company for nearly twenty years.

As my husband and I face the adventures of retirement, I hope to concentrate even more on my writing while we travel to see friends and family.

http://www.marioncornett.com

Thank you for purchasing
this publication of The Wild Rose Press, Inc.

If you enjoyed the story, we would appreciate your
letting others know by leaving a review.

For other wonderful stories,
please visit our on-line bookstore at
www.thewildrosepress.com.

For questions or more information
contact us at
info@thewildrosepress.com.

The Wild Rose Press, Inc.
www.thewildrosepress.com

Stay current with The Wild Rose Press, Inc.

Like us on Facebook

https://www.facebook.com/TheWildRosePress

And Follow us on Twitter
https://twitter.com/WildRosePress